Withdrawn Stock
Dorset Libraries

BUTTON HOLED

BUTTON HOLED

Kylie Logan

CHIVERS

British Library Cataloguing in Publication Data available

This Large Print edition published by AudioGO Ltd, Bath, 2012.

Published by arrangement with the Author

U.K.	Hardcover	ISBN	978 1 4713 0670 9
U.K.	Softcover	ISBN	978 1 4713 0671 6

Printed and bound in Great Britain by
MPG Books Group Limited

For David,
who never pictured himself
at button shows or button museums,
but who is always along for the ride!

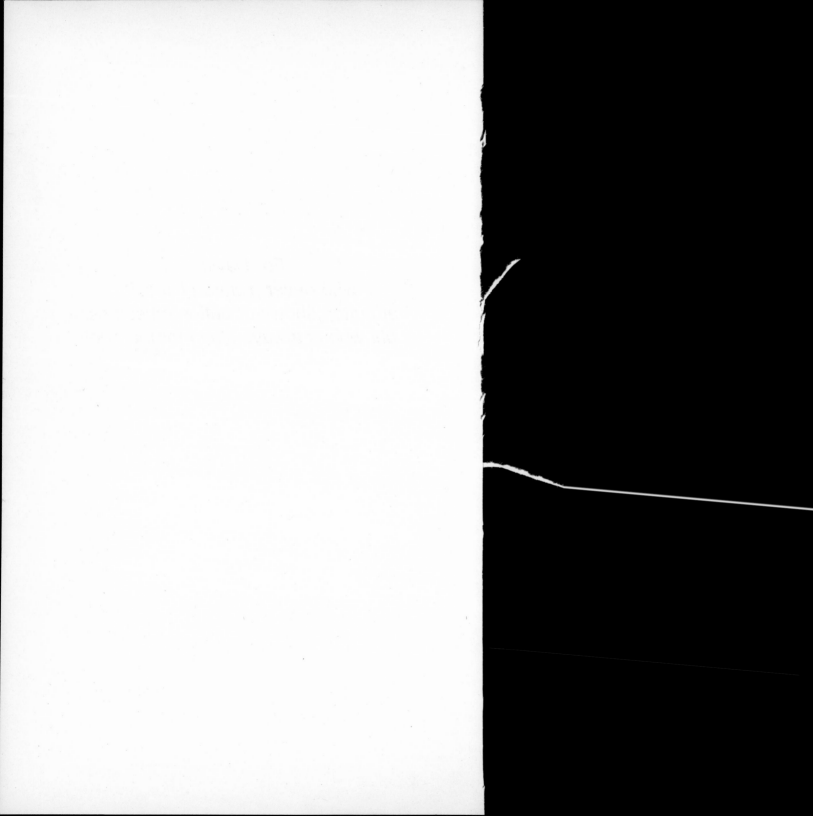

CHAPTER ONE

Here's the thing about walking into your button shop at five in the morning and running smack into a hulk of a guy wearing a black ski mask: it tends to catch a girl a little off guard.

Off guard, I sucked in a breath that was half surprise, half gasp of terror; and just inside the door of the Button Box, I froze.

For exactly two seconds.

That was when my instincts kicked in. No big surprise, they told me to turn and run like hell.

I would have done it, too, if there wasn't another guy — the twin of the giant who greeted me before I even had a chance to turn on the lights — right behind me. Even as I watched, he snapped the door closed, crossed his arms over a chest the size of Soldier Field, and braced his legs. He didn't say a word. He didn't have to. The message was loud and painfully clear — no way I was going to escape in that direction.

Trapped, my heart pounded a furious rhythm, and my blood whooshed inside my head. There was no use screaming. Five in the morning, remember. And even though my shop had only been open for a week and I had yet to meet all my fellow merchants in the other converted brownstones there in Old Town, I was pretty sure nobody but me loved their jobs so much that they came into work before the sun was up.

Too bad. At least if somebody was around to find it, my body wouldn't lie there for hours until my assistant, Brina Martingale, decided to show up. She'd be late — as usual — and I was betting that by then, I'd be stone-cold and as gray as the twinset I was wearing that day with my best pair of black pants.

Oh yeah, things looked pretty grim. I told myself panic would get me nowhere, and while I was at it, I reminded myself that if I just stayed calm, I'd find a way out of this mess. It couldn't/wouldn't/shouldn't be a stretch. After all, I am notoriously level-headed, composed, and oh-so sensible.

Levelheaded, composed, and sensible, huh?

I did my best to ignore the mocking voice inside my head. The one that sounded a whole bunch like my ex and reminded me that what were clearly assets to me added up to a big ol' *b-o-r-i-n-g* from his point of view.

And that's when it hit.

And that's when I groaned.

It was the first sound any of us had made, and in the deathlike silence, my groan reverberated through the shop like a voice from the grave.

So not a pretty simile considering the situation.

Rather than think about it, I looked from Giant #1 to Giant #2.

"Come on, guys," I said, and reminding myself of the above-mentioned assets, I skirted the edges of whiny. But just barely. "I know what this is about. It's Kaz, isn't it? Damn the man! He owes somebody money. Again. But here's the thing, see — we're not married anymore. Get it? I divorced the turkey almost a year ago. Which means I'm no longer responsible for his gambling debts. So if you came here expecting me to make good on his bad luck, it's not going to happen. And if you think you're going to find something valuable here that you can take and pawn, you're wasting your time."

Oh, yes, this last bit was a big, fat lie, but then, I was counting on the fact that goons in black ski masks don't know that much

9

about antique and collectible buttons. Besides, desperate times, desperate measures, and all that.

"I sell buttons," I pointed out, and I downplayed the whole antique and collectible aspect by adding, "Nothing but old buttons. There's not one thing here that's worth very much, and —"

"Shut up!" The guy behind me shuffled closer, and just that fast, my false bravado melted like a dollop of whipped cream floating in a hot cup of latte. My eyes were finally adjusting to the play of light and shadow, and I looked up just in time to see Giant #1 look down at me. There was nothing about this man that wasn't sinister, from the shoulders bigger than the antique rosewood writing desk at the back of the shop to the long and jagged scar I could see just at the place where the ski mask ended and his shirt collar began. Against the black ski mask, his eyes were sunken and menacing. "Cooperate," he growled, with a sort of Arnold Schwarzenegger accent I knew was phony. And no less terrifying because of it. "Cooperate, and nobody will get hurt."

He didn't need to elaborate. When he said *nobody*, he wasn't talking about himself or his friend.

"Nobody needs to get hurt. Not ever!"

Oh yeah, that was me, all right, teetering on the edge of panic and sounding like I'd stepped straight out of some can't-we-all-get-along protest march. I darted a look around the shop. When I left there Saturday afternoon, the place was pristine. The oak floor had been swept, the display cases gleamed, and the entire place had the clean, comfy scent of lemon furniture polish. I loved my shop, all twelve hundred square feet of it, with its antique tin ceiling and the sagey-green colored walls. I loved it so much that over the last weeks before I officially opened my door to business, I'd meticulously cataloged every one of the nearly one hundred thousand buttons in my collection and tucked them away in the old library-card-catalog file cabinets along the wall to my left. Now, the trickle of light from out on the street glinted against metal buttons and glass buttons and jeweled buttons.

Drawer after drawer of them, removed from the cabinets, dumped on the glass-topped display cases over on my right.

And on the two wingback chairs in front of my desk.

And on the floor.

Just like that, my fear was forgotten, and the button-collecting, order-loving, chaos-avoiding side of me kicked in. So did the

11

memory of how much effort it had taken to get all those buttons moved from my apartment here to the shop and how many hours I'd spent getting everything organized and looking just so.

"Damn! Do you have any idea how long it took me to put those buttons away? You can't just toss them around. Old, remember, I said they were old. Which doesn't mean they're worth anything," I added, reinforcing my earlier assertion that there wasn't anything there worth stealing. "But buttons are little pieces of art, you know. And little chunks of history. They have to be treated carefully. Bad enough I've got to deal with Brina all day long. The girl doesn't know a glass button from a gumball. And now I've got this mess to clean up, too? And today! Today of all days! What gives you the right to —"

"Is there some part of *shut up* you don't understand?" This came from Giant #2, the same guy who'd told me to keep quiet in the first place. He came up behind me so fast, I didn't have a chance to try and get out of his way. Once his arm went around my throat, I couldn't have moved if I wanted to. His grip was iron. He yanked me back against a body that felt as if it was made out of poured concrete.

"I said keep quiet." The touch of his breath against my ear turned my knees to rubber — and not in the good way that kind of thing happened back in the day when Kaz whispered sweet nothin's and I turned ·into a puddle of mush. This man's breath was damp and as chilling as a touch of fog. It smelled like a food I couldn't identify, and that, mingled with the earthy scent of his black leather jacket, sent shock waves through me.

He took advantage of my helplessness to ratchet up my fear, tightening his hold. "You put up a fight and you're dead," he growled, and I guess the way he was holding me, he could feel my feeble attempt at sucking in a breath to inflate my lungs, because he made sure to add, "You scream, and I'm going to snap your little body in half so fast, you won't know what hit you."

Oh yeah, right about this time, I was so freakin' scared, my mind started playing tricks on me. That was the only thing that would explain why I almost thanked him for the "little body" compliment. I mean, it was only natural considering I am a middle-sized, average-looking woman of thirty-three who had been known to be called *cute* but is not, on anybody's size chart, what might be termed *little*.

I dragged myself out of these crazy thoughts and tried to talk myself — and these two goons — down.

"Not going to scream," I swore. "If you guys want some help carrying buttons out to the car —"

"Buttons!" The guy who had ahold of me snorted the word and said to his friend, "You take care of everything you were supposed to?"

Giant #1 shook his head, not like he was disagreeing, but more like he couldn't believe his fellow burglar had the nerve to ask. "You wanna tell me how I'm supposed to know?" Had he been a little less civilized, I'm pretty sure he would have emphasized his point by spitting on my newly refinished hardwood floor. His hands out at his sides, he pivoted to look around the shop. "There's so much crap here —"

"Watch it, buddy." I squirmed, because squirming wasn't screaming, and all I had agreed to do was not scream. I had also not agreed to stand by and listen to my life's work disparaged by some creep who had to hide behind a ski mask. "Those are my buttons you're talking about. And my buttons are not crap. In fact, they are —"

Apparently, listening to me was not high on the to-do list of the guy who had ahold

14

of me. At the end of his rope, he lifted me off the floor and shook me. Not such a good thing considering that my head snapped back and forth, and the world skipped and wobbled before my eyes. But, as it turned out, all was not lost. At the exact moment my toes touched the floor, his grip on my throat eased up.

It's the Boy Scouts who are always prepared, right? Well, I'd obviously never been a Boy Scout. Or a Girl Scout, either, for that matter. But I knew an opportunity when I saw one, and I was as prepared as I would ever be.

The second I slipped just a bit more out of his grasp and my feet hit the floor, I folded like a cheap lawn chair in the close-out aisle. I landed on my knees before Giant #2 realized he'd lost his hold on me, and before he could snatch me up again, I took off as fast as a woman can who's crawling across a floor strewn with buttons.

I didn't yelp or yip, not even when I brought a knee down on a metal button. I didn't complain, either (though I prayed it wasn't one that was too valuable), when I heard a glass button crunch beneath me. All I did was scramble as fast as I could, trusting that the dark would cover my moves and that I knew the shop better than the two burglars ever could.

While they were shuffling around, banging into each other and the display cases as they tried to catch hold of me, I scurried like a sand crab into the back storage room, jumped to my feet, and slammed the door behind me. There was a lock in the doorknob, and I fumbled for it. No easy thing considering my fingers were slick with sweat.

Even once I'd flicked the lock, I knew it was only a matter of moments — and the inconsiderable width of one door — before I was in big trouble again. I raced to the work table, where I'd imagined never doing anything more strenuous than spending endless quiet hours researching, cleaning, and packing buttons for shipment, and it's a good thing I wasn't the kind of little woman the burglar had hinted I was, because I got behind that table and pushed for all I was worth. Once it was against the door, I dared to take a breath and think through my next move.

Light or no lights? In a flash, I decided I'd keep them off to buy some time in case I needed to hide once the burglars burst through the door. Besides, I'd spent plenty of hours in the back room these last weeks since I leased the shop, and I knew the place like the back of my hand. I didn't need the

16

lights to grab the phone.

Goons in ski masks might be pretty brave when it comes to intimidating a lone woman, but apparently, they aren't stupid. They were long gone by the time the cops arrived, and the cops were long gone by the time Brina did me the honor of showing up.

I explained what had happened as best — and as quickly — as I could. Then I laid out my plan. Fortunately, I didn't have to go into the bit about how this was a special day and we had a special client coming in. Brina remembered it all on her own. I knew this the moment I laid eyes on her because she'd added new (and very bright) stripes of red and pink to her inky hair, and she was wearing a black tank and a black mini that — believe it or not — were far more presentable than the holey jeans and rock-band T-shirts she usually wore. The outfit showed to perfection (and oh, how I use that term lightly) the tattooed, multicolored dragon draped over her left shoulder and the blood-red Celtic warrior spike band around her right wrist.

Somehow, even in the face of that much body art, I managed to keep focused. We needed to get the shop cleaned up, I told her. And we needed to do it fast.

"You mean you don't want me to be careful about sorting out the buttons?"

"Not today." I said this as I was scooping up moonglow, paperweight, and Bimini buttons all into one pile. This should have been Brina's first clue that, for once, I was willing to relax my exacting standards when it came to my collection. Moonglow, paperweight, and Bimini buttons are all made of glass, see, but they are all different. In the best of all possible worlds, they'd never get jumbled together.

But then, the best of all possible worlds had lost a little of its luster the moment I stepped through the door and found the Button Box getting burglarized.

"The cops want me to inventory everything so I can tell them what's missing," I explained, my voice a little breathy because I was zooming into the back room with handful after handful of buttons, dropping them (carefully, of course) on the table in there, then coming back into the shop for more. This, obviously, should have been Brina's second clue that it was time to move away from the doorway and get to work. I gave her a look that conveyed exactly that, picked up more buttons, and pointed out, "I can't tell the police what was taken until I figure out exactly what's left."

She thought this over for a minute before her cheeks went pale beneath their coating of purplish blusher. "You mean we're going to have to go through all the buttons?" she squeaked. "Again?"

I would have sympathized

1. if I saw the prospect of spending long hours with my collection as anything less than a blessing

and

2. if I had the time.

Instead, I kept scooping and piling. "Think of this as a chance to do a little continuing education," I told Brina, resisting the urge to add enough sarcasm to make it clear that in Brina's case, *any* education would be a real plus. "You'll have another opportunity to go through the buttons so you can learn how to classify and store them correctly."

"Yeah." She slipped her oversize hobo bag off her shoulder and plopped it on the floor. "That's exactly what I was afraid of."

Maybe it was the shock of my early-morning encounter. Or the fault of the adrenaline still pouring through my body like vodka and Red Bull at a sorority party. Rather than comment on the way she rolled her eyes, I gave Brina a smile and assured her with words that would have certainly brightened my day back when I was her age. "You'll get to learn more about buttons."

Her eyes scrunched and her nose wrinkled; she thought this over and sniffed. No easy thing considering there was a silver stud sticking out of the left side of her nose.

"No way there can be that much to know about buttons," she said, as sure of herself as only a twenty-year-old can be. "They're just buttons, and I've worked here two whole weeks, so I gotta already know everything there is to know about buttons. Shit, Josie, it's just like my grandma said when she told me about this job and made me apply for it. It's not like you know anything about real life; buttons are the only thing you ever talk about!"

This time, Brina's cheeks didn't just get pale; they turned a sickly green. Who would have guessed the kid actually had a conscience? "Sorry," she squeaked. "I didn't mean that the way it sounded."

"And I'm not offended, so don't worry about it." It was a lie. I was the tiniest bit miffed; I just didn't have the luxury of wallowing in my miffedness. "We've got to get moving, Brina. There's a lot to clean up. And it's nearly ten o'clock."

"Oh my gosh!" Brina took a look at the clock on the wall, and her eyes lit like bottle rockets. "She's going to be here soon!"

I didn't need the reminder, but that didn't stop a splurt of excitement from jumping around my insides. I doubled my pace, and finally, Brina joined in. Within fifteen minutes, things looked better. Not perfect. Just better. Another fifteen minutes and I would have been happy. Another thirty and I would have been thrilled. A couple days, a case of Pledge to remove the black dust left behind by the cops and their fingerprinting powder, a couple bottles of Windex to polish things up, and the luxury of having everything finally back in order . . . it wasn't until then that I would be a happy camper.

"What about these . . ." I had just come out of the back room, and I found Brina standing at the table near the front door where I kept a basket of tasteful business cards, a bowl filled with those red-and-white striped mints, and a book for guests to sign. She looked even more confused than usual. "These . . ." She pointed. "These thingies."

"Those *thingies* are buttonhooks," I told her at the same time I thanked whatever lucky stars shone on antique button dealers.

I'd just gotten the hooks in from a collector in St. Louis, and they were old, lovely, and valuable. I was grateful they'd gone unnoticed — and untouched — in the burglary. There were three hooks. The longest featured a silver handle modeled into a gorgeous swan's head with garnet eyes. The other two were less spectacular and less pricey, but that didn't mean I wouldn't be able to find buyers for them. One was made of mahogany, and the other was tortoiseshell with a gold-inlay monogram. "They were used back in Victorian times," I told Brina. "That's when there were lots of buttons on clothing and gloves and shoes. Buttonhooks made it easier and faster to do up all those buttons."

Eventually, the buttonhooks, too, would need to be cataloged and put away. For now, the little table between the door and front display window was as good a place as any for them. I nudged them so they were straight and equally spaced and stooped to retrieve the couple dozen buttons that had rolled under the table.

"No way we're going to be ready on time," I groaned, and as if I needed the reminder, the phone on my desk rang. I was all set to haul myself to my feet and answer it when Brina charged past me. "I'm your assistant,

remember. It's my job to answer the phone."
And she did, with a cheery, "This is the Button Box. Brina, Ms. Giancola's assistant, speaking."

Big points for Brina. She sounded efficient and professional.

For exactly the space of three heartbeats.

Then her jaw dropped and her voice went breathy when she squeaked, "Hugh Weaver? *The* Hugh Weaver? The Hollywood producer who made *For Whom the Trolls Troll?* I just saw the movie last week! Again. I mean, like, I saw it again. I've seen it at least a dozen times. Maybe more. And, of course, I wear a costume like everybody else who goes to see it. I always go as Princess Paula and — what's that? Oh. OK." Her face as red as the stripe of hair above her right ear, she waved me over, handed me the phone, and said in a stage whisper, "It's Hugh Weaver! Oh my God! I saw him on *Entertainment Tonight* last week! I can't believe you actually know him, just like you said you did. When you said you did, I thought —"

I am self-aware enough to be certain I was better off not knowing exactly what Brina thought of me. Before she could elucidate, I took the phone. "Hey, Hugh." I tried not to sound too anxious even though I was juggling a handful of buttons — and I knew what he was calling about. "What's up?"

"The sun, the moon, and the stars! Like the ones in your eyes!" Hugh hadn't changed from the fast-talking guy who sat next to me in every college theater class I'd ever taken. "Kate's on her way," he said, cutting to the chase.

I handed the buttons to Brina and with a shooing sort of wave, instructed her to pick up the pace and whatever other buttons she could find.

"We've finished shooting for the morning, and she's not in any of the scenes we're working on this afternoon. She just got in the limo. You ready for her, Josie?"

Yes, of course I could have told him about the burglary and admitted that this was a very bad time. Sure, I could have begged him to use his influence to get the appointment rescheduled. But I wasn't willing to take the chance.

Not when the client who was headed in to see me was going to solidify my reputation as the country's premier dealer in antique buttons.

Maybe I had learned something from Kaz, after all. I mean something more than just how I was never, ever again going to trust a single word that came out of a man's mouth. I assured Hugh that all was well, lying like the pro Kaz was at the same time I fished the bits and pieces of a crushed glass calico button out from a tiny crack between two of the oak floorboards.

"You're not going to let me down about this, are you, baby girl?"

I hated when Hugh called me that. "Hey, I did the costumes for *Trolls,* didn't I? And you've come to me how many times since then for buttons for the costumes in your other movies?" I asked him all this on my way over to the garbage can to get rid of the calico. On the way back, I reminded him, "And Kate Franciscus . . . Thanks to your recommendation, she's already ordered buttons from me, too. Buttons to match those outlandish stainless-steel stilettoes of hers. And buttons to replace the ones that were missing on that vintage fur coat she found in Budapest and couldn't live without. Even buttons that matched the exact color and markings on her dog. Come on, Hugh, you think I can't handle this?"

On the other end of the phone, Hugh grunted. "Don't get me wrong, honey. I know you're reliable. Always have been, always will be. Good ol' Josie Giancola, reliable, dependable, predictable."

He made me sound like a cocker spaniel. I might have been offended if I didn't re-

25

alize the three trays of buttons I'd laid out over the weekend to show Kate first were upended on my desk. I flipped the trays over and hurried to retrieve each glorious antique button I'd chosen to show her just as Hugh was saying, "You've always dealt with Kate's assistant, never with la grande dame herself. You don't know what you're getting into. Kate Franciscus in person is nothing like Kate Franciscus in the movies."

I was pretty sure I realized that, and pretty sure Hugh should have realized I realized it. Before I could point it out, he went right on. "Margot will have the '66 Dom with her in an ice bucket, and believe me, Kate is going to want a glass of that champagne the moment she steps into your store. Margot has the crystal flute, too, so don't worry about that. Or the raspberries. Hell, I hope Margot remembered the raspberries! I don't suppose you could just run out and —"

"No." I couldn't be any clearer, so I didn't even try. "We'll get by," I assured Hugh.

"God, I hope so." I imagined him with his hands folded in supplication and discarded the thought as soon as it formed. Hugh is not the praying type. "It's hot out today. You've got air-conditioning, right? You said your shop was new, and —"

"Earth to Hugh!" I used the old catch-phrase I'd had to pull out so many times in college when Hugh the artiste got carried away by whatever new ideas filled his head. "This is Josie you're dealing with. And Josie is —"

"Reliable, dependable, predictable."

I resisted the urge to bark. As for being predictable . . .

I was grateful he couldn't see the chaos that was my workspace. "She's coming to buy buttons from me, Hugh. Buttons, I can handle."

"I know you can," he said, but at this point, I was barely paying attention. A few of the buttons I'd selected for Kate had rolled under the glass display case behind my desk, and I bent to pluck them to safety.

"These aren't just regular buttons, remember," Hugh said, ignoring the grunt I made when I braced a hand against the display case and pulled myself to my feet again. "They're buttons for Kate's —"

"Wedding gown. Yes, I know. Everyone knows. Every time I turn on the TV or open a newspaper, I see stories about her and that king she's marrying."

"He's a prince." Hugh wasn't impressed. "Prince Roland of Ruritania. Blowhard billionaire playboy. Kate is absolutely going bonkers planning this wedding. Why do you think she insists on choosing her own buttons? She doesn't trust her designers to do it. Or her assistants. Or anybody else. There hasn't been this much hype about a Hollywood wedding since Princess Grace sailed off to Monaco."

"And had Princess Grace wanted antique buttons for her wedding gown and had I been around back in the fifties, I could have handled that, too." I caught sight of more buttons under my desk, and there was no way I was going to let them stay there. "Relax, Hugh," I told him by way of saying I had to go. "I've got everything under control."

I actually might have believed the fib myself if at that moment I didn't see a shadow outside the front window. Long, dark, sleek. Either Shamu had decided to make an appearance on the streets of Chicago or a limo had just pulled to a stop in front of the shop.

The blood drained out of my face. A rumba rhythm started up inside my ribs.

Kate Franciscus was here.

Sure, my day had started out as bad as any day can. But things were about to change. Thanks to a Hollywood starlet with a load of glamour, a bigger-than-life personality, and the chops to have the paparazzi

28

following at her heels, my reputation as one of the country's leading purveyors of antique buttons was about to morph into the stuff of legends.

CHAPTER TWO

Buttons still littered the place like snow-flakes.

The gorgeous antiques I'd selected to show Kate Franciscus were still in a jumble on my desk.

My chestnut brown curls were hanging in my eyes; my twinset was up around my hips.

And now, it was too late!

Gulping down a breath to calm myself, I brushed my hair and tugged my twinset. Tugged my hair and brushed my twinset.

In honor of the occasion, I'd worn Grandma Roba's pearls, and what with all the lifting, bending, and retrieving I'd been up to — not to mention the escaping from bad guys — they were twisted as tight around my neck as Giant #2's iron grip had been.

Rather than chance thinking about the burglary and risking a full-fledged case of the screaming meemies, I reminded myself that it was time to start acting like the totally together businesswoman I am.

Tell that to the cha-cha-cha going on inside my chest.

I held my breath, the better to quiet the crazy rhythm. While I was at it, I pulled back my shoulders and waited for the biggest star in Hollywood to walk into the Button Box.

But instead of Kate Franciscus, a young woman stuck her head into the shop.

"Are you Josie?" She looked at Brina when she said this, and I was pretty sure if Brina had said *yes,* the girl would have run screeching down the sidewalk, so I took pity on her and stepped forward. When I stomped on a button, I acted like it was no big deal, bent to pick it up, and said, "I'm Josie."

"I'm Wynona. Wynona Redfern." The girl took a tentative step inside, and if she noticed the chaos, she didn't let on. But then, she was too busy looking terrified. She was about Brina's age, a short, rectangular kid with strawberry-blonde hair, a square jaw, and a flat chest. Her voice wasn't much more than a whisper. "I'm Blake's assistant."

Button in hand, I gave her a probing look. "And Blake is . . ."

Wynona's face flushed with color. "I'm so

sorry, ma'am." She clutched her hands together at the waist of a suit coat that didn't quite match her black skirt. "It's my first week on the job, and I'm trying so hard to keep everything straight, but there's so much to remember, and Miss Franciscus, she isn't all that easy to deal with like what I thought she'd be and . . ." Wynona gulped. So not a pretty sound, but then, Wynona wasn't a pretty girl. "Blake is Sloan's assistant," she said. "And Sloan is Margot's assistant."

"And Margot is Kate Franciscus's assistant." Suddenly, it all made sense. In a weird, Hollywood sort of way.

Wynona was grateful I'd caught on so quickly. Her expression cleared, and her grin revealed teeth that didn't fit her mouth. They were toppled against each other like tombstones in an abandoned graveyard. "I'm supposed to make sure that everything's ready." Most of Wynona's pink lipstick had already been chewed off. She gnawed at the rest of it. "I'm new and all, but I already know, Miss Franciscus . . . She likes everything to be ready."

"Oh, we're ready, all right!" Brina scooted up from behind me, as hopped up as a Mexican jumping bean on a hot sidewalk. "You can tell Miss Franciscus that everything here at the Button Box is shipshape. A-one. Top-notch. Ready as ready can be!" Brina swept out an arm to demonstrate.

Too bad she didn't look where she was waving. At the same time Wynona stuck her head outside to tell Blake (or was it Sloan?) that it was OK for Miss Franciscus to get out of the limo, Brina knocked against the buttons — those glorious, antique, expensive buttons — that I'd just picked up off the floor.

They went flying.

So did I.

Eager to make a good first impression, I got right to work gathering up those beautiful buttons, and to give her her due, Brina was right there with me, though what with all the muttering and apologizing, she was more of a hindrance than a help. No matter. I was on a mission, and so intent, I hardly even noticed the commotion when it started up outside on the sidewalk.

That is, until my robin's-egg-blue shop door popped open and Kate Franciscus arrived with a flourish and in a cloud of expensive perfume.

She found me on my hands and knees, searching for the buttons with my butt sticking out from under my desk.

Embarrassing?

It might have been.

If anyone was paying the least bit of attention to me.

The way it was, the world stopped spinning and time stood still. Kate Franciscus, even more gorgeous in person than she was on the silver screen, was suddenly the bright sun in a universe that included nothing more significant than the rest of us — dull, colorless planets whose very existence had no point except to orbit around her.

Yes, she was that impressive. And I was that obligated to stop acting less like a starstruck groupie and more like the recognized button expert I am. In fact, I'm pretty convinced I would have recovered sooner and gotten everything under control if I could see straight. The way it was, in the second between when the shop door opened and Kate swept in, a couple dozen camera flashes exploded from the phalanx of paparazzi out on the sidewalk, and I was blinded. I blinked against the fireworks that popped behind my eyes and, disoriented, sat up and banged my head into my desk.

Heedless of the sound of skull hitting wood, Kate kept smiling and waving to the photographers, who kept snapping picture after picture.

Kate's assistants kept scurrying. Between

shots, Margot set a silver ice bucket with a bottle of champagne in it on my desk. Sloan adjusted the azure and amber silk scarf around Kate's neck, which looked spectacular with her Tabasco-colored silk shantung suit. Blake plastered herself against the library card files to keep out of the pictures, and little Wynona wrung her hands and looked as if she was about to burst into tears. Brina, it should be noted, had been struck dumb (it wasn't much of a stretch) the moment our guest of honor arrived. She pulled herself to her feet and stood there wide-eyed, openmouthed, and completely in awe at being in the presence of the woman the media didn't need a surname to talk about. They simply called her Kate the Great.

"You are really too kind. All of you." Kate's voice was husky and as seductive as the little wave she threw at the photographers. Her smile was sleek and gracious; her teeth were even and as blindingly white as the pyrotechnics still twinkling in my eyes.

"One more picture, Miss Franciscus," one of the paparazzi shouted, and as stunningly beautiful as a Greek goddess, she lifted her chin and posed, ever gracious.

That is, until Margot signaled Sloan, who

nudged Blake, who told Wynona in no uncertain terms that enough was enough, and it was time to close the door.

Wynona snapped to and did as instructed, and as soon as the door clicked shut, Kate turned away from the front display window and the reporters who had their noses pressed there. Her shoulders fell, along with her smile.

She slid off her sunglasses and tucked them into a leather purse I had no doubt cost more than my monthly rent — on both the shop and my apartment. Combined. Without even looking her way, she thrust the bag at Margot, who took it out of her hands and, without looking, passed it on to Sloan. This was, apparently, where this buck stopped, because Sloan backed against those old library catalog files, wrapped her arms around the purse, and held on tight.

I watched all this through eyes that were slowly returning to normal, blinked, and figured it was time to make my move. I got to my feet, and it wasn't until I stuck out my right hand by way of introduction that I remembered I had a fistful of buttons in it. I transferred them to my left, and gave it another try. "Miss Franciscus, it's so nice to finally meet you in person. I'm Josie Giancola. I'm glad you could —"

My greeting dissolved beneath a look that could have paralyzed multitudes. Kate Franciscus had ebony hair and porcelain skin. She was taller than me, and she was wearing shoes that added four inches to her already impressive height. Somewhere, an alligator was mourning the loss of a fallen comrade. Kate was no bigger around than a thread of angel-hair pasta, and when she looked me over, one perfectly shaped eyebrow lifted ever so slightly. Without glancing at Margot or any of her other anxious minions, she snapped her fingers. "Where the hell is my champagne?"

Margot flinched and jumped into action. She retrieved a crystal flute from her own leather tote, and a container of fresh raspberries. I swear, the dew was still on them. Margot looked to Blake to fetch the champagne, but poor little Wynona was as nervous as a cat in a room full of rocking chairs and too antsy to keep still. Eager to please, she raced to the silver ice bucket on my desk, scooped up the Dom, and thrust the bottle into Kate's hands.

A collective gasp went up from the assistants, and at the same time that Margot plucked the cold, wet bottle out of Kate's hands, she gave me a pleading look and mouthed the words, "Linen towel."

I didn't have one, but no worries; there was a roll of Bounty nearby. I'd been using the paper towels to wipe up the fingerprinting powder, the better to keep it from spreading to my inventory. I set down the buttons I was holding, ripped off a paper towel, and handed one to Kate, whose look told me she wasn't quite sure what so common a thing might be. She was, though, game, and she touched it to her damp hands, tossed the paper towel at Margot, and swiveled a look at Wynona. It would have knocked the kid dead if not for the fact that Wynona was so embarrassed, she refused to meet Kate's eyes.

"Who are you?" Kate asked.

Wynona was on the spot and she knew it.

And I was hostess of this little party. I reminded myself that one of the jobs of a hostess is to smooth muddles and ruffled feathers, so I stepped forward. "This is Wynona Redfern, Miss Franciscus," I explained. "She's your new assistant."

Apparently, I do not have as trusting of a face as I always thought. Kate swung toward Margot. "Where's the other one? That Shannon girl?"

"Shawna." Margot corrected her, but in a way that made it clear it wasn't important anyway. "Shawna took suddenly ill, and

Wynona came along right in time." She tried for a smile that matched the enthusiasm of her voice. It didn't work. Margot, ever penitent, cast down her eyes. "I'll have a talk with Sloan."

"And I'll have a talk with Blake," Sloan chirped from her perch by the wall.

"And you can be sure I'll have a talk with Wynona," Blake snapped.

"And now that that's all taken care of, we can all talk about buttons!"

Was that me sounding like a cheerleader? It's so not my style, but for the second time in a day that was already feeling too long, I had no choice but to scramble and punt.

I motioned toward the wing chairs near my desk, but it was clear that Kate didn't make a move unless it was her idea. She held out a hand, and as if by magic, Margot had a raspberry in a flute and the champagne, too. She handed it to Kate, who took an appreciative sip. It wasn't until she swallowed that she looked my way. "Well, what are you waiting for?" she demanded. "I don't have all day. Let's get down to business."

Stan Marzcak, who lives across the hall from me, has a hairline that receded long ago; a long, thin nose; and a faraway look in his rheumy blue eyes that people who don't know him mistake for senility. If they paid attention, they would realize that though Stan is old enough to be retired from the Chicago Police Department, he's nobody's stereotype of a little old man.

And nobody's fool.

Sure, Stan always looks like his mind is wandering. Because it is. Usually straight to the heart of a problem.

He proved it once again when he stopped by for coffee the next morning and completely ignored the subject of Kate the Great. I was grateful, and that was no big surprise. My other neighbors had peppered me from the time I walked into my apartment building to the time I went to bed with the usual who, what, when, and what was she wearing questions.

Stan? Not so much. He got right down to business.

"Here's what's got me baffled." He drummed his fingers against my kitchen table, trying to work through the problem. "Why would a couple burglars bother with a place like yours?"

He didn't apologize for what sounded almost like an insult.

He didn't need to.

I knew exactly what Stan was getting at.

But then, I'd spent all night thinking the same thing. That is, when I wasn't tossing and turning my way through dreams about a giant in a black leather jacket who was sipping a glass of champagne while he did a flamenco dance atop my button inventory.

"What you're saying is that there are plenty of other shops in the neighborhood, and any self-respecting burglar would find any one of them more appealing," I said, and Stan nodded. There was nothing he appreciated more than logic. Except maybe the fact that I was easy to beat at the monthly poker games he hosted.

My finger drumming echoed his. "There are a few doctor's offices down the street," I said.

"And doctors always have drugs."

"And there's a jeweler two stores down from me."

"Jewelry." Stan was on his way over to his weekly senior softball game. He sat back and crossed his arms over his gray uniform shirt. "Jewelry is easy to carry and easy to pawn. No offense, kiddo, but I don't know a hock shop in the city that would give you fifty cents for a boatload of buttons."

This, too, was something I'd considered in the hours between flamenco dreams when I couldn't sleep.

"It doesn't make sense," I said.

Understatement.

Stan was nice enough not to point it out.

"So the cops who came to check things out . . . Who did you say they were?"

I'd already told Stan the story, but I wasn't surprised he asked again. Stan is an all-ducks-in-a-row kind of guy. "Gonzalez," I said. "And Morzowski. And the guy who dusted for fingerprints was —"

"Don't know them anymore." Stan waved away the fact as inconsequential. "Brand-spanking-new college graduates who watch too many cop shows on TV and think that's what it's really like to be on the job. Gonzalez, though, I remember him. Good man. Talks too much, but he's got a head on his shoulders. And he said —"

I shrugged. "What you said. That he couldn't imagine why any burglar would bother with buttons." There was one theory that had occurred to me in the wee small hours of the morning, and truth be told, I was rooting for it to be true. If it was, it would mean I had nothing to worry about when it came to running into not-so-jolly giants again.

Which means I'd look like a total doofus if anyone found out I'd pushed my couch against my front door as soon as I'd returned to my apartment the evening of the break-in.

I ran my idea up the flagpole for Stan to consider.

"Unless those two goons were in the wrong place?"

"Possible."

I breathed a sigh of relief.

"But not likely."

My stomach instantly retied itself into a couple dozen knots.

"From what you said, they weren't punks," Stan pointed out, working through his reasoning when he saw that I wasn't able — or willing — to do it myself. "Punks would have taken one look around your place, seen there was nothing there worth stealing, and gotten the hell out of Dodge. I mean, it's pretty obvious that all you've got in that store of yours is buttons, buttons, and more buttons. Or maybe they would have at least grabbed something. Your computer, maybe. Something so that breaking into your place wasn't a complete waste of time. These guys stuck around. And like you said, they trashed your shop and they assaulted you. You're not going to know exactly what's missing until you start sorting those buttons of yours, but whether they made off with some or not, the question is why? What were they doing there in the first place?"

It was the same question that had been pounding through my head for twenty-four hours.

Fortunately, I got a reprieve from all that thumping when I heard my newspaper hit the front door. I went to get it, not so much because I cared what was happening in Chicagoland that morning, but because the familiar action of walking to the front door, opening it, and finding that, as it always did, my paper had bounced halfway between my apartment and Adele Cruikshank's next door was soothing and ordinary.

Something the last twenty-four hours definitely had not been.

On my way back to the kitchen, I glanced over the front page, confirming to myself that there wasn't much of anything new in the world that I wanted to know more about, and opened the paper to page two.

"Hey!" A smile cracked the solemn expression I'd been wearing, and I tipped the paper toward Stan so he could see the photo of Kate Franciscus in all her glory there at the top of the page. "Take a look at the headline. *Kate the Great Visits Local Button Emporium.* Cool! I couldn't pay for advertising like that."

"Congrats." Stan drained his cup of coffee. I knew he wouldn't say yes to a second one, so I didn't bother to offer. He plucked the newspaper out of my hands, looked at the photo, and whistled low under his breath. "I'd say she looks like a million bucks, only my guess is that a million isn't nearly enough. She's some hot number, huh?"

"They don't come hotter." I picked up Stan's coffee mug and took it over to the sink along with my own. "And . . ." Since we'd been focused on the burglary and the subject of Kate hadn't come up, Stan didn't know this part of the story. "She's coming back. Tomorrow evening after the movie is done shooting for the day. She was really taken with a few of the antique porcelain studs I showed her." I rinsed the coffee mugs, smiling all the while. But then, thinking about buttons always brought out the best in me. "And those jewel buttons I got in a couple months ago," I added. "You remember, the openwork metal with the faceted center stone surrounded by three diamonds."

Stan didn't remember. Or maybe he did and he was so enthralled with the photo of Kate in the paper, he just wasn't paying attention. His eyes were glued to the picture, and honestly, I guess I couldn't blame him.

Kate was a striking woman. A striking woman who also happened to be the biggest mover and shaker in Hollywood.

I pretended not to be offended that he'd rather look at Kate the Great than listen to me ramble, and just to prove it, I kept right on rambling. "I encouraged her to look at a few old carved ivory buttons, too. At least the ones I could find. She took thirty-six different buttons with her to look at and consider. You know, so the designer she's flying in from Paris can look them over, too."

"Uh-huh. Yeah. Sure." Stan's mind was still a million miles away.

I guess I couldn't blame him. He was a man, after all, and I mean, what woman on the face of the earth could even begin to compete with Kate the Great? It was small-minded of me to be offended. Which didn't mean I didn't deserve a little revenge.

"I think when she comes back, I'll show her some of the other buttons I keep in that treasure chest I have buried in the back courtyard between my building and the ones on the next street," I said, as innocent as can be even though I was pulling Stan's chain. "You know, right near that outdoor pen where I keep the elephants. And that herd of dinosaurs I found roaming in Lin-

46

coln Park and brought to the shop with me."

"Anything you say, kiddo." Stan closed the newspaper, folded it, and tucked it under his arm. He popped out of his chair faster than any man his age should have been able to. "I've got to get going, Josie. See you later. Bye."

He made it to my front door in record time, and call me crazy, but something told me all this dodging and scrambling was more than simply a sudden case of Kate Franciscus appreciation.

I stepped into his path to keep him from getting away, and looked from Stan to that newspaper tucked securely under his arm.

Securely being the operative word.

I am not the suspicious type. At least I never had been until Kaz gave me so much to be suspicious of. Now, my suspicion radar triggered, I motioned for the newspaper.

"Hand it over," I said, and even though Stan gave me a vacant look designed to make me think he was as innocent as the driven snow, I knew he knew what I was talking about; he tightened his grip on the paper.

"I'm going to be late for my softball game. See you later, Josie."

I let him get past me. All the better to slide

the newspaper out from under his arm. "What's the deal?" I asked at the same time I flipped back to Kate's picture.

Stan made a move to snatch the newspaper out of my hands. "You don't want to see that."

"Oh, yes I do."

Note to self: a thirty-three-year-old woman in her flannel sleep pants, her Chicago Bears T-shirt, and her Crocs can move faster than a seventysomething guy. Over near the window and far enough from Stan so that I didn't have to worry he'd grab the newspaper back from me, I took a closer look at the photograph and saw what Stan had seen. What I hadn't had a chance to see the first time I looked at the picture.

Pikestaffed, I stood there with my eyes wide and my mouth open. Oh yeah, I looked like a Lake Michigan carp, all right, and at that point, I didn't even care.

Because the only thing I could do was stare.

At Kate in the center of the picture, the light catching the highlights in her hair and accenting the sparkle of her smile.

And at me, over in the corner.

With my head under my desk.

And my butt sticking out.

Stan came up behind me and put a reassuring hand on my shoulder. "Hey, kiddo, sure, a million or more people are going to see that picture this morning. But look at the bright side. At least you've got a nice butt!"

CHAPTER THREE

Sometimes, Mitchell Kazlowski still shows up in my dreams.

Though there are certain . . . er . . . benefits that can result from the situation (like the night I had that vivid dream about how we were back in Barbados on our honeymoon . . . in that cute little hotel with the ocean view . . . in that darling little tropical-colored suite . . . in that big ol' bed we hardly ever left except when we needed food, rum drinks, or the night we dared a little sex on the beach), this is not necessarily good news.

Having warm and fuzzy thoughts about Kaz is like dealing with a not-so-reputable collector for an entire too-good-to-be-true-priced box of buttons.

Sure, there are some tantalizing things at the top. But as I learned back when I first got into the button business, when I dug deeper, I found out I'd been sold a bill of goods.

Just like with Kaz.

I admit, over the years, he'd made my heart dance around plenty.

Mostly, it was just from annoyance.

I hung onto the thought and reminded myself I could no way, no how let go of it (at least not without completely losing both my self-respect and my mind) when I rounded the corner on North Wells Street the next evening and caught sight of Kaz coming the other way.

Oh yeah, my heart started dancing, all right.

Damned heart.

Didn't it know I didn't have time to tango? I had just run out to pick up a turkey sandwich and was on my way back to the shop for my follow-up appointment with Kate Franciscus. I didn't need to get distracted.

And there is no distraction quite like Kaz.

"Hey, Jo!" He closed in on me fast, but then, that's the way Kaz does everything. Well, almost everything. There was that sweet little room in Barbados, and —

I batted the thought as far away as it was possible for it to get. Not so easy because before I knew it, Kaz was two feet from me, a smile in his brown eyes and his face lit with the sizzling grin that had been known to make even the most levelheaded button diva forget herself.

"I just stopped by your store," he said, tilting his head back the way he'd come. "Some girl was there. She said she didn't know when you were coming back."

"Brina." I supplied the name, not so much because it mattered that Kaz knew, but because when he was standing there looking me over and I caught a whiff of the aftershave I used to buy him every Christmas simply because it magically seeped into my brain and made me nuts from wanting him, I knew it was wiser for me to concentrate on work than on Kaz.

Kaz in nicely worn, butt-hugging jeans.

And a dusky blue shirt, open at the collar, the sleeves rolled up above his elbows.

I forced myself to watch a passing bus, the better to keep my mind on other things, and said, "Brina is my assistant. I left her in charge." I lifted the white carryout bag in my right hand. "While I went out to grab some dinner."

It was all I was willing to say. In fact, as soon as I got back to the Button Box, I was going to send Brina home. It was only five-thirty, and Kate wasn't scheduled to arrive for this evening's appointment until eight, but I wasn't taking any chances. When Kate made this appointment, she'd insisted we meet alone. None of her assistants, and no sign of mine. Apparently, after looking over my buttons, she was ready to make her choice, and like everything else about her royal wedding, she wanted this detail to be a surprise. For everybody.

"An assistant, huh? You've come up in the world." I didn't have to look at Kaz. I could hear the amusement coloring his words. "She sure doesn't look like an assistant. She doesn't even look like your typical button nerd." He didn't bother saying he was sorry for the slam. But then, Kaz never does. In the long line of things that had pushed me over the edge from Mrs. to ex, it was the one that still grated the most. "She looks like she should be working at some biker bar."

"She's Adele Cruikshank's granddaughter." Kaz didn't need to know that Adele had begged and I had given in. Kaz already knew I gave in far too often. It was the only thing that could possibly explain why we'd stayed married for three years.

As for what had finally forced us apart . . .

It wasn't much of a mental leap for me to remember the two goons in my shop. Or

53

that just about the first thing I'd thought of when I ran into them (after the whole terror/panic/scared-senseless thing) was Kaz.

The thought threw ice water on the heat that had been building since I set eyes on him. When I looked Kaz up and down, I'm surprised goose bumps didn't blossom on his arms.

"Who are you in trouble with now?" I asked him.

Kaz has a way of stepping back, throwing up his hands, and proclaiming his innocence. It's a great act. Too bad I'd seen it so many times, I know it means he's as guilty as hell. He did it now, and when I didn't immediately cave, he looked genuinely disappointed.

"Come on, Jo." He poked his hands into his pockets and rocked back on his heels. "You know me better than that."

"Yes, I do."

One heartbeat.

Two.

When you're married to a man like Kaz, you learn how to work a punch line.

"That's why I'm asking."

There was no point in waiting for him to tell me I was wrong. Of course, that's exactly what he was going to do. Of course, he'd be lying through his teeth. I started walking. It was the un-subtlest way I could think to show Kaz we had nothing to say to each other. Not anymore.

He tagged along. Just like I was afraid he would.

"You think I'm here to ask for money, don't you?"

I didn't even bother to give him so much as a sidelong look. But then, I could afford to act like I wasn't concerned. For one thing, because I wasn't. For another, it was exactly what I expected him to say. "I think somebody you owe money to is looking for money," I said. "And since they didn't find any in the Button Box the other night —"

"What the frig!" He clapped a hand on my arm and stopped me so fast that, before I knew it, we were toe-to-toe. Kaz is a heavy-equipment operator at the Port of Chicago, and he looks the part. Wide shoulders. Slim hips. Abs that won't quit and biceps that owe their definition not to some fancy equipment at some fancy gym, but to long days of hard work.

That is, when he isn't dodging that hard work so he can place his next bet.

He cocked his head to give me a probing look. When I saw a wave of concern cloud his expression and actually thought it might be genuine, I gave myself a mental slap. "You mean somebody broke into your shop?"

"Come on, Kaz." I ripped my arm out of his grasp. It was that or fall into the trap of remembering how good it felt to be skin to skin. Believe me, this wasn't the time or the place for that. Or the century. Or the universe. "You're telling me you're not into somebody for big bucks?"

"That's not what we were talking about. We were talking about somebody breaking into your store. How much did they take?"

"How much did they need to take to cover your losses?"

He flinched, and honestly, I might have fallen for the whole wounded-animal look if I hadn't seen it . . . oh . . . about a million times before. My exasperated sigh pretty much said it all, but just in case he wasn't into nuances, I spelled it out for him. "I don't know what they took. Not yet. I'm putting my inventory back in order and I worked on it all day today and I'm tired and I've got an appointment I have to keep so maybe I'll just see you around some-time."

Nuances aren't Kaz's thing. Neither is the oh-so-obvious. When I started up again, he didn't get the message; he was right at my

56

side. "I had nothing to do with any burglary, Jo. I swear."

Honest to Pete, I wished I could believe him.

And I knew if I did, I'd only be proving that I never learned my lesson. This time, I did look at him, out of the corner of my eye. "You didn't answer my question. I asked if you were into somebody for big bucks. Then again, I don't suppose I need an answer. Why else would you stop to see me? It's always all about the money, isn't it?"

"Just happened to be in the area." There was that grin again, hotter than the sun in Barbados and just as dangerous to those who were foolish enough to go out without plenty of protection. "Who says I can't stop in to see my favorite button collector?"

"I'm the only button collector you know. You made sure of that because you made sure you kept far, far away from my business."

"Oh, come on. If you're going to start in on me again because I never went to any of those stupid button shows with you —"

"I'm not starting in on you. Not again. Because I never did in the first place. And this has nothing to do with you not going to button shows with me." We were at a cross street, and the light was against us. I'd rather have taken a chance on an encounter with a Yellow Cab than continue our conversation, but traffic was heavy, and though I talk a good game, I'm really not much of a risk taker. Except, of course, when it came to Kaz. "I'm not stupid, Kaz," I pointed out. I shouldn't have had to. "We both know this is the time of the month I get my royalty check."

Oh yeah, he is quite the actor. If I didn't know better, I actually would have believed that fleeting look of surprise. "Royalty?" His eyes lit. "Oh, you mean for that movie you worked on with that Hugh Weaver guy. You're still getting money from that?"

I bit my tongue. After all, we were on a public street and there were children nearby. They didn't need to hear what I was thinking, which was pretty much that Kaz was the lousiest liar I'd ever met. Only the words that pounded around inside my head weren't nearly that nice.

"You know I get a check every month," I said instead, skirting the whole nuance thing again and laying it on the line. "You know this, Kaz, because back when I got my first few royalty checks, I put all the money in the bank to save it for the down payment on a house. And you withdrew all that money because you knew in your heart of hearts that the Colts were going to beat the Saints in the Super Bowl. Let's see . . ." I tipped my head, thinking. Or maybe one side of my head was just heavy from all the sarcasm I was storing up and ready to let loose. "The way I remember it, you lost all that money and you didn't care. You figured you'd just get more the next month."

"For richer or for poorer!" He was the only one I knew who could make that part of the wedding vows sound like a joke.

The light changed and I crossed the street. It wasn't hard for Kaz to keep up. I am, after all, a short woman with short legs.

"It's just a couple thousand bucks, Jo, and I wouldn't ask at all if it was for me. But I've got this friend, see, this guy down at the port. He's been sick, and he hasn't been able to work. And he's got a wife who's on disability. And kids. Three of them."

Yes, he talked a good game, and I would have been a noble and charitable person had I listened. But I'd heard it all before. Always a sick friend. Or a relative in need. Always a story. Over the years, I'd learned that none of them were ever true. "No," was all I said.

"But that movie you worked on with Hugh Weaver, the one you did the costumes for all those years ago . . . . it's hotter than ever. I saw DVDs in a bookstore the other day and —"

"No. I sunk all the money I could afford into the shop. And I need some money to live on until things finally take off. How else do you think I was able to quit my job at the insurance company?"

"My point exactly!" Kaz's eyes were the color of a cup of double espresso. They packed the same wallop. "You've got enough money to quit your job. And enough to start this crazy business of yours. And thanks to that goofy movie, you'll have more coming in next month."

We were in front of the Button Box, and I stopped and said, "Yes, I will. And you won't be getting any of that, either."

"Ah, come on, Jo." Kaz was brazen enough to skim a finger up my arm.

I was shameless enough to let him.

That is, right before I said no again, and turned to walk into the shop.

"But you're going to be more successful than ever. You know, after this."

I turned around just in time to see him pull a newspaper out of his back pocket. He unfolded it, and I wasn't surprised to see the photo of Kate from the previous day's paper. He waved it back and forth in front of my nose.

"Once word gets out that you're catering to the stars, you're going to be one hot button dealer."

It was my turn to smile. Now that I thought of it, it was the first time I'd bothered since I ran into Kaz. "I'm counting on it," I told him.

"So you'll have more customers than ever, and you'll sell more buttons than ever, and the money will just keep rolling in."

"I'm counting on that, too."

"Which means all that royalty money is just gravy, and here's this guy, this friend of mine, who can hardly afford to put groceries on the table, and it's only a couple thousand lousy bucks, and —"

This time, I didn't even bother to answer, I just groaned.

And I guess Kaz took pity on me, because he gave me a quick peck on the cheek and turned to walk away. Right before he disappeared around the corner, I heard his parting comment. "By the way." He grinned and waved the newspaper. "Nice butt!"

The fact that I was breathing hard had nothing to do with my walk down North Wells. Or the fact that the clock was ticking and Kate was scheduled to arrive in just a

61

couple hours.

It had everything to do with Kaz.

Attraction or repulsion?

I was so busy trying not to think about it so I didn't have to decide that I wasn't paying attention. That would explain why I jumped when I heard a man say, "Hey, you're the button lady."

I turned just in time to see him round the corner of the alley that led between my brownstone and the one next door and back to the common courtyard shared by the nearby buildings. He was middle-aged, average height, and as bald as a baby's backside. He had a camera slung over one shoulder. Just the hint I needed — paparazzi.

He obviously recognized me.

I hoped it wasn't because my butt looked familiar.

"So, she's coming back, huh?" The man had a round face and heavy jowls. There was a single gold stud in his left earlobe. He couldn't possibly have known I was busy rehashing the close encounter of the shake-my-resolve kind with my ex so he assumed I was either being coy or I was offended by his question. Covering his bases, he smiled an apology. "I can understand you don't want to say anything. After all, you don't know me from Adam."

62

"I don't know Adam, either."

He laughed. "Hey, it's like this . . ." He took a couple steps closer. Like it or not — and I didn't like it one bit — I had an automatic and gut-wrenching flashback to the morning of the burglary; I took a couple steps back. He reached into his pocket and handed me a business card. "Mike Homolka," he said, pointing to the name printed on it. "I'm a journalist."

"You're one of the paparazzi."

"You say *tomato;* I say *tomahto.*" He shrugged. "What matters is that I make my living getting the story. Get my drift? And I know you've got a story to tell. I've done my homework, see, and I know you worked with Hugh Weaver on *Trolls.*" He chuckled. "Whoever thought that goofy movie would make Weaver some sort of Hollywood god! And you were the one who did the costumes for that movie, right? From rags to riches! And all because of some cult hit. That makes you grist for the ol' gossip mill. Know what I mean?"

I didn't, but then, Homolka didn't give me time to tell him that. He was as fast-talking as he was loud. And he was plenty loud.

"But hey, I'm not going to hassle you about the whole *Trolls* thing. Not today.

We'll talk about that another time. You know, when things are slower and I'm hard up for a story."

This was supposed to make me feel better?

I had no plans to sit outside and eat my turkey sandwich, but I didn't like the idea of Homolka hanging around outside my shop. Maybe if I headed to the courtyard and sat out there for a while, he'd get bored. And leave.

No such luck.

He followed right along.

"So . . ." One of Homolka's eyebrows slid up his forehead. "What's it like working with Kate the Great? And what did she say about that wedding gown of hers? Did she look at white buttons? Ivory buttons? Or is she going to be less traditional and go with a color?"

When I sat down on one of the park benches the local merchants had donated to our little courtyard oasis and didn't answer, he leaned in closer and lowered his voice, like he was sharing a secret. "Hey, honey, I've got people who are willing to pay for this information. You're a businesswoman. You understand, right? You can't blame me for trying."

"I can't." I opened the bag with my

sandwich in it, took one look inside, and changed my mind. Somehow, being with Homolka had robbed me of my appetite. "But you can't blame someone who has a professional relationship with someone else for refusing to betray a confidence."

"Is that what it is? A confidence? So, she wants you to keep it all hush-hush? Of course she does. That's just like Kate. She knows the more she keeps those luscious lips of hers shut, the more people will talk about what she might be thinking. See, she's a smart businesswoman, too."

I reclosed the bag.

"Kate loves the spotlight," he said. "And oh, how she loves letting us take her picture. But then when any of us tries to get her to talk so we can get our stories straight and make sure we're publishing nothin' but the truth, she clams up like one of them marble statues. Claims it's all about her right to privacy. That's why stuff gets published sometimes that isn't quite . . . well . . . stuff that isn't totally true. But you . . ." Homolka looked me up and down, and I felt a chill. "With your help, I won't have to make anything up, and then my editor won't end up printing a bunch of lies. So you see what I'm getting at here, right? Talk to me, and you'll be doing Kate a favor in the long run.

The truth will get out, and no one will have to speculate."

I knew whatever I said, my words were going to be twisted around and turned into a quote I wouldn't want to see in the papers any more than I wanted to see that photo of my butt again. I stood. But apparently, even a closemouthed button dealer wasn't enough to put off a guy as pushy as Homolka. When I made my way back down the redbrick alley and onto North Wells, he was right behind me.

"You're working late." He tried one last ploy. He'd obviously been on this sort of fishing expedition a couple billion times before, and he knew that according to the law of averages, the normal person would eventually cave.

What he didn't know was that I'm not normal.

Not when it comes to this sort of schmoozing, anyway.

There was Kaz, after all.

"Seems funny that you'd be working late the same week Kate was here to visit. I mean, if she already ordered buttons from you, that sale would be all wrapped up, right? And you wouldn't need to still be hanging around. Unless she's coming back, of course. This evening?"

I was back in front of the Button Box, and I tossed him a look that would have warned a smarter man to back off.

"I'll pay you a thousand dollars if you'll talk to me."

I guess he wasn't one of those smarter men. I froze and turned to stare at Homolka, but only because I was so knocked for a loop by his offer, I needed time to process it. Processing over, I whirled around the other way, anxious to get into the shop, praying he wouldn't be bold enough to follow, and worried about what Kate would say (and do) if she got there and found Mike Homolka lying in wait for her. I couldn't tell him to go away. That would only make him more suspicious. But I hated the thought of Kate getting ambushed.

Torn between appealing to Mike's human side and wondering if *human* and *paparazzi* were oxymorons, I turned one last time when I had my hand on the shop door. He had walked away. He was watching me from in front of the blues club two doors down. The only thing I could do was go into the shop and hope that by the time Kate arrived, it wouldn't look like my problem.

I pushed the door open and stopped dead in my tracks. The bag with my turkey sandwich in it slipped from my hand and hit the floor with a splat.

Too stunned to move a muscle, I stared at the chaos, which reminded me of the chaos of the burglary.

The chaos I'd finally cleaned up and had under control when I left the shop not an hour earlier.

Like the hiccup of a bad dream, there were buttons spilled all over the floor. But this dream contained another grisly component — in the center of all those buttons, there was Kate Franciscus, dressed in skinny leather pants and an emerald green jacket that would have looked spectacular with her coloring — if she wasn't so ashen.

That silver swan-head buttonhook I'd arranged so neatly on my door-side table only a couple days earlier was sticking out of her chest, and blood curlicued down her side and puddled on the hardwood floor.

My breath gurgled on the bile that rose in my throat, and I jumped back onto the sidewalk. But I didn't get the door closed fast enough.

That was why Mike Homolka was able to get a couple dozen photos of Kate's body and a couple dozen more of me, staring in horror and screaming like a banshee.

CHAPTER FOUR

"Good thing Mankowski down at the end of the street remembered me. Otherwise, I never would have been able to get near this place."

I heard Stan's voice just a nanosecond before a Starbucks cup appeared right under my nose. The unmistakable aroma of Caffè Misto streamed out of the little hole on the to-go lid, tickling my senses and coaxing me back to reality.

"Drink." The cup was in my hand before I could respond, and Stan was looking at me over it. "I put plenty of sugar in it. You know, to help with the shock."

Shock.

Now that he put a name to it, what I was feeling made sense: the numbness that coiled in my stomach and made my arms and legs feel as if they were made of lead, my clammy skin, the way my breaths were so fast and so shallow that I wheezed like I had a five-pack-a-day habit.

"Go on; take a sip." Somehow, Stan understood that expecting me to accomplish something even that simple was akin to asking me to leap tall buildings in a single bound. He reached over, popped the lid off the coffee cup, and put a hand under mine to lift it to my mouth. "It will make you feel better, kiddo. I promise."

I wasn't sure anything ever could, but I knew Stan; he wasn't going to let me off the hook. A sip, and I felt some of the tightness in my chest uncurl. Another, and I somehow managed to draw in a long, slow breath.

"There you go." He patted me on the shoulder. "Keep it up and you'll be feeling like yourself in no time."

"Can you promise that, too?" My voice was gravel. We were outside the shop on the park bench near the street, but the door was open, and I looked past Stan to the commotion that was once my tidy button emporium. The last hour or so was pretty much a blur. I sort of remembered jumping back out on the sidewalk, scrambling for my cell phone, and — for the second time in less than a week — dialing 911. I had a vague recollection of Brina and Dr. Levine, the optometrist who occupied the brownstone directly across from me, racing across the street at the sound of my screaming, of the cops arriving, of the questions and the confusion. I had a foggy sort of flashback that included all of us being told to wait outside and stay out of the way.

The memory of Kate's body on the floor of the Button Box, her blood pooling around her — that was as clear as day, and something I would never forget.

I shivered.

Stan draped a Cubs sweatshirt over my shoulders and gruffly explained away the kindness. "I had it in the car. I figured I might as well bring it with me."

"But how . . ." Even my favorite coffee wasn't strong enough to completely order my brain. I took another gulp and shook my head to clear it. "What are you doing here?" I asked Stan. "How did you know?"

"I was watching TV at home, and all the first report said was something about the body of a woman in a shop on North Wells. I knew you were supposed to be here to-night, and I thought about everything that happened on Monday morning, and well, you know . . ." Stan cleared his throat.

"Hey, I'm fine." I grabbed for his hand. "Just a little shaken, that's all."

He kept his poker face firmly in place. "Now, hell . . . As soon as Kate the Great's name was mentioned, the media went into an uproar! It's all over the news." Stan turned and craned his neck, the better to see what was going on in the shop. "I wonder if those bozos in there know what they're doing. I'd hate to see them mess up an investigation this important."

The cops in the shop looked efficient enough to me. But then, before the night of the burglary, the only thing I knew about crimes and investigations was what I'd seen on TV. Now, I watched a couple uniformed officers cordon off the sidewalk outside my shop with yellow tape, while a couple more peered down at Kate's body, taking notes and making phone calls. A technician bustled by and went inside, kicked aside a couple dozen buttons to make room, and flopped a hard-sided briefcase onto the floor. He popped it open and dug through it.

I groaned. "More fingerprinting powder. More to clean up."

"Makes me wonder who's in charge." Shaking his head, Stan got up and walked to the door. "Hey! You need to be careful. Those are Josie's buttons all over the place, and this is her shop and —"

"Yes, sir. Thank you for the suggestion." Just as Stan was about to step into the shop, a cop blocked his path. She was a tiny thing, dark-skinned and as pretty as a model, but there was a glint in her eyes that said she wasn't about to take any guff. Not from anybody. "We're being as careful as possible."

"Not when those guys in there are bumbling around like they're wearing concrete shoes." Stan made a face. "Didn't they teach you anything at the academy?"

"Yes, sir. You can be sure they did."

"Then you should know that the first thing you need to do —"

"Yes, sir." When Stan stepped over the threshold, the cop put out a hand. "You'll need to go back and sit down," she said, an edge of iron in her voice. "When the detectives get here, they'll talk to each of you."

"By the time they get here, these guys are going to make a mess of the evidence." Stan looked past the woman. "Dryer, is that you?" he called, and one of the uniformed cops spun around.

"Hey, if it isn't the man leading the life of leisure! Stosh, how's it going?" My guess was Dryer was nearing retirement himself. He was overweight, and what little hair he had left was as silvery as that swan-head buttonhook used to be. Before it was thrust into Kate Franciscus's heart and covered

73

with her blood. He put out a hand to shake Stan's. "What are you doing in a weird place like this?"

Stan cocked his head in my direction. "She's a neighbor. And a nice kid. It's her place. You know, when you're collecting evidence, you should start —"

"Great to see you, Stan." Dryer clapped him on the shoulder. "But you know how it is. You're a civilian now, and you can't get involved. You just go sit down and we'll be with you in a couple minutes."

Stan opened his mouth to say something. But since Dryer smoothly back-stepped him onto the sidewalk and closed the door in his face, he never had the chance.

When Stan came to sit down next to me on the bench, he was grumbling.

Me? I was grateful someone had finally thought to shut the door. At least now I didn't have to look at Kate's body and the mess that was once my life's work.

Depressing.

But at least the thoughts were enough to shake me out of my daze.

It was the first I saw that Dr. Levine, the optometrist from across the street, was sitting on a bench in front of the shop next door. He was busy texting, no doubt getting word out about how he'd suddenly found himself smack in the middle of what was bound to be the most sensational murder to hit Chicago since the St. Valentine's Day massacre. Brina was sitting next to him. She was hugging herself and sobbing softly.

Brina, who was supposed to be in charge when I ran out for a sandwich.

Like I said, I don't know much about murders or investigations. But I knew enough to suddenly wonder if I might have a star witness on my hands.

My knees were rubber. I managed to pull myself off the park bench anyway and make my way over to her. There was still coffee in my cup. I handed it to her.

"You OK?" I asked.

She took a drink and sniffed. Her nose stud winked at me. "It's just like in the movies," she said, looking past me toward the shop. No doubt she was picturing exactly what I was picturing: Kate's ashen face; her open, staring eyes; the blood. "Only . . . only, it's real, you know? And . . . and she was so pretty and so rich and so famous and she was going to be a princess and now . . ." A new cascade of tears started, and I plucked a tissue out of my pocket and handed it to her.

I made sure I kept my voice down so Dr. Levine didn't get wind of what we were talking about and start spreading the news. "You were supposed to be in the shop," I reminded Brina. "But when I got here . . . when I screamed . . . I saw you coming out of Dr. Levine's. Did you —"

She shook her head so hard I thought it was going to come loose and go bouncing down the street. "It wasn't my fault, Josie. Not exactly, anyway. Bert . . ." She looked over at the optometrist, and I realized I didn't have to worry about him; he was so busy sending messages that he wasn't paying the least bit of attention to us. "Dr. Levine, he's got a new computer and it's really fast and not like the clunker I have at home and he doesn't have Internet sites blocked on his like you do on the one on your desk, and things were slow over at his place, so he came by and we started chatting, and he, like, mentioned the new computer, you know, and then he asked if I would like to see it, and there was nothing much happening here and you never told me Kate was even supposed to be here tonight and —"

"And you weren't watching the shop after all." My shoulders drooped. Kate had been able to walk right in unnoticed. So had her killer. The fact that Brina was a big zero when it came to keeping an eye on my inventory paled in comparison. "Brina, you were supposed to —"

"I know, I know. But, Josie, don't you see, if I was here like I was supposed to be, I would have been there when Kate the Great got here and —"

"You would have called me. You would have told me she was early. And I would have raced over here, and she wouldn't have been here alone, and . . ."

And I wouldn't have allowed myself to get distracted.

By Kaz.

My shoulders drooped some more.

Brina's eyes got wide. "That's not what I was thinking, Josie. I was thinking more like, you know, what if I was here? I might be dead, too. Or . . . or what if I was able to escape? You know, by bobbing and weaving." Still seated, she did a weird sort of version of that. "That would make me, like, a witness. You know? Just like in the movies. And then . . . and then the killer would come after me, and I would have to go into hiding, and there would be Witness Protection and a new identity and I'd need to move to a new city and get a new job and —"

All right, I admit it — that sounded pretty appealing.

I didn't mention it. But then that was

77

because a dark sedan pulled up and Nevin Riley got out.

"Finally!" Stan threw his hands in the air. "Somebody with brains. You know he's got brains," he added for the benefit of the true civilians in the area. "I heard since I left, they gave Riley my old job. Hey, Riley!" Stan popped off the bench. "I was just telling Josie here that those guys in her shop, they should be —"

"Nice to see you, too, Stan." They shook hands. "But Josie's the one I need to talk to."

My stomach clutched. And not because I get anxious talking to those in authority or anything.

Let me explain. See, after my divorce, my friends and neighbors decided to do me a favor and get me out and dating again. Only it wasn't exactly a favor. And not because I was pining for Kaz or anything. I mean, sure, there are times I still think about that honeymoon in Barbados and . . .

Anyway, that's not what I'm talking about.

I'm talking about friends who fix up their friend and they think they're doing this fabulous thing for her, only they never stop to think that the friend they're trying to help is a button nerd who doesn't get out much, and always has her nose in a book about

78

buttons or is writing an article about buttons for the local or the national button society newsletters or is busy studying the buttons she already owns or dreaming about the ones she'd like to get her hands on. That means that friend isn't very good at discussing the weather or current events or . . . well, or much of anything except buttons.

The accountant Adele Cruikshank fixed me up with? He didn't notice; he was even more boring than me.

The advertising executive my ex-sister-in-law insisted was just right for me? He talked so much that he didn't have a chance to find out how dull I was.

As for the guys Stan found for me . . .

Well, no big surprise there. The guys Stan arranged for me to meet were always cops, and cops are hard-charging, quick thinking, and macho. The last thing they want to hear about is buttons. I did a couple quick mental calculations (which was pretty impressive considering my current emotional state), and figured out that thanks to Stan, I had had three such dates from hell.

And none was more horrible, more uncomfortable, and more downright disastrous than the one I had with Nevin Riley.

The curt nod he sent my way gave me a quick moment of hope — he didn't remember. No such luck. Cops have steel-trap minds. Which means Nevin remembered, all right — the long, uncomfortable silences in the restaurant, the couple times I brought up buttons, his resulting attempts to change the subject, fast. I wondered if he also remembered that phone call he got just as the pizza came to the table, the call I knew was a setup. Sure, he claimed it was so important, he had to cut our date short and get back to the office, but I knew better. Nevin Riley couldn't wait to get away from me.

"Ms. Giancola." Nevin is a tad over six feet tall and has a runner's body, lean and athletic. He gave me a cursory once-over and took a small leather notebook out of the pocket of his charcoal-gray suit. "You found the body?"

So much for small talk. But then, I guess he remembered I wasn't very good at it anyway.

I nodded. "We had an appointment, Kate and I and —"

He stopped me with a quick shake of his head that mussed his shaggy, sandy-colored hair.

"Is there some place we can talk? Alone?"

This was not a come-on and I knew it. For one thing, he'd run out on our one and only date with nothing more than a flimsy excuse. For another, he'd never called after that one, awful date, so I guess it was pretty clear that Nevin wasn't interested. For a third . . . Well, I'm logical enough to know he couldn't take the chance of my statement contaminating what anyone else had to say. Of course we had to talk alone.

I guess Dr. Levine was paying more attention than I thought. Typing with one hand, he pointed across the street to his office. "Door's unlocked," he said, fingers flying. No doubt, the fact that the statements were taken in his office would make his texts hotter than ever.

"I could help," Stan offered before we crossed the street. I'll give him credit: Nevin thanked him for the offer. Then he kept on walking.

I followed him, but not before I took one last look into the front display window of the shop I had once dreamed of as my home away from home. I watched what the cops and technicians were up to and tried hard not to look at Kate's body. I guess it didn't work, because before I knew it, I was rooted to the spot, staring at the two crime-scene technicians who were slipping bags over Kate's hands. Nevin gripped my elbow, urging me to get a move on.

"Sorry," I croaked.

"No need." We walked across the street between a phalanx of police cars with their lights flashing and crowds of people who were gathered around, and he opened Dr. Levine's door and stepped aside to allow me into the office first. All the lights were still on, and so was the computer that had been so tempting, it made Brina abandon her duties. It was open to the web page of a local tattoo artist.

Nevin turned off the screen. "Have a seat."

I chose the one on the customer side of the table where glasses were fitted. Nevin took the one opposite me, the optometrist's side. "You had a burglary at your place earlier this week."

So much for chitchat, but then, what did I expect? I'd already proven myself incapable. I shifted uncomfortably in the metal chair. "You don't think —"

"I don't think anything, because I don't know anything yet. About that burglary . . ."

I told him everything I remembered and watched him scratch notes as I spoke, which was fine with me, because it gave me a chance to look him over. I'd never describe Nevin as drop-dead handsome. His blue eyes were a little too far apart. His nose was a tad too pointy. His mouth was far from generous. Still, I remembered walking into the pizzeria where we'd first met and thinking he was nice looking. Maybe that's what had doomed our date from the start. He was cute, and I — for the first time since I gave Kaz the heave-ho — was interested. I tried too hard — to be funny, to be clever, to be interesting.

Interesting and buttons.

Two words that don't go together in most people's vocabulary.

Then again, Nevin wasn't all that flashy himself. He didn't have Kaz's swagger, Kaz's dazzling smile, or that sexy aura that pulsed around Kaz like a neon come-and-get-it sign.

No doubt, that's why I was attracted to Nevin in the first place.

And now?

He was efficient, organized, and completely impersonal, and just in case he could read my mind and knew I still thought he was cute, I clasped my hands together in my lap and forced myself to concentrate on the investigation, not the investigator.

"You didn't recognize the two men you found in your store the other morning?"

I snapped back to reality to find him watching me carefully. In a very coplike, business-y way.

"They were wearing ski masks," I said, even though I was sure that detail had been included in the report he'd obviously read. "One of them had a scar on his neck and one of them — I don't remember which — had a funny, phony accent. You know, Arnold Schwarzenegger meets Dr. Frankenstein."

"So you're saying you didn't know them?"

A polite way of reminding me he didn't appreciate my editorial comments. I told myself not to forget it and stuck to the cold, hard facts. "No. Neither one. They were burly and tall." This wasn't exactly editorializing because it was true, and because I justified the comment with, "I'd remember guys that beefy."

He nodded and made a note. "And you haven't seen them since?"

"No."

"And even though your store had just been burglarized, you went out and left the door open."

When he put it like that, it did sound dumb. I looked away, hoping he wouldn't notice that my cheeks were suddenly flaming. "It wasn't as stupid as it sounds."

"I didn't say it was stupid."

I dared a look at him. "Still, you don't understand."

He gave in with a tip of his head. "I will admit to that."

It wasn't until I ordered my thoughts that I attempted to explain. "Kate Franciscus was supposed to come in and see me this evening. At eight. I ran out a little before five-thirty to get something to eat." I thought of the to-go sandwich in the white bag, wondered what had become of it, and decided I didn't care. I'd long since lost my appetite. "I was planning on telling Brina she could leave as soon as I got back. Leaving her in charge while I was out, that was the stupid part."

He pursed his lips. "Because . . ."

"Because Brina's not responsible, and I should have realized that. I mean, I do realize it; it's just that it was only for a few minutes and I figured it wouldn't hurt. I was hungry, and Kate was early, and Brina . . ."

"The girl with the weird hair and the tattoos."

I nodded.

"According to the first officer on the scene, Ms. Martingale was here, in Dr. Levine's office."

I nodded. "Like I said, not very responsible. And easily distracted. And not very —"

"Bright?"

I was grateful for the assist, and I smiled my thanks. It was the first I'd even tried for a smile since I found Kate, and my face was stiff. That would explain why the expression didn't last long. "Kate showed up way early, and Brina, she said she was keeping an eye on the place but apparently, she wasn't. She says she didn't see Kate, or anyone else, come in."

At least he didn't point out that trusting Brina was my first mistake.

Instead, he blindsided me. "Unless she's lying about what she saw."

I sat up so fast, the Cubs sweatshirt slithered off my shoulders. "You don't think —"

"Can't say. Not yet. So, Ms. Franciscus, she was dead when you got here?"

I tugged the sweatshirt back in place, toying with the sleeves, tugging them closer around me. "I've never seen a dead body before, not outside a funeral home," I said. "But there was all that blood, and . . ."

"Did you touch her? Anything in the store?"

I shook my head. "I went outside and called the cops."

"And that's it."

I nodded. "Dr. Levine and Brina ran out

86

to the street and I told them what happened and we waited for the police to arrive. You know the rest."

Nevin flipped his notebook shut. "Then that's it. You can go."

"Home?" I thought about the chaos in the Button Box. "I'd rather wait until everyone is gone. I guess I'm feeling a little possessive when it comes to the shop. There's a lot that needs to be cleaned up, and a whole lot of recataloging and re-sorting and cleaning. My poor buttons!"

Too late, I realized I'd used the *B* word.

I didn't wait to see Nevin's eyes glaze over. Once in a lifetime is enough for that.

Instead, I got up and hurried to the door. I was already there when I heard him say, "You know, Josie . . ."

I spun around to find him tapping his notebook against the table.

"Not that it matters or anything . . ." His shrug emphasized his point. "I just want you to know that last time I saw you . . . that phone call I got from the office . . ." He tugged his left earlobe. "I mean, I know that looked pretty fishy and all, but . . ."

What else could I do but deny I'd had my suspicions? "I never thought —"

"Yeah. Sure. I just thought —"

"No, really." I managed a fleeting smile.

"I hope you didn't think —"

"I wondered. I mean, it really was pretty awkward and —"

"No problem." I turned back to the door.

"Josie."

I looked at him over my shoulder.

"It was legit," Nevin said. "And important."

"I figured." It was another lie, but I was rewarded for it by the look of relief that swept over his face and the one-sided smile that made him look cuter than ever.

"I should have called to explain," he said. "I meant to. It's just . . ."

"Yeah, I understand." That was stretching the truth a tad, too. But then, he didn't have to know that.

I still wasn't sure I believed him, I mean, about the phone call and all, but I did have to give him points for at least trying his hand at damage control. I guess that's why when I went back across the street, where cops still swarmed like bees around a hive and a team from the coroner's office was just putting Kate's body onto a stretcher, I might have been smiling, just a little bit.

CHAPTER FIVE

"So what do you think? Did you see them checking things out over here?"

I knew Stan was standing near the front display window, but I barely looked up when he asked the question. Then again, I was a little busy scooping buttons off the floor, all the while avoiding the spot where, just a few short hours earlier, Kate Franciscus had bled all over my newly sanded and varnished floor. It was the day after the murder, and finally, the cops, the technicians — and Kate — were gone.

Now if only the rest of the world would leave me alone!

As if on cue, the phone rang. Since I'd seen neither hide nor hair of Brina that morning, I cupped the fistful of buttons close to my heart and answered the phone myself. I didn't wait for the caller to say anything; the words just spilled right out of my mouth. Then again, I'd already gotten six phone calls that morning; I knew what was coming.

"The Button Box," I answered pleasantly enough; then, practically before the tabloid reporter on the other end of the line had a chance to introduce himself, I said, "No, I'm not interested in selling my story. I don't have anything to say."

"Of course you do!" He sounded young and eager. I almost felt guilty about hanging up on him.

Almost.

I looked around, grumbling, and even I wasn't sure if it was because I was overwhelmed by the sheer enormity of the job ahead of me or if it was a comment on the ghoulish obsession of the public in general. Already, news of Kate's murder had gone viral on the web. It was all over TV, too, and in the newspapers. Kate Franciscus, the hottest thing in Hollywood, was twice as much a star dead than she had ever been when she was alive.

The thoughts pounded through my head, just like my sneakers slapped the floor when I made a trip to the back room to deposit the buttons on the work table. When I came out into the shop, Stan was still stationed near the window. In the morning light, his face looked pale. His eyes, though . . . His eyes were sharp, the fire in them as blinding as the morning sun.

"Did they look upstairs?" he asked, and I knew he was talking about the cops who'd been on the scene the night before. " 'Cause I'll tell you what, Josie . . ." He leaned over to peer up to the second floor of the brownstone. "A good cat burglar with the right tools and a little luck —"

"Would not be able to rappel down from upstairs and not have anyone see him, not on a busy street. Besides, Emilie — she owns the travel agency upstairs — was in her office at the time. I think she would have noticed." I shouldn't have had to point this out, but then, it had been a stressful twelve hours for all of us so I cut Stan some slack. What with him insisting on staying at the shop until I left the night before, and me insisting on staying until the cops were done looking over the scene, we hadn't gotten home until well after midnight. If Stan was thinking more like himself and less like a bored retiree who watched too many movies and who'd gotten too little sleep, I wouldn't have had to state the obvious. "And even if that was possible, there's no way to open the front display window, not without breaking it. Which means the killer didn't need to rappel anywhere. All he had

91

to do was walk in the front door." I made a vague sort of gesture toward the fine film of fingerprinting dust that coated the window like sand in the desert, and when I was done, I picked up a pile of buttons at my feet. "Nothing was touched. The cops didn't find any fingerprints at all, none except Brina's and mine, of course."

"Dang." Stan scraped a hand through what was left of his hair. "The whole thing about the murderer coming in through the window, that sure would have cracked open this case. And that would have shown them, huh? Civilian!" He had a steel-trap mind, and not being acknowledged as on a par with the cops at the scene was one insult he was never going to forget. "I was on the job when most of those guys were still in elementary school. They got a lot of nerve." He pushed away from the window, his eagle-eye gaze sweeping the room. "How about secret passages? Is there an old dumbwaiter that's been walled over? Or a secret room?"

"No. And no." He knew all this, of course. Stan had insisted on checking out the area before I signed the lease. He wanted to be sure the neighborhood was safe, he'd said, and that Emilie, upstairs, was trustworthy, and that the brownstone was as secure as it could possibly be. Apparently, secure hadn't been secure enough, but I wasn't going to point that out. I knew that Stan being Stan, he was just trying to cover all his bases. "You heard what the cops said. Whoever killed Kate must have followed her here." A shiver snaked up my spine. "I just wish . . ."

"Baloney!" He waved away my concerns. "You wish you woulda been here so that maybe you coulda been a victim, too? Stop beating yourself up over something you can't change, Josie. Yeah, sure —" Like the street-corner traffic cop he'd started his career as, he stuck out a hand to stop what he knew I was going to say. "Sure, if you were here, the killer might not have tried anything. But I know how these guys think. This one? He wanted Kate the Great dead plenty bad. The force of that stab wound proves that much. If he didn't kill her last night, he just would have done it some other time, some other place."

The phone rang again, and just in case it was an actual customer and not a reporter or a photographer or a macabre fan looking for details about Kate's death I was never, ever going to provide, I piled the buttons I was holding on the desk. "Some other place is sounding pretty good right about now," I said. I answered the phone with an efficient

"The Button Box," and I was all set to launch into my I-have-nothing-to-say-and-I'm-sticking-to-it story when I was cut short by a familiar voice.

"Talk about taking this whole famous thing to a new level!"

It was enough to get me grumbling all over again. "What do you want, Kaz?"

"Hey, a guy can't call and check on his favorite button collector?" The tone of his voice told me he was smiling. "You're all over the news, Jo. What kind of husband would I be if I didn't call to see what was up?"

"An ex-husband?"

He chuckled. "You always said you were going to be the most famous button dealer in America. I guess you're on your way, huh?"

I shifted the phone to my other ear. "What do you want, Kaz?"

"You're having a bad day."

Understatement.

I didn't point it out. He didn't press.

In fact, Kaz breezed right on. "I had to call. You know, after I saw your picture on the front page of the paper this morning."

It was the first I remembered that Mike Homolka had met me outside the evening before. I'd been so busy being shocked —

not to mention grossed out and scared silly — when I found Kate's body, I'd forgotten all about the machine-gun fire of camera flashes. Come to think of it, I didn't recall Homolka being there when the cops arrived. But then, I guess the photographs he took before anyone else even knew Kate was dead were worth a premium. He would have wanted to get them into the hands of the highest bidder, ASAP.

I could only imagine how I looked in that one instant.

Then I realized that me looking like a fool . . . Well, that might not be the worst of it.

"He didn't . . ." I gulped. "The picture in the paper didn't show Kate's body, did it? That would be . . ." No word I thought of was sufficient to express my outrage.

Kaz supplied one. "Obscene? You bet it would be, and you can bet the guy who took the picture will get it printed somewhere else, and no doubt make a fortune on it, too. But today's paper . . ." I heard a noise, as if he was flipping through the pages of the newspaper. "The editors showed a little restraint. It pretty much just shows her shoes and a little bit of her legs."

"And a lot of me."

"You were upset."

I tipped back my head and closed my eyes. "Do I look that bad?"

"You look . . ." He paused, and I knew that for once, Kaz was trying to spare my feelings. I might have marked the day on the calendar as momentous if there weren't bigger, more important things to overshadow even this unusual occurrence. "Upset," Kaz said. "And who can blame you? Except I was sitting here reading about the whole thing this morning and watching the news, and I'm thinking now that it's all over . . ."

A familiar prickle of suspicion tickled along my shoulders. "Now that it's all over *what?*"

He gave in in the space of a heartbeat. "Heck, Jo, you're going to be more famous than ever after this! I'll bet the reporters are calling. Am I right? You're going to end up making a lot of money off this, what with the movie rights and a book deal and —"

What's the definition of insanity? Doing things the same way and expecting a different outcome?

I guess it was official, and I was truly insane, because the only thing I could think to say was no.

"No?" I pictured Kaz with that same gee-whiz look on his face that I'd been tempted to smack off more than a time or two. "What are you talking about?"

"I'm talking about how this seems to be exactly the right moment for you to ask for money. My answer is the same today as it was yesterday. Yesterday, as you no doubt remember, it was no."

"But I have this friend who's in trouble, see, and —"

"No, you don't."

"And yesterday, that was before —"

"Yes, it was. Good-bye, Kaz."

"But, Jo, I —"

He was still talking when I hung up.

And I was still shaking my head in wonder at the audacity of the man when the phone rang again. I grabbed it. "What are you, a bonehead?" I demanded. "No means no, Kaz. Not maybe, or I'll think about it, or —"

"Is this the Button Box?" The woman's voice stopped me cold. "Estelle, here. Estelle Marvin."

I froze. Right before I cringed.

Boy, did I cringe.

Estelle Marvin was a legend, a woman who'd built a beautiful-living empire on the cornerstone of her phenomenally successful cable TV crafts show. Scrapbooking? It may not have been her idea originally, but Estelle

97

had transformed it to high art. Knitting? With Estelle's encouragement, thousands of women had picked up needles. Quilting? Crafters everywhere looked forward to her monthly patterns and bought her books and her calendars and the line of greeting cards that featured her bold designs.

Estelle did it all, and she did it all with sass and spunk and a flair for promotion that gave new meaning to the word.

Estelle was to the genteel world of crafting what a hurricane was to the Caribbean. Not exactly a refreshing breeze, but one that sure made people sit up and take notice. We'd met a time or two, and I had always been appropriately awestruck.

Now I'd called her a bonehead.

I whispered a prayer of thanksgiving; at least she couldn't see my fiery cheeks. "Hello, Estelle." I forced myself to be all business. "I'm sorry. I thought you were someone else. Of course, you're not —"

"A bonehead?" She barked out a laugh. "I've been called worse. Don't worry about it. Listen, I was taking a look at this morning's paper and thinking that maybe now you'll reconsider my offer."

I should have known this was coming, but I'd been so distracted — by the murder and the mess and the phone calls — I guess I wasn't thinking straight. Now, a curl of ice wound its way through my insides. By now, I should have been used to the sensation. Every time Estelle and I talked, I ended up feeling like I'd just been put through the Slurpee machine at the local 7-Eleven.

"Offer?" I squeaked out the word. "You mean, about me being on your show?"

"You make it sound like a death sentence or something. Sorry!" She didn't sound it; another laugh burst out of her. "I guess that's not exactly an appropriate word to use considering what happened to poor Kate."

"But what happened to poor Kate, that's exactly why you're calling."

"Of course it is! What, you think I really am a bonehead?" My guess is that the majority of her adoring fans didn't know the well-dressed, perfectly coifed, gorgeously turned out doyen of do-it-yourselfers smoked like a chimney. I heard her haul in a breath along with a lungful of cigarette smoke. "Come on, I've been asking you to do this button segment on my show for months. Now is the perfect opportunity. You and those damn buttons of yours . . . Well, after this, you're going to be hotter than ever."

"I don't want to be hot. Not because of a

murder."

"Of course you do. Everybody wants to be famous and successful. It doesn't matter how you get there; what matters is making it to the top. If that's not what you want, why are you in business?"

She was right. Of course, she was. But . . .

I braced myself for the fight I knew was coming. "You know I'd be happy to do it, Estelle. I've told you that before. If we could just rework your concept for the segment and . . . and find another name for it."

I pictured her words whooshing out of her along with a stream of smoke. "What's wrong with *the Button Babe?* My God, Josie, it's not like anybody takes any of this life-can-be-beautiful shit seriously."

"I take my buttons seriously. And my business." I'd told her this before; maybe that's why I thought I shouldn't have had to mention it again. Why I sounded tentative and intimidated. "I want to be thought of as an authority, not as a babe. And that whole idea of yours, about having a sort of cabana boy bring out the trays of buttons, and about me lounging there, sipping a drink and talking about buttons . . ." Just thinking about it made my knees weak. If there was a chair around not piled with buttons, I would have flopped into it.

"Oh, come on! You're young. You've got nice hair, decent skin, that adorable little bowed mouth. You're cute." Facts were facts. At least that's what Estelle's tone of voice said. "As cute as a button. And I've told you before, the whole setup is perfect. People will love the idea of a nerdy little button babe being waited on hand and foot by a handsome hunk. Let's face it, most people hear *button collector* and they think old fuddy-duddy. We could give buttons a whole new image!"

We certainly could. And I was 100 percent certain it wasn't the one I wanted to present to my fellow collectors or my customers. Rather than argue a point I knew she'd never understand, I went for the obvious. "I've told you, Estelle, just thinking about getting in front of the cameras makes me stutter and stammer. Add a hunky guy in a loincloth and —"

"Ooh, loincloth! I hadn't thought of that. We could give it a sort of ancient empire theme. I'm making a note of that now. Loincloth — you're a genius!"

"No, I'm not. I'm an introvert."

"Yeah, me too." She didn't give me a chance to respond to this barefaced lie; she stormed right on. "A little coaching from our producer, and you'll sound like a pro. A little makeup will work wonders, too."

Oh yeah, that was plenty encouraging.

"My customers won't like it if I don't come across as studious and serious."

"Overrated." I couldn't help but picture her flicking one perfectly manicured hand in my direction. "We'll make it fun. Hey, I hear there are actually old buttons that show pornographic scenes. We could —"

"No. Really, Estelle, you know I'd be thrilled. You know I'll think about it. But not until we can handle the segment with style and class. And this is really coming at a bad time, anyway, what with Kate —"

"Hell, half of what I know about publicity, I learned from Kate. She was a good friend of mine, you know, God rest her soul. In fact, we're doing a show on the perfect wedding, and she was going to be my guest."

This was news, but Estelle didn't give me the opportunity to stop and think about it.

"Good God!" she roared. "Nobody was more uppity than Kate, and even she recognized the value of cutting loose and having some fun on my show."

"Was there a cabana boy involved?"

Estelle thought this was very funny. It took a minute or more for her to stop laughing and hacking. "You'll think about it, won't you?" she asked, and before I could respond, she answered herself. "Of course you will. You're a smart cookie, and you've got a good business head on your shoulders. You're not going to pass up an opportunity this juicy." She didn't wait for me to answer. Before I knew it, I was listening to the buzz of a dial tone in my ear.

I hung up. "I'm turning off the phone," I told Stan, and I did just that. "If anyone needs to say something to me, they can leave a message. At least this way I can have a little peace and quiet and get this place back in shape."

Yeah. Right. For about three seconds.

That would have been right about when Nevin Riley plowed through the door.

He was wearing the same suit he'd had on the night before, and by the looks of its wrinkles, the same shirt, too. That, along with the smudges of sleeplessness under his eyes and the way his hair hung over his forehead, convinced me he hadn't had a moment's rest since he'd gotten the call about the murder.

I knew how he felt. But even my own weariness wasn't enough to make me forget that the night before, he'd just about come out and apologized for abandoning me on our first date. Maybe that's why a little ribbon of warmth curled around my heart.

That is, until I saw that he was carrying the morning's newspaper rolled up in his left hand. He slapped it into his right palm. "Why didn't you tell me about this?" he demanded. Nevin's just about the least intimidating looking guy I've ever met, but there was steel in his voice, and I knew in that moment that, like me, plenty of bad guys had been fooled by his little-boy good looks. I bet plenty of them felt like I did right about then, too. Like my stomach had jumped up into my throat.

"About . . ." It took a moment for my brain to catch up with what was going on and another few seconds for my tongue to coherently form the words. "Oh, you mean about the photograph."

"I mean about the photographer."

There was no use offering him any excuses. He wasn't in the mood, and I shouldn't have had to justify my actions by reminding him that I was not exactly myself the night before. Dead bodies will do that to a girl. Instead, I went into the back room, grabbed for my purse, took Homolka's card out of it, and came back into the shop to hand it to Nevin. "He was outside when I got here yesterday evening," I told him.

He snapped the card out of my hands and turned to the door. "Next time, don't keep important information from me."

"There's not going to be a next time." I guess it was a little confrontational to come back at him like that, but hey, I was exhausted and out of sorts myself. "And I wasn't trying to keep anything from you. The last thing I was thinking of last night was paparazzi."

"Right." He slipped the card into his breast pocket. "That's the sort of flimsy excuse that's going to make my superiors very happy."

Just that fast, he was gone.

And just like that, I was fuming.

"Son of a —" I forgot Stan was even there until he cleared his throat. "Sorry," I mumbled.

He sloughed off the apology. "Don't hold it against the kid. He's getting it from all sides. Guaranteed, his lieutenant is all over him, the top brass are hounding him, and the press is after him like dogs with the scent of a raccoon in their noses."

"Yeah, well, he doesn't need to take it out on me." My insides were roiling, and it was either work and get rid of the feeling or race down the street to a nearby fabric shop, buy the supplies, and make a Nevin Riley voodoo doll. Sanity prevailed, and I stooped to retrieve the nearest buttons. It wasn't until I did that I realized I was standing at the spot where Kate had been killed. Right about then, even that wasn't going to stop me.

"You know," I told Stan, "the first time I met him, I thought Nevin was a real loser. Then last night . . ." I deposited a small mountain of buttons on the nearest display case, then bent to pick up more. At least if I concentrated on buttons, I wouldn't be tempted to think about how the night before, I'd found myself thinking Nevin wasn't so bad after all. "Last night he seemed like a regular guy. Now today . . ." More buttons, and I set them down and went after another cache. "I'll tell you what, Stan, overworked or not, that doesn't excuse how he just treated me. I don't care if I ever talk to the man again for as long as I —"

I stopped, my hand poised over one of the buttons on the floor. It was what we in the business call a medium. That is, it was about an inch from side to side, and from what I could tell, made of boxwood. The carving on it was exquisite. It was an owl . . . No, I told myself, tipping my head and examining the button from a different perspective. It was a hawk, each detail of the bird's feathers carefully rendered, its eyes bits of onyx.

My hand frozen, I looked over my shoulder at Stan. "Get Nevin on the phone for me," I said.

He wrinkled his nose. "But you just said —"

"I know what I said. And I meant it. But . . ." My hand was trembling, and I pulled it to my side and wiped my suddenly damp palm on the leg of my jeans. "He left a stack of his cards here last night. They're on my desk. Get him on the phone, will you, Stan? He just left; he can't have gotten far. Get him back here, ASAP."

"Sure, Josie. Anything you say. Only I wish I knew what was going through your head."

"That's easy enough." By now, I was down on my knees, my nose close to the button I didn't dare touch. "I think he needs to see this button. Because, Stan, it's a real beauty. And it isn't one of mine."

CHAPTER SIX

It was one of the most beautiful boxwood buttons I'd ever seen. I was itching to take a soft cloth and a little mineral oil to it, to clean it and polish it, and drink in the wonderful fragrance of the wood. I was itching to touch the button, too, but . . . Well, the Chicago police had other ideas.

Waiting for Nevin to arrive for this appointment he'd called to schedule, I looked longingly at the plastic evidence bag sitting on his desk, and the gorgeous button inside.

"Sorry I'm late." I'd been so focused on the button, I didn't notice he'd finally showed up until he was all set to sit down. It was the day after I found the button, and he was wearing a freshly pressed shirt and a brown tie that didn't exactly go with his navy wool suit. His eyes were alert. His hair was still mussed. "Sorry about yesterday, too," he said, taking his seat. "I was —"

"Rude and abrupt?" Oh, sure, I could

have cut him a break. But why? If there was one thing I'd learned from Kaz (OK, so I'd learned a lot of things from Kaz, but this was one of them), it was that guys who act like jerks don't deserve my understanding. Or my forgiveness. "In case you haven't noticed, you're sorry a lot."

He made a face. "I screw up a lot. Personally, I mean. Not professionally. Professionally, I'm a damn good cop."

"And a lousy person?" I made sure I kept my words light. There was no use hitting him over the head with the message.

He winced as if I had, and scratched a finger behind his ear. "I'm not a lousy person. Not all the time, anyway. At least I don't like to think so. You just keep catching me at bad times."

"Apparently." I hoped the small talk was over, and sat up a little straighter, a signal that I was ready to get to the meat of this meeting, whatever it was.

Nevin apparently didn't share my desire to get it over and get it over quickly. He shuffled a stack of papers on his desk, tapped them into a neat pile, and set them back exactly where they'd come from. When he was done, he sat back and cleared his throat. "I thought we could try again," he said.

"You mean like a date?" The words whooshed out of me a little too loudly, I guess, because a couple of the cops at their desks in the bullpen-like office looked over and grinned. I lowered my voice. "You're kidding, right?"

"Not really." One corner of his mouth pulled into a wry grin. "Unless you want me to be."

The ball was in my court, and I guess I wasn't willing to play, because even before I knew it, I found myself with my arms crossed over my chest. Defensive? Oh yeah. And when I realized it, my embarrassment morphed into full-blown mortification. It was déjà vu all over again, and I had an ugly flashback to that night at the pizza place. There was Nevin, trying to make conversation. And there I was, rambling like a lunatic. Only this time when I started rambling, it wasn't about buttons. "I sure hope you didn't ask me to come all the way down here just to talk about going out again," I snapped.

"Of course not."

"Because if you felt bad about what happened yesterday and the way you burst into the shop and how you didn't even stop to say hello to Stan or to ask how I was doing or to think that the reason I didn't tell you about Mike Homolka in the first place was that some of us aren't used to finding dead bodies and some of us aren't immune to the blood and the gore and some of us . . ." I stopped for air. But not for long. "Some of us were just a tad upset the night of the murder and not exactly thinking straight, and if you thought of any of that, then maybe rather than making me close the shop early today and schlep over to the El and come all the way down here, you could have just called and maybe apologized and explained why you acted like such a jerk in the first place and then you could have just asked me out on the phone."

OK, so now I did sound like a full-blown lunatic, and I didn't even regret it. I'd said what he needed to hear, and I guess he got the message; the tips of his ears got pink.

"Sorry!" he said. "Again."

While I struggled to settle my heartbeat and the breaths that were coming too hard and too fast, Nevin reached for the evidence bag.

"Actually what I called about was this." He lifted the bag, the better to show off the button inside. "Thank you for calling me when you found it."

I forced myself to sound like the reasonable woman I usually am. "You're welcome.

I thought it might be important."

"And thank you for having the sense not to touch it. Unfortunately —"

"No fingerprints?" Like I might actually see them if I looked closely enough, I peered through the plastic at the button. "That's too bad."

"It is." He set the button on the desk. "It's left us at a dead end."

He didn't have to elaborate. When he said *us,* he was talking about the police in general. But I knew what he really meant to say was *me. It's left me at a dead end.*

"Buttons are your business." He jumped in with an argument so smooth, I knew he must have practiced it before I got there. I wondered if that's why he'd come to our meeting late. Was he standing in the men's room, reciting this speech in front of the mirror? I'd never know, and he'd never admit it, but the visual was enough to relieve some of the tension wound inside me. "From what I've been told," he said, "you're one of the country's most-respected experts on buttons."

"Yes." Admitting it, I felt more like myself and less like the crazy woman who'd just taken him to task. "I am."

Nevin's smile lasted as long as it took for him to set the bag back where it came from.

He folded his hands on the desk in front of him. "That's why I asked you to come down here today. Josie, I need your help. To solve this murder."

I was on my way back from the El to my apartment when I ran into Stan, just coming out of the grocery store. Maybe it was a mistake to mention my meeting with Nevin and the not-so-small fact that he wanted me to help out with the investigation. Stan pounced right on it.

"So I'm thinking a stakeout," he said, shifting the reusable grocery bag he refused to let me carry for him from his left hand to his right. "We can follow each of the suspects. You know, for a week or two. What do you think?"

"I think . . ." It was late in the afternoon, and my head was swimming. As I've already admitted, my wildest dreams usually center on Kaz. Or buttons. I never thought they'd include murder, or me helping to find a killer. "I really don't think that's the kind of help Nevin was talking about," I said. "He wants me to do some research. And talk to my contacts in the button-collecting world. He wants to know more about the button and where it came from and how it got to my shop. He doesn't need help with the actual police work."

"Yeah. Right." Stan kept walking, even though when we rounded the corner, we saw there was some commotion going on a little farther up the street. A crowd of thirty or so people was gathered on the sidewalk, and the commotion looked to be happening near our building. He narrowed his eyes and tipped his head, walking a little slower, sizing up the situation.

I slowed my pace, too. I'm not nearly as tall as Stan, and I had to crane my neck. Whatever was happening, it looked to be peaceful enough. "I'm going to investigate," I said, telling him exactly what I'd told Nevin. "In books. I'm going to make phone calls. To button people. No stakeouts. And what do you mean, anyway?" Now that I had time to process it, what he said struck me as more than a little odd. "What are you talking about when you say *suspects?* We have suspects?"

"There are always suspects. You'll learn that fast enough."

"But I don't want to learn that. I don't need to learn it." Nevin had given me close-up and detailed photographs of the button. He'd had an evidence technician join us who slid the button out of its protective bag and made all the measurements I

114

asked for. I patted my purse where I had all the information safely stored away. "All I need to do is tell Nevin everything I find out about the button."

We were closer to the crowd now and I stopped to try and get some sense of what was happening. "So . . ." I dangled the word like a fat worm on the end of a hook. "Our suspects are . . ."

Stan chuckled. "Think about it."

"I have." Not technically true since I was pretty sure this part of the investigation wasn't any of my business and I hadn't spent even a moment considering it. "Kate was alone in the shop and —"

"And that photographer was outside when you got there."

I nodded. If I was thinking more like the careful investigator Nevin wanted me to be and less like a woman with her head in a cloud of buttons, I suppose I would have thought of that. "Mike Homolka. OK, yeah, I can see how he might be a suspect. Right time, right place. But it seems to me a guy who just killed somebody wouldn't stick around."

"Unless he wanted to get pictures of that someone he just killed."

"But he could have done that before I got there."

"Except that he might not have wanted to take the chance of anybody seeing him or of some sharp-eyed cop taking a look at the photos and seeing some little clue that indicated they'd been taken before you got back to the shop. On the other hand, if he arrived at the Button Box with you . . ."

It all made sense. Even if it didn't prove anything.

"And then there's Brina and Dr. Levine, of course," Stan said. "They were right across the street."

"Of course they were. But you can't possibly think —"

"When you eliminate people right off the bat like that, that's called jumping to conclusions, and it's as dangerous as deciding who's guilty before you have all the facts."

It was a valid point, even though there was no way he could ever convince me Brina or Dr. Levine might have been involved.

We walked along quietly for a bit before Stan said, "Then there's that husband of yours."

"Ex-husband," I reminded him. Right before I stopped cold, whirled to face him, and blurted out, "What?"

He shrugged. "You said it yourself; he told you he'd been to the shop."

"And saw Brina while he was there. Which

means Brina hadn't gone across the street yet. Which means Kate hadn't arrived."

"Yeah, sure. That's what he says."

"And you think I shouldn't believe him?" The second the words were out of my mouth, I realized how ridiculous they were. "Of course I can't believe him. He's Kaz."

"Which doesn't mean he's lying about this. It just means we've got to be careful, that's all. You know, we've got to look at the facts, and get a time line down, and consider alibis and motives."

"Which pretty much eliminates Kaz." I felt a little funny standing up for the guy who'd given me nothing but grief, but the order-loving side of me couldn't let Stan get carried away. Facts were facts, just like he'd said, and this one was inescapable. "Kaz didn't have any reason to kill Kate. He didn't even know Kate."

"Ah, motive!" Stan nodded. "Now you're thinking like a cop. It's all important, the who and the what and the where. But the why . . . The why is always the heart of the matter. Figure that out, and the rest just falls into place."

For all I knew, he was right. Then again, we didn't exactly have a chance to talk about it. We were close to our apartment building, and from someone in the knot of

117

people, I heard, "There she is!" The crowd surged toward me.

"Stan?" I gripped his sleeve. "Who are they? And what do they want?"

I found out as soon as the first camera flash went off. The next second, a woman in a gray suit shoved a microphone in my face. "You were the first one on the scene," she said. "So you must have heard Kate's dying words. Tell us, Josie. The people of America deserve to know what she said. Did she name her killer? Did she talk about Roland? About their doomed love?"

"I . . . I . . ." I blinked, looking around at the crowd of reporters and photographers like a stunned rabbit and wondering how, since I had an unlisted phone number, they'd found out where I lived in the first place. "I have nothing to say."

"But you must have seen the murderer." This time, it was a tape recorder that got shoved at me. There was a middle-aged man in a plaid sport coat on the other end of it. "Is that why you're trying to keep out of the investigation, Josie? Have the cops told you to keep your mouth shut? They have, haven't they? They want to make sure the killer doesn't know that you got a good look at him."

"But I . . . I didn't . . . I . . ."

A young guy with long hair and bad skin pushed his way to the front of the crowd. "Maybe you don't want to say anything because you're not much of a liar. Maybe you were the first one on the scene because you had something to do with the murder yourself. Why did you hate Kate so much, Josie? Was it her money? Her beauty? Her power? What made you kill her?"

"OK, that's enough." Stan gripped my forearm and pushed through the crowd and went straight for the door of the apartment. "Josie's got nothing to say to any of you clowns." He unlocked the door and pushed me into the lobby ahead of him.

"Thanks!" I pressed my back to the wall and closed my eyes, hoping to calm myself. "That was awful!"

"Fools!" Stan was glaring out the window, and I saw a few flashes go off. No doubt, one of these days soon, some tabloid would feature his picture on the front page. He would not be happy about that.

"I can't believe they'd care that much about me," I groaned. "I don't know anything. I can't tell them anything."

He scraped a hand along his chin. "I guess they're just doing their jobs," he admitted a second before his eyes narrowed. "But if they ever get pushy like that with you again,

I'm going to show them a thing or two."

I knew he would. Which is why I smiled.

I'd just shifted away from the wall and was headed toward the elevator when the doors opened and Brina stepped into our postage-stamp-sized lobby — Brina and Mike Homolka.

"So, yeah, this is the elevator she rides every day," Brina was saying. "And you saw her door and talked to her neighbors and —" She caught sight of me, and her face went as pale as the silvery streak she'd added to her hair since last I saw her. "Oh, hi, Josie."

Homolka flashed a picture.

"You?" I guess I wasn't all that surprised, but I was plenty outraged. "You're the one who told these jackals where to find me?"

"Oh, come on, Josie." When Brina squinched up her nose, that stud in it sparkled in the overhead lights. "It's business. You understand about business. You're the one who's always saying —"

"They paid you?" I could barely swallow around my outrage. "Well, of course they did. That's why you sold me out." I swung toward Homolka. "You looking for an exclusive?" I asked him.

His eyes shone with excitement. "You bet! What have you got to say?"

"You can tell the world loud and clear. Brina here? She just got fired."

It took a couple hours, a long shower, and a glass of wine to get me settled down. Once I was feeling more like myself and less like a zebra carcass left on the Serengeti for the hyenas to feast on, I pulled out every button reference book I owned (there were a lot of them), settled myself on the couch, and got to work.

"Wooden buttons," I mumbled to myself, flipping through the pages of the first book. I found the chapter I was looking for, skimmed it, found nothing that was even vaguely helpful, and went on to the second book.

And the third.

And the fourth.

And the fifth.

It wasn't until I'd been through all my books and done a thorough Internet search that I realized my eyes burned and my neck felt like it was in a vise. That's the first I bothered to check the clock. It was past nine, and my rumbling stomach reminded me that I hadn't had dinner. I stretched, rubbed the small of my back, and dragged into the kitchen for a yogurt. Just so I didn't sit there and accomplish nothing while I was eating it, I grabbed a couple of the books I'd already looked through and flopped them on the kitchen table.

"Carved buttons, wooden buttons, realistic buttons," I mumbled to myself, paging through the books. I got nowhere fast, and aside from some antique boxwood buttons from China, I didn't see anything that even came close to the boxwood hawk in style or workmanship.

Just to be sure, I checked the photographs Nevin had provided for me. Again.

I nodded, confirming something to myself. "Good work, kiddo," I told myself, just like Stan would have if he were there. In fact, he would have been proud of me. I'd refused to let myself jump to conclusions, checking and rechecking all the references and all the facts before I made up my mind, even though I'd been tempted to do just that the moment I saw the button.

All along, I suspected it was what we in the button biz call a studio button, that is, a button made in limited quantities and not by a factory or a manufacturer, but by an artist. Studio buttons aren't really even intended to go on clothing. Most of them are snapped up by collectors.

Trouble is, the style and craftsmanship of this studio button didn't ring any bells.

I rifled through the photographs the police had taken, including the one I'd insisted on that showed the back side of the button. "No artist's signature, no marking, nothing to indicate who made it or where it came from."

I propped my elbows on the table and cradled my chin in my hands. If I was going to figure out where the button came from and — more importantly — why it was on the floor right where Kate's body had been found, I was going to need more to go on. It was late, and unlike a certain button dealer who pretty much lived and breathed her business, most of the other dealers and collectors I knew had actual lives. It was too late to call them, and I promised myself I'd do it in the morning. For now, all I could do was wonder. About the button and its maker. About whoever had brought it to the shop.

About those suspects Stan had mentioned.
Mike Homolka.
Brina, my first and now my former employee.
Dr. Levine.
Why any of them would have the button was as much of a mystery as why it had ended up being left with Kate's body.

"And none of it's getting me anywhere," I

mumbled to myself. Right before my cell phone rang.

I would have kept on mumbling and let the call go to voice mail, but as far as I knew, nobody but friends had the number. Whispering a silent prayer that I hadn't, in a moment of weakness, given it to Brina, I answered.

"Josie, is that you?" I barely recognized Hugh's voice. But then, he was sobbing. "Josie, baby girl, I need to talk to you. Now. Josie . . ." He gulped. "You've got to help me out. Like you always do. It's about Kate, see, and . . ." He let go a shaky breath. "I think I did something really, really stupid."

CHAPTER SEVEN

I was carded at the front desk of Hugh's luxury hotel and again outside the elevator that was for the sole use of those staying in its priciest suites. Up on the thirty-first floor, my ID was checked once more, this time by a strapping guy in a dark suit who walked me to a set of double doors and handed me off to a trim and efficient-looking woman in black who introduced herself as Lucia. She told me to have a seat and that Hugh would be with me in a moment. Even though it was after ten o'clock, Lucia didn't seem fazed by my visit, and I imagined I knew why; I pictured Hugh's opinion of me in neon lights, flashing over my head.

Good ol' Josie — reliable, dependable, predictable.

No wonder Lucia wasn't surprised. If she knew that much, I figured she also knew that things had always been this way between Hugh and me, even back in college. He needed help — with anything from homework to laundry — and I pitched in. At first, it was because I had an aching crush on Hugh and I was hoping to get him to notice me. But even a button nerd is not completely dense. It didn't take longer than the first semester for me to realize I was out of his league. Hugh liked his women tall, busty, and gorgeous. I was none of those things, but he liked me, anyway. As a friend. A friend who could get things done.

Good ol' Josie always pitched in, and always without a complaint.

Only this time . . .

Lucia excused herself, and waiting for Hugh, I glanced around the incredible living room, with its startling postmodern furniture, the white and plum decor, and an amazing view of Lake Michigan out the floor-to-ceiling windows that took the place of two walls.

This time, I had to admit, I was worried. About Hugh's phone call and that problem he said he had. About what he expected me to do about it.

There was more than a thread of panic in his voice when we talked, and I couldn't get that, or what he said, out of my head.

You've got to help me out. Like you always

do. It's about Kate . . . I did something really, really stupid.

I wondered how stupid really, really stupid was.

And if that really, really stupid had something to do with murder.

"Hey, baby girl!" Hugh's voice zapped me out of my thoughts and back to reality. I looked up just in time to see him walk out of what must have been the bedroom of the suite. Hugh had always been good-looking, in a film-student, artsy sort of way. It was the long dark hair and the soulful eyes that had gotten to me years before along with the ragged jeans, the secondhand denim jackets, and the endless supply of T-shirts he borrowed from the endless one-night stands who were only too happy to share. These days, he preferred Dior to denim and a corporate haircut that made him look every inch the Hollywood power broker he was.

None of that could disguise the furrows of worry on his forehead. The forced cheeriness in his voice didn't fool me, either. Hugh's eyes were red. So was his nose. His hair stuck up at odd angles like he'd been tugging at it.

Instinctively, I stood, prepared — as always — to offer him comfort and a shoulder to cry on.

He didn't give me a chance. Before I could move away from the couch, he was right up in my face. He grabbed both my hands and squeezed tight.

"I didn't do it. You know that, don't you, Josie? You know I had nothing to do with Kate's murder."

Startled by his intensity, I gathered my thoughts, hung onto my composure, and took a moment to study Hugh. Though we chatted on the phone occasionally, it had been years since we'd been face-to-face, since that first summer after college, in fact, when we worked on *Trolls* together, and I could see there was more to his transformation than pricey clothes and designer hair.

Hugh's teeth were unnaturally white, and they'd been straightened since last I saw him. So had his nose. Come to think of it, I remembered his chin being rounder and fuller. At this point, I guess none of that mattered. Not as much as the way he hung onto me. Yeah, the phrase *for dear life* popped into my head.

"You believe me, don't you, Josie?" His words shivered from trembling lips.

Too bad I wasn't in any shape to offer reassurance. Listening to Hugh, seeing the desperation that shone in his eyes, my stomach flipped.

I commanded it to settle down and extricated myself from his grip. I might not have been feeling it, but in an effort to at least look calm, I sat back down, and said, "Apparently, we have a lot to talk about."

He nodded. Took my lead and sat down. Stood up again. "There were lots of people who wanted Kate dead," he announced.

OK. Have I mentioned this was getting weird?

Clearing my throat, I ordered my thoughts and gave him the kind of stare I'd once seen a trainer use on an unruly Jack Russell terrier. "Maybe you better start from the beginning," I said. "I'm a little confused."

"Yeah. Sure." Hugh did a spin around the room. Sort of like that Jack Russell did when the trainer made an effort to control him. "It's just that . . . The police called. They want to talk. To me." Even though the suite was bigger than the entire fourth floor of my apartment building, he was moving a mile a minute, and by this time, he was already back in front of me.

I knew Nevin was the one who must have made the call since he was lead investigator on the case, and really, it wasn't hard to think like Nevin. Nevin Riley might be more than a little rough around the edges when it came to personal relationships, but as he'd pointed out the last time we talked, he was a professional. With him, a case was bound to be all about the logic.

I held on tight to the thought and clutched my hands together on my lap. "Of course they called you," I told Hugh. "You and Kate were working on a movie together, and they're going to want to understand what Kate was up to in the days before she died. They talked to me, too. They're putting together a time line. Your work with her and her visit to my shop, that's all part of that time line."

"Yeah. Sure. Of course." For the space of a few heartbeats, relief swept across his face. Right before he fell to pieces again. "But what if they ask questions I can't answer?"

"Then you'll tell them you can't answer. It's better than concocting a lie."

He didn't respond, so I tipped my head, trying to catch his eye.

"Did you hear me, Hugh? There's nothing to be gained from lying to the police. They'll find out eventually. And what . . ." A new and very disturbing thought hit. I sat back and swallowed hard, and when I forced myself to ask the question burning in my brain, my voice was breathy. "What do you . . . Is there something you need to lie about?"

He paced to the bar, poured Scotch into a crystal glass, and slugged it down. "*Charlie*, the movie we were shooting . . . *Charlie*'s shot to hell," he grumbled. "A third of the way through, and Kate is in just about every scene. How the hell can anybody expect me to finish a movie about the most famous madam in Victorian-era Chicago when the madam in question has gone and gotten herself killed?"

I laced my fingers together. "You didn't call me for business advice, Hugh. If I can believe what I've been reading in the papers these days, nobody knows the movie business better than you do. Besides, I'm sure this sort of thing has happened before. The production company must have insurance."

"Yeah. Sure. Right." He poured another drink and took his time with this one, sipping and studying me over the rim of the glass. "That's not what I'm worried about," he said. His chest rose and fell. "Josie . . . You're the only one who can help me."

Maybe.

Before I could point that out, he was pacing again. "I can't believe she's gone," he sobbed. "I mean, Kate's name is synonymous with beauty and youth and glamour and to think about her body stone-cold and dead . . ." When he swallowed, his Adam's apple bobbed. "People are stunned. They're holding candlelight vigils outside her homes in Maui and Paris. They're screening retrospectives of her work. Already, there are rumors that the whole thing is a put-on, that she faked her death to get out of the limelight. Like it was even remotely possible for Kate not to be the center of everyone's attention!" His laugh teetered on the edge of hysteria. "I know there's not a snowball's chance in hell that the whole thing is a hoax. I mean, really, I know in my heart of hearts that she's dead, but I keep waking up in the middle of the night thinking what if . . ." His eyes went glassy, his thoughts no doubt flying a million miles away to some happier place that still had Kate in it. He washed away the fantasy with a drink. "I guess it's only natural not to believe she's gone. I mean, how could any of us believe it? Could you? Could you believe it when you heard she was dead?"

I am never surprised to realize Hugh is being insensible. Again.

I am, though, always disappointed.

Disappointed, I leaned forward, my elbows on my knees, and a funny thing happened. Maybe it was my experience with Kaz (or more specifically, with divorcing Kaz) that had prepared me for this moment. Suddenly, I saw Hugh in a whole, new light.

It was not all that flattering.

"Kate was killed in the Button Box, my new shop," I said. I wasn't so much hoping to jog his memory as I was trying to make a point. As colleagues, he and Kate were close, and I understood how upset he was. But as the person who walked in and saw that buttonhook plunged into her heart . . .

I pulled in a long, shaky breath.

"I was the one who found her, Hugh. You know that."

He finished his drink. "Then maybe you can understand a little of what I'm going through. The emptiness. The despair."

More like the bad dreams, the creepy feelings.

I didn't mention it. There was, apparently, no point. Once a narcissist, always a narcissist, and it looked as if Hugh had found his niche.

I tamped down my irritation but only because I remembered that studio button and the job Nevin had charged me with. I ignored Hugh's neediness for once, and concentrated on my own. I needed information. And he just might be the one who could give it to me.

My acting skills were never all that good to begin with, but I pulled out all the stops, hoping to sound more like I was making conversation than searching for clues. "I didn't realize Kate was as much of a button collector as I am," I said. "She brought a button to the shop with her. A really nice, handmade button. I'd love to get more of them, but I need to figure out where it came from. Did she ever show it to you?"

"Kate and buttons?" Thinking about it, he puffed out his cheeks. "Come on, Josie, you know Kate was way too chic for —"

"Something that nerdy?"

"No. That's not what I meant. I . . ." He scrambled to save face. Not mine, his. My irritation ratcheted up a notch.

"It doesn't matter." I stood. "If the button didn't belong to Kate, maybe someone else working on the movie —"

"Not likely."

He didn't need to elaborate. Hollywood types were too trendy, too swank, and way too in to be out of this world about buttons.

I knew a dead end when I saw it. Which didn't mean I was ready to throw in the towel. There was more than one road to the information I was looking for, and I took a sharp turn and headed in another direction.

Literally and figuratively.

I strolled over to the bar. "What did you mean, Hugh, when you said plenty of people wanted Kate dead?"

He shrugged and looked away. "Just a figure of speech."

"No, it wasn't. Not the way you said it. Like you really believed it. If you know something . . ."

He glanced at me out of the corner of his eye. "Those assistants of hers . . ." Hugh curled a lip. "Ungrateful, every single one of them. Kate did wonderful things for them."

"And she treated them like indentured servants."

Obviously, the thought had never occurred to him. "The chance to live and work with Kate . . . That should have been a dream come true for every single one of them. How many girls get that kind of opportunity? All the limelight, none of the work."

"None of the acting." Hugh didn't understand the subtle difference so I added, "Kate used them as her personal robots. I saw that much the day she stopped at the shop. But if any of them was unhappy, why not just quit? I can't imagine one of them might have —"

"I don't know. Really." He stepped back from the accusation. "But I heard grumbling. You know, when Kate wasn't around."

"And when she was?"

"When she was, they did their jobs and they did them without whining. They'd better, or Kate would have had them tossed out in a heartbeat."

"You said there were plenty of people. The assistants, they're not the only ones."

He didn't even need to stop and think about it. "There's Estelle, of course."

"Estelle Marvin?" He nodded, confirming my thought. "Estelle told me she and Kate were friends."

"Yeah, like oil and the Gulf of Mexico are friends."

I pictured Estelle, always elegantly turned out. And never a wallflower. I thought about Kate, powerful and assured.

"I can see that," I said. "Estelle and Kate were both hard-driving, successful women. Those qualities would draw them together. And their egos . . . Well, I can see how they'd butt heads."

"It wasn't just that. After all, Kate knew that when it came to beauty and style, nobody could compete with her. She wasn't threatened in that way, not by Estelle. Not by anybody. But there was that silly TV show."

"Estelle's craft show?" I thought back to everything Estelle had told me. "She was doing a wedding segment. And Kate had agreed to —"

"Had. Had agreed." Like it would help drive home his message, Hugh stared at me.

Maybe I'm not as perceptive as he thinks. I still wasn't sure what he was getting at, and I felt my way through, reluctant to put words in his mouth. "So Kate agreed to be on the show, and then . . ."

"And then Estelle was so sure she had a mega-hit segment on her hands, she sunk a boatload of her own money into promoting Kate's appearance. I'm talking scheduled print ads, TV, you know the drill. That can't have been easy because word has it that Estelle lost a ton of money in the most recent market downturn. And what she's got left, she spends like a drunken sailor. Estelle loves to live the good life. And Kate . . ." *Trolls* aside, Hugh knew a thing or two about drama. He leaned forward, capturing my gaze, drawing out the moment. "First she told Estelle she'd be happy to appear on the show; then Kate changed her mind and pulled out."

This was news — and not what Estelle

had told me — and I tipped back my head, considering it. Knowing Estelle, Kate's sudden decision could only mean one thing. "Estelle was mad."

"As a wet hen!" Hugh pushed away from the bar. "She showed up on the set last week and ranted and raved and carried on. We had to have security escort her back to her limo. I've never seen anybody that angry."

"Was she mad enough to kill Kate?"

"God, I hope so!"

I looked at him in wonder. "You think Estelle killed Kate?"

"Frankly, my dear . . ." His lips thinned. "I don't care if she did it or not. I just want the police to think she did. Then at least they won't think it was me."

I wasn't surprised that Hugh was looking to save his own skin. After all, it was one of the things he did best. I was shocked to think he'd do it at any expense.

My stomach turned into a block of ice. Hugh was standing near the windows with his back to me, and slowly, I closed the distance between us. "Is there a reason they might think it's you, Hugh? Does this have something to do with what you said on the phone? You said you'd done something stupid. You didn't —"

"Kill Kate?" When he spun to face me, his

eyes were wild. "See, even you think it's possible. They're going to be breathing down my neck, hounding me, taking apart my life bit by bit to try and get at what they think is the truth. They're going to make my life a living hell, and you've got to do something about it, Josie."

He caught my arm, and one finger at a time, I loosened his hold. "I can't do anything until I know what really happened."

He nodded like he understood, but it took him a while to pull himself together. When he did, his voice shook. "Kate and I were lovers."

I am not a compulsive reader of the supermarket tabloids, but this I would have noticed, and I told him as much.

He flopped onto the couch. "It is amazing, isn't it? We were actually able to keep our affair under the radar. Even I'm not sure how. It was . . ." He closed his eyes, and for a moment, his expression cleared and a smile touched his lips. "She was wonderful."

"She was engaged to Prince Roland."

One corner of his mouth pulled into a thin line. "Roland. Yeah. At first when I heard the news, I figured it was all just a publicity stunt. That's how Kate was. She'd do just about anything to get her name in the headlines. She had a movie coming out, and being engaged to a prince, that's the kind of publicity money can't buy. So when I saw her name associated with Roland's, well, I just assumed it was something she'd arranged to get her picture on the front page of the paper. Then about six months ago, she came back from a trip to Europe and . . . well . . ." His shrug said it all: he still didn't understand.

"We were supposed to spend a week on Cerf Island together. You know, a sort of reunion. That's when . . ." His voice clogged. "That's when she told me it was all true. All those headlines. All that gossip. She said she was in love with Roland, and that . . . that it was over between us."

I had no choice but to ask the inevitable. "You were angry?"

He closed his eyes. "Beyond angry. She breezed into the resort on Cerf, told me the news, and breezed out again. There I was, looking like a fool in the middle of the Indian Ocean with my heart in about sixty million pieces."

Yeah, except for the Indian Ocean part, I could relate. I'd once been married to Kaz.

Rather than dwell on it and get caught up in the emotional undertow, I stuck with the facts. Something told me I wasn't going to like what I was about to hear, but I was there for information, wasn't I? There was only one way to get it.

"What did you do?" I asked Hugh.

His words escaped on a stuttering sigh. "Called her. Hundreds of times. I tried to reason with her. I begged." He bounded off the couch. "I would have sold my soul to the devil if I had his cell number. When none of that worked . . ." He pressed his fingers to his temples. "I hired somebody to follow Kate."

The *stupid* part of the equation was starting to come into focus.

"What were you thinking?" I asked. "What did you hope to accomplish?"

He lifted his chin. "I was hoping to get her back, that's what I was hoping. I was hoping she'd see that she'd made a mistake. Roland over me? I was hoping she'd come to her senses, and I thought if I kept tabs on her . . . What?" His eyes were blazing now, challenging. "You've never been that much in love? I was jealous, all right? I thought about her day and night, and I had to know what she was up to."

This kind of crazy jealousy was something I didn't understand. But then, Kaz's only mistress had been his gambling habit.

"And that person, was he still following Kate?" I asked Hugh. "This past week?"

Instead of answering, Hugh ducked into a room on the other side of the dining room. When he came back, he was carrying a stack of photographs. He handed me the eight-by-ten pictures.

They were photographs of Kate on the set, and Kate shopping in one of the boutiques along Michigan Avenue's the Magnificent Mile, and Kate eating at Alinea.

Tabloid stuff and not all that interesting.

Until I found the ones taken of her outside the Button Box on the day she'd originally come to see me, with the assistants, all except Winona, trailing behind her.

There were more — Kate in the shop before she instructed whatever hapless assistant was in charge of doors to close mine. Kate on the floor wearing those leather pants, her lifeless eyes staring at the ceiling and me staring at her, my eyes wide with terror, my mouth open in a silent scream.

My head came up. "Mike Homolka. He was the one you hired to follow Kate?"

"Mike's always up for a little double-dipping. I paid him top dollar to keep tabs on Kate. He sold the pictures he took of her while he was following her."

"And he followed her that night. The night

142

she was —"

He nodded.

"Are you telling me . . . ?" The words stuck in my throat. "Did he see who did it?"

"You're not getting this, are you, Josie?" Hugh snatched the photos out of my hands. "Number one, no, Mike didn't see who did it. That's because I told him what time Kate was supposed to arrive at your office. I had no idea she was going to get there early, so Mike had no idea, either. He told me he was hanging around the area, but he wasn't paying a whole lot of attention. He didn't think he needed to. In fact, he went into that little club down the street and had a beer. Leave it to Kate!" His laugh was anything but humorous. "She probably thought he was going to follow her later; that's why she ducked out and went to your place early to begin with." Hugh's chest heaved. "Kate wasn't used to going places on her own. She always had her assistants with her to take care of all the little details. Yeah, yeah . . . I know what you're going to say. You're going to say she was spoiled. Of course she was!" He threw his hands in the air. "Kate was the most glorious woman on earth; she deserved to be spoiled. If only she didn't insist that every little detail of that damned wedding of hers be kept a secret. Then she would have had someone with her."

I nodded. "Our appointment was supposed to be private. But if you told Mike to go there, you knew she was coming to see me."

Hugh's gaze darted to mine. "That doesn't mean anything."

"That's not what the police are going to think, and you know it. If she knew you were having her followed, why would she tell you —" I gave myself a mental slap. "She didn't tell you she was coming to my place. You found out. How?"

Anybody with a smidgen of a conscience would have at least blushed when he said, "I hacked her e-mail."

"Hugh!" I groaned. "When the cops find out you were a jealous ex-lover . . ."

He nodded. "Yes, there's that. That, and the e-mail I sent her the day she was killed."

"And let me guess, in it, you threatened her."

"Threatened? Don't be ridiculous." He waved an arm, taking in the luxurious suite. "Do I look like a guy who needs to threaten a woman to get her to come to her senses? I'm not the nobody I was when you knew me back in college, Josie. I've got a name, and I've got a reputation, and I'm not going to have it dragged through the mud if word gets out to the press about any of this. I didn't threaten Kate." If hard looks could have convinced me, his would have worked. "Not exactly, anyway. I just told her . . . I pointed out what she should have known. That she was never going to be happy with Roland. And that if I couldn't have her . . ." His jaw was so tight, I waited to hear it snap. "I might have mentioned that if I couldn't have her, I didn't think anybody should."

I'd heard enough. Without another word, I headed for the door.

"Josie!" Hugh rushed to follow me. "Where are you going? What are you going to do?" He grabbed my arm and spun me around. "You're going to help me, aren't you?"

"I'm going to search for the truth."

"The hell with the truth. You think that's really more important than saving my neck?"

"My guess is you should think it's more important to find out who killed the woman you say you loved."

"Kate's dead, and I miss her so much, but the fact is, nothing can bring her back. Right now, I've got to worry about myself."

I managed a smile. It hurt. "That

shouldn't be too hard. It's always what you've done best."

"You're kidding me, right? Josie!" He reached for my arm, but I stepped back, away from his grasp. "Are you telling me — ?"

"I'm telling you that you were right, Hugh. What you did was stupid. And I'm telling you the cops are going to find out. You know they are. About the affair, and about how you paid Mike to follow Kate. About that e-mail."

"But you're going to help me get out of it, right? I mean, it's what you do. Good ol' Josie, reliable, dependable —"

"Don't you get it, Hugh? I'm not going to lie for you. You just admitted it; you were crazy jealous. And you were angry. Were you angry enough to kill Kate?"

His jaw slack, he stepped back. "Do you . . . You mean you think . . . Come on, Josie, you know me better than that."

I shouldn't have had to point it out, but hey, Hugh couldn't see past his cosmetically altered nose. I yanked open the door and stepped out into the hallway. "That's just it, Hugh," I told him. "I don't really know you at all. Not anymore."

CHAPTER EIGHT

Having worked on *Trolls* with Hugh, I am not some wide-eyed, easily awed, mouth-hanging-open-to-see-a-movie-set type.

At least I never had been before.

Until that next Monday, that is, when I left Stan in charge of the Button Box and went to the grand old lakefront brownstone where *Charlie* was being filmed.

What with the Victorian-era building's original stained-glass windows, the gorgeous wood moldings, and the fireplaces (I counted seven, but then, I never did have a chance to see the entire place), I was more than impressed. Maybe Hugh had every right to be uppity and self-centered. He'd definitely come up in the world. No more cardboard backdrops, discount-store costumes, or half-baked actors. Not like we'd had with *Trolls.* This was the real deal, and even before I was no farther than the foyer, with its marble inlay floor and a chandelier that sparkled in the morning sun, my eyes were wide and my jaw, gaping.

That is, until a security guard stopped me.

"The set is closed. No press," he said.

"I'm not."

"No gawkers."

"I'm not that, either." Not true. Not technically, anyway, since gawking was exactly what I was doing. I snapped my mouth shut. But only until I told the man, "I have an appointment with Margot, Kate Franciscus's assistant. That's why the guard outside . . ." I poked a thumb over my shoulder toward the twelve-foot-tall oak doors that led out to the front stoop. "He said it was OK for me to come in. Kate had some of my buttons. She was going to show them to her designer and now . . . well . . ." I didn't need to explain. "I'm here to pick them up."

Was it obvious that I was telling the truth, but not the whole truth and nothing but? I had an ulterior motive, see. When it came to the mystery button I'd found in the shop, I'd struck out with Hugh, but I wasn't ready to give up. The way I figured it, nobody knew Kate better than her assistants, whether they wanted to or not. They were the next logical step in my investigation. Lucky for me, there were those buttons

Kate had taken with her when she visited me the week before. The ones she hadn't brought with her to the shop the night she was killed. Those buttons provided me the perfect excuse to dig a little deeper.

While I was thinking these things, the security guard was busy edging to the side, the better to check me out from every angle. His eyes lit with recognition. "Hey, you are that button lady," he crooned. "Your picture was in the paper. I recognized your —"

I was grateful when the door swung open and interrupted the man. Not so grateful to see we'd been joined by —

"Kaz?" I rubbed my eyes. I must be hallucinating.

No such luck.

In spite of temperatures outside that were quickly skyrocketing from hot and sticky to hotter and unbearable, Kaz looked as fresh as if he'd just stepped out of the shower. He was dressed in his usual jeans and a polo shirt that looked familiar. It should. I'd bought it for him for his birthday two years before. The chocolaty color of the shirt perfectly matched his eyes. No surprise. That's why I'd bought it in the first place.

Like he belonged there, he strolled over, gave me a peck on the cheek, and shook the security guard's hand. He introduced himself and added, "I'm Ms. Giancola's assistant."

I nearly choked. "You're —"

"Late? Yes, I know. I'm sorry." I knew something was up the moment that last word was out of his mouth. Or maybe it just sounded weird because it was a word I'd never heard Kaz use before.

"You can both go on up," the security guard told us. "Fourth floor. They weren't using any of those rooms up there for the filming, so they gave them to Ms. Franciscus. You know, for like an office and a dressing room."

I was too stunned by Kaz's sudden appearance to do anything else but what I was told, so I went the way the security guard directed. Kaz walked along at my side. We'd already climbed the elegant winding staircase and were on the second-floor landing before I trusted myself to speak.

"I don't like getting blindsided," I told Kaz, refusing to look at him. I did a hairpin left turn to the next staircase — less ornate than the one that led up from the first floor. "What are you doing here? And how did you know where I was in the first place?"

"That's a no-brainer. All I had to do is follow that crowd of paparazzi that's been tailing you."

I grumbled. The reporters and photographers had been waiting outside my apartment building when I left there that morning — again. I would have thought that by now, they'd be tired of trying to get me to talk, and me saying nothing. I'd seen a couple of them hop into cabs and follow me when I headed to the movie set. "All I want is to be left alone," I grumbled. "I'm starting to feel like a zoo animal."

"You could always come stay with me for a while."

My right foot on the step ahead of me, my left on the one below, I froze and looked over my shoulder at Kaz.

"What?" Mr. Wide-Eyed-and-Innocent had the nerve to look . . . well, wide-eyed and innocent. "I'm just saying, if you need a place to crash —"

"I'll drag a cardboard box under the North Wabash Avenue Bridge and hope I don't roll over in my sleep and land in the river."

"If you say so. I only thought that if you came to my place —"

"What?" I steadied myself, my fingers in a death grip around the banister, and I made sure my glare was searing — and as no-nonsense as it was possible to get. "What did you think was going to happen if I came

151

to stay with you? We're not married any-more, in case you forgot."

"Like I could."

I wasn't exactly sure what he was getting at. I was sure I didn't want to know.

I turned around and clomped up another few steps.

"I thought if I followed you I could . . . you know . . . protect you from those reporters and photographers who are after you."

For all his faults — and believe me when I say there are many — I could never ac-cuse Kaz of not being chivalrous. It was one of the things that made me fall in love with him in the first place and, ironically, one of the things that doomed our marriage. Nobody dreamed the impossible dream quite like Kaz. Especially when that dream involved scoring big on his next sure bet.

Which wasn't what we were talking about.

Which meant my jaw shouldn't be tight and my stomach shouldn't be lurching into my throat.

I forced myself to relax, and at the third landing, I stopped and turned to face him. "Thank you," I said. "I appreciate the offer. But I don't need a bodyguard."

"Except that those guys won't leave you alone. Who knows what they might do to get at you." This landing ended in a blank wall, and knowing what I know about history (a natural offshoot of learning about buttons, who wore them, and the times in which they were made), I wasn't surprised. Like so many others of its vintage, a house this grand was sure to have a servants' stairway at the back of the building.

I was already heading that way when Kaz snatched my hand. "Jo, if you won't come stay at my place for a while, at least let me stay with you at your apartment. You know, just to make sure you're all right. Once I walk out of the building with you a couple times and tell those jerks where to get off, they'll stop bothering you."

Warning! Danger!

Oh yeah, I recognized that voice inside my head. It was the one that cautioned against getting tempted by the heady feel of my hand in Kaz's.

It was also the one that told me there was more to his offer than met the eye.

I shook away my chocolate-induced fantasies, narrowed my eyes, and gave Kaz a careful once-over. "You knew I'd never agree to stay at your place with you. Admit it, Kaz. You threw that out just to make yourself look good. As for you staying with me . . . You're trying to dodge somebody, and my guess is it's somebody you owe money to. Who's looking for you? And what is it this time? They're going to bug you until you pay? Or have they graduated to the break-your-legs stage?"

I didn't wait for him to answer. But then, I didn't really care what his answer was. I stomped down the hallway, searching for the servants' stairs, and when I found them, I took the steps two at a time. No easy thing considering my heart was already pounding and my breaths were coming fast.

I honestly didn't care if Kaz followed me or not, and frankly, now that I'd seen through his lie about caring about my well-being, I figured he wouldn't. I reminded myself that I had more important things to think about than Kaz's bad habits, and I stepped out of the narrow stairwell into a room that ran the length of the building. Through the oriel window at the front of the brownstone, there was a killer view of the lake. Through the windows at the back, a look at the third-floor roof garden. At this time of the year, the place was alive with color and blooms. A fountain trickled at its center.

Although the rest of the building had been carefully nurtured to be true to its Victorian roots, this entire level was different. The floors were bleached oak. The furniture was black leather, accented with stainless steel. The walls were painted a color that reminded me of sterling.

I wouldn't have been surprised to hear that Kate had demanded the fourth floor be remodeled and turned over to her before she ever agreed to do the movie, nor would I have been shocked to find that Hugh had caved in to her demands and begged the building's owner to comply. No doubt there was a construction crew in here the very next day.

Kate always got what she wanted.

Except she never wanted to get murdered.

The thought settled inside me like a rock, and I reminded myself not to forget it. That was exactly the same moment Margot and Sloan came bustling out of a room over on my right. Between them, they were carrying a cardboard box the size of an easy chair. Margot had her back to me. Sloan saw me, gurgled out a noise of surprise, and stopped.

"Forgot you were coming." With a grunt and a glance over her shoulder, Margot dropped her end of the box on the floor. Sloan followed suit. I heard a dull, clinking sound like breaking glass. Neither young woman seemed concerned.

Margot brushed her hands together.

"You're here for your buttons."

I'd hoped not to be dismissed so quickly, so I glanced around the room and tried to make small talk. "It's beautiful here, so different from the first three floors, but just as spectacular in its own way."

Margot's shrug was designed to show me just how much she didn't care. Last time I'd seen her, she'd been perfectly turned out in a trim, black business suit and pumps. Today she was wearing skinny jeans and a purple T-shirt, and her blonde hair was pushed back and held off her face by a green headband. Sloan was similarly dressed, in jeans and a flamingo-pink tank. Her dark hair was pulled into a ponytail. One blindingly pink fingernail was broken to the quick, and Sloan looked at it and moaned, "It will all look a hell of a lot better once we're standing outside waving good-bye to this place."

I glanced past them and toward the room they'd just come out of. From where I was standing, I could see a couple of rolling clothing racks. One was packed to the gills with designer outfits in a very small size. The other was filled with costumes so incredible, they took my breath away. Back in college, where I majored in theater with the hope of someday doing the costumes for movies or plays, I would have given my right arm to work with garments so authentic looking and so fabulous. Blouses with leg-of-mutton sleeves, ball gowns with deep-veed bodices and nipped waists. Skirts designed to hug hips, then flare out just above the knee. Above-the-elbow kid gloves in white and ivory and black.

I thought about the mystery button — the one that didn't have any fingerprints on it — and swiveled my gaze from the costumes to the assistants. "Have any of the costumes gone missing? Like the gloves?"

"Gloves?" Sloan made a face. "You're kidding, right? Who in their right mind would want them?"

"Of course." There was no use tipping my hand. Instead, I glanced at the box Margot and Sloan had brought in from the other room. "There must be a lot of details to take care of," I said. "All Kate's things. You're packing them to go to —"

"Paris," Sloan said, at the same time Margot said, "Maui."

Maybe Margot was right. Or maybe since she was on top of the assistant totem pole, she always won out. "Maui, of course," Sloan mumbled.

No way I was getting in the middle of that. Hoping that the farther I was from the doorway, the longer I could get away with hanging around, I edged toward the sofa and the glossy metal table next to it. "There must be buttons, too, of course. I don't mean mine. I mean —"

"Buttons, sure." I should have known someone as well trained as Margot wouldn't let any grass grow under her feet. She zipped off and came back in a jiffy, holding the small leather briefcase I knew contained the buttons I'd given to Kate for her consideration. "Kate called. The night she was killed. I was still here, and she'd already left and when I heard the phone ring . . . Well, I checked caller ID and when I saw it was her, I didn't answer. I was already off the clock that day. She left a message, said she'd forgotten those buttons she was supposed to get back to you and said I should drop whatever I was doing and run them over. On my night off!" Margot sniffed.

I took the briefcase from her and gave myself a mental kick in the pants. This investigating stuff wasn't as easy as it looked on TV, and I wasn't going to find out anything if I didn't take it easy, take my time, and get the assistants to talk.

Stalling for time, I snapped open the case. The buttons I'd given Kate were mounted just as they would be if I was taking them to a show for sale or entering them in a competition, on what we in the business call trays, nine-by-twelve-inch white, acid-free matt board. Normally, I would have just slipped each tray into a heavy plastic sleeve to prevent the buttons from rubbing against each other. For Kate, I'd used the plastic sleeves, then wrapped each tray in velvet and set all three trays in the briefcase. No, I was not playing favorites. In fact, this was the way all my most prized buttons traveled.

As I knew they would be, all the buttons were present and accounted for, and I closed the case and wondered what a real detective would do next. That lasted maybe half a second before I reminded myself that I wasn't a real detective; I was a button dealer. Buttons were, are, and will always be the only thing I know how to talk about.

I looked from Margot to Sloan. "I found a button in my shop, and it doesn't belong to me. I thought Kate might have left it there."

"Kate didn't even remember to take those buttons with her when she went to see you the other night," Margot said with a look toward the briefcase. "You really think she would have brought buttons of her own?"

"You really think she'd have any? I mean, any that weren't attached to clothing?"

Sloan didn't need to elaborate. The unspoken words hung in the air between us. Like Hugh, Margot and Sloan believed buttons were for nerds.

And Kate Franciscus was anything but.

Another dead end. And another chance to prove I wasn't going to give up. I sat down, the better to send the message that I wasn't going anywhere anytime soon. "So if Kate didn't drop that button, maybe one of you did the day you were at the Button Box."

"A button?" Blake appeared out of the back room, her short-cropped hair a mess and smudges of dirt across her cheek. Clearly, as third in line, she'd been given the less tasteful of the cleanup and packing tasks. I could only imagine what poor little Wynona would be left to deal with. "You're not serious, are you?" Blake dragged a garbage bag behind her. She plopped it down in the middle of the living room floor. "Buttons aren't exactly our thing."

"But one of you might have lost it off a piece of clothing." I was prepared; I had a photo of the button with me, and I slipped it out of my purse and showed it all around. "It's an unusual button, probably hand-crafted. If it was on one of your suit coats or purses or —"

Margot leaned over for a better look.

160

So did Sloan, who sneered. "It looks like somebody made it out of some old tree." She didn't need to elaborate. Clearly, handmade was akin to so-not cool.

"Like any of us would buy anything like that." Blake rolled her eyes.

"If it doesn't belong to one of you . . ." I glanced at the assistants gathered around me. "Maybe you've seen it someplace? Maybe someone else would know? How about Wynona?"

"Wynona!" I didn't realize names could be associated with tastes until I heard the sour twist Margot gave this one. She answered me, sure, but she was looking hard at Blake when she did. "Wynona isn't with us anymore. Is she, Blake?"

"Hey, it's not my fault." Blake threw up her hands. "How was I supposed to know the girl wasn't on the up-and-up?"

"She wasn't?" I sat up. Sure, it had nothing to do with buttons, or more specifically, with the button I needed to learn more about, but this was definitely interesting. I leaned forward, and because I knew Margot would take the lead, I looked her way. "What happened?"

The smile she threw at Blake was scorching. "Blake didn't do a background check like she was supposed to."

Blake flopped down on the chair opposite mine and crossed her arms over her chest. "When Shawna got sick, we needed another assistant fast. You didn't expect me to do the things we had Shawna doing, did you?"

"And look where trying to dodge a little work got you," Sloan crooned. "Sweet little Wynona wasn't all that sweet after all. She had a taste for jewelry."

"Pearls, specifically. Antique and valuable," Margot said. "Too bad they were Kate's."

The day I'd met her, Wynona was painfully shy. The thought of her as a thief . . .

It didn't jibe. "Are you sure?"

"Kate was." This from Margot, who nodded. "Otherwise, she wouldn't have fired the little twit."

Another spot of news. "When?" I asked.

While Margot was still thinking about it, Blake piped up. "The day after we came to see the buttons."

"The day before Kate was killed," I mumbled.

Margot, Sloan, and Blake exchanged glances, but they left it to Margot to speak. "You're not saying —"

"A single thing." I made that clear by getting to my feet. "I don't know anything about pearls, and I sure don't know anything about murder. Buttons are my business."

"She was hopping mad," Sloan threw in.

"Kate?" I asked.

"Wynona." As if reliving the scene, Sloan narrowed her eyes. "Wynona looked innocent enough, all right, but after Kate called her in for a meeting . . ." She shivered. "I was here when Wynona walked out of the back room Kate used as an office. She had tears streaming down her cheeks, and she was so damned mad, her face was on fire."

"Maybe she was just embarrassed at having been caught," I suggested. "Or grateful? After all, Kate apparently just fired her; she didn't have her arrested."

"Or maybe she was mad enough to kill her!" This from Blake, whose eyes shone with excitement.

I wasn't so sure she was on the right track. "Wynona doesn't exactly strike me as the murderous type."

"And she hadn't even started yet when Kate did all that stuff with security."

I turned to Blake who'd dropped that bombshell. "Security? Like . . . ?"

Blake glanced at Margot, who gave her the go-ahead with a gesture that pretty much said it didn't matter anymore what anyone knew. "A month or so ago," she said.

"Of course, Kate has always had security, but she hired another couple guys. And she had us screen her calls more thoroughly. Margot, you asked —"

"What was up, that's right." Margot nodded. "And Kate told me that with the wedding coming up, she couldn't be too careful."

"She was afraid of someone," I said. "Who? Was there anyone who didn't like Kate?"

Blake laughed. "What you should be asking is if there was anyone who liked her. It would be a hell of a lot easier to find that out, and your list would be a lot shorter."

It reminded me of what Hugh had said: plenty of people wanted Kate dead.

I asked them what I'd asked him. "Who?"

"Who hated Kate?" Margot looked at her coworkers. "Well, all of us, for starters, but then, that's no big surprise. You don't get bossed around day and night by a woman who thinks she's God's gift to the world and not get just the teeniest bit resentful. But like I told that cute cop, that doesn't mean any of us killed her."

"What you mean to say is that it doesn't mean any of us . . ." Sloan pointed a finger between Blake and herself. "Neither of us killed her. What about you, Margot?" Her smile was as brittle as ice. "Were you still pissed at Kate because you wanted time off to go visit that boy toy of yours in San Diego and Kate said —"

"That was business, and once she explained to me how she couldn't spare me before the wedding, I understood. It was nothing to get mad about." Margot's words were convincing enough, but the muscle that jumped at the base of her jaw said otherwise. "The way I remember it, Sloan, you were a little miffed at Kate yourself. You were the one —"

"I didn't use her stupid lipstick." Sloan's smile dissolved in an instant, and she booted the garbage bag just for good measure. "And even if I did, she didn't have to mention it in front of Hugh and the rest of the production staff. You know she only did it because she'd heard that I was thinking of applying for that administrative job Hugh has available. Kate wanted to make sure I couldn't leave, and she figured if she made me look incompetent, Hugh wouldn't touch me. Right in front of all of them . . ." She turned my way to explain. "Right in front of everybody, Kate said I was lucky to be working for her, because I was so untrustworthy, anybody else would have canned me on the spot. How ridiculous is that? If she was looking to fire anybody . . ." Her gaze swung to Blake, who instantly turned the color of the ashen walls.

"I told you, it wasn't my fault," she said. "Kate shouldn't have blamed me for Wynona."

"But she did, didn't she?" Margot leaned in close, challenging Blake. "Did she threaten to fire you, too, Blake? Is that why you were grumbling about her that morning and saying how much you would like to see her —"

"I never said dead." Blake popped out of her chair. She was a hair shorter than Margot, and when she folded her arms across her chest and tipped her chin up, her eyes spit fire. "I said I couldn't believe how narrow-minded she was."

"And Kate heard you and reamed you out." Sloan joined in the fray. "And you just got madder and madder at her. When I saw you at lunchtime that day —"

"I said I was thinking about quitting."

"Maybe you decided quitting wasn't a good-enough revenge."

"That's just crazy." Blake stomped away. "It's all just crazy." She poked a thumb into her chest. "I sure didn't kill her. I don't know about you two."

"Well, I didn't, either," Sloan huffed.

Margot pulled herself up to her full height. "I'm not even going to say it. I shouldn't have to."

I was feeling a bit like a preschool teacher caught in the middle of toddlers in tantrums. Bad enough these three were going at it; worse, if they were so busy sniping at each other, they couldn't give me any useful information.

"I'm sure you told the police all that." Yeah, that was me, sounding a little too chipper and so worried this was going to turn into a full-scale melee, I didn't care. "They must have asked you."

"The cute cop did." First Margot, now Sloan. What cop needs social skills when he can get by on his looks? If we ever had another semi-civilized conversation, I'd be sure to mention it to Nevin. "He asked about alibis, too." Her smile inched up a notch. "I have one. I was at dinner with my cousin who lives here in town. What about you, Margot? Blake? Were you able to tell him you had an alibi?"

Margot's cheeks turned pink. "I was at the hotel. Alone."

"I went to dinner," Blake grumbled. "And I was alone, too, which pretty much proves I didn't do it, because if I did, I would have come up with a better alibi than that." She swung her gaze to me. "Right?"

I couldn't say. But then, with my ears ringing and my head spinning, it was kind of hard to get a grip. Instead, I hung on tight to the briefcase with my buttons in it and headed for the stairs. If the assistants wanted to eat each other alive, at least I wouldn't have to watch.

I was back in the glorious marble foyer when Kaz walked out of a back room.

"No luck," he said.

So maybe my head was still spinning from all the infighting upstairs. I gave him a questioning look.

"With security," he explained. "You heard what that one assistant said —"

"What surprises me is that you heard."

"Does it?" He grinned. "You didn't think I was going to miss out on something like that, did you? I was on the stairs, listening, only then that one chick said something about security, and I figured I'd help you out. You know, to show you what a great guy I am." He winked.

I stayed strong. "And you found out . . ."

Kaz held the front door open for me. "Pretty much nothing. Kate Franciscus added some extra people to her security staff. That part was true. But nobody knows why and there was never any trouble.

So . . ." We were on the stoop in the punishing sunlight. I slipped my sunglasses out of my purse and put them on just as Mike Homolka dashed to the bottom of the steps and snapped a few shots.

Kaz took my arm, and we walked to the sidewalk. "Told you you needed protection."

"I really don't," I said, and in my head, I had all the reasons why I didn't lined up. I was going to tell him that I was a big girl and I could take care of myself. I was going to point out that Kate was the one who'd obviously been in danger and there was no reason for me to worry about my safety. And if Kaz didn't back off even then, I was all set to mention that a woman who's been betrayed by the man she thought she could depend on has got to learn to fend for herself.

Too bad I never had the chance.

But then, that was because a twelve-speed mountain bike careened around the corner and headed right for me.

"Watch out!" Kaz yelled and pushed me out of the way, and it was a good thing he did. Instead of slamming right into me, the bike swerved. The front tire grazed my right leg, and the driver threw out an arm.

The last thing I remembered was bouncing off the curb and landing in the street.

CHAPTER NINE

"I don't need it." I pushed Kaz's hands — and the SpongeBob Band-Aid he was holding in them — away. It actually might have been a good move if Stan wasn't leaning over from the other side of me, all set to pounce with a Spider-Man bandage.

I angled between them and got off the guest chair in front of my desk at the Button Box. "Honest, guys, I appreciate the help, but a cartoon character across the bridge of my nose . . ." I touched a tentative finger to the scrape there and winced.

"Told you you needed it!" I watched SpongeBob and Kaz come nearer and ducked out of the way just in time to avoid them both.

Thanks to Kaz and Stan, I already had Barbie on my knees, Dora the Explorer on my elbow, and Scooby-Doo on my wrist.

That's what I got for having bandages on hand in case of any accidents when Kaz's sister's kids came to the shop to visit.

Kaz knew better than to push. Or at least he should have. That didn't stop him from pulling out his cell. "If you won't let us help, at least let me —"

"Call 911?" I plucked the phone out of his hands just as he was about to dial. "I told you when it happened, Kaz, I'm fine except for a few bumps and bruises and scrapes, so I don't need paramedics. And I don't need the cops, either. They're not going to come running just because some careless teenager —"

"Is that who you think did this?" Stan hadn't moved from his spot near the desk, but I could tell his brain was working a mile a minute. His eyes narrowed and glinting, he swung his gaze to Kaz. "Let's go over it again. Just to see if I have all the details down pat. When you got back here, you said she walked out of that fancy brownstone and —"

"Yeah. That's right." Thank goodness Stan had distracted him. Kaz put SpongeBob down. "We were barely on the sidewalk. And this bike comes careening around the corner right at her and —"

"Man or woman riding it?"

Kaz didn't spend more than a nanosecond thinking about Stan's question. "Man," he said. "I think. Maybe. Yeah, a man. He was wearing a red sweatshirt and jeans. And I'm pretty sure a bike helmet, too, but it's hard to say. His sweatshirt hood was pulled up over his head."

Stan took it all in. "And Josie was on the sidewalk? Or out in the street?"

"Sidewalk." Kaz nodded. "Definitely."

"She was standing . . ." Stan grabbed my hand and dragged me over to stand next to Kaz. "On your right? Or your left?"

"Left." Kaz switched locations to be on the proper side and once he did, Stan looked over our relative positions and his eyes narrowed a little more.

He swung one arm out. "If the biker was coming from that direction like you said . . ." He pointed and arced his arm back the other way, closer and closer toward where I was standing. "You see what I'm getting at here?" he asked Kaz.

Kaz nodded. "He should have run into me, not Jo. So the guy in the sweatshirt, he was either the worst biker in the world or just plain stupid and careless or —"

"What?" Since they were talking about me like I wasn't there, I stepped forward to remind them, ignoring the pain that shot up my hip when I did. Yes, I'd refused Kaz's offer to call the paramedics. That's because

I knew nothing was broken. But that didn't mean nothing hurt. Including my ribs and hip at the spot where I came down splat on that briefcase with my buttons in it. Fortunately, the briefcase was sturdy, and though one side of it was mashed in and the latch had been nearly impossible to open, I'd managed.

Thank goodness, none of the buttons had been damaged.

I couldn't say the same for me.

I rubbed a hand on the hip I knew would be a lurid shade of purple by morning. "If you two are cooking up some kind of loony conspiracy theory . . ." I looked from Kaz to Stan. "Don't. It was an accident. That biker was probably some mindless teenager who wasn't watching where he was going. No doubt, by now he's hiding out somewhere, hoping he didn't really hurt me and he doesn't really get in trouble."

Stan stuck out his chin. "Loony, huh? Don't forget, you did have that burglary here."

"And then someone got murdered here." Kaz put in his two cents' worth.

"And now this?" Stan gave me that eagle-eye stare of his. If I wasn't so busy repositioning Barbie where they'd stuck her, right on raw skin, I might have cared. "If you ask me, this is looking pretty fishy."

"Which means someone should definitely be going home with you and staying there."

I pretended not to hear Kaz and, instead, thought back to the split second before I realized that bike was about to slam into me. I remembered feeling the front tire graze my leg. That was right before the biker raised an arm, smashed into me, and sent me flying.

"All right. Sure. He stuck out an arm. But that was because he was trying to keep himself from falling," I said, even though Stan and Kaz had no idea what I was thinking. "There was no way he hit me on purpose."

Kaz wasn't buying it. He stepped back and stared at me, his arms crossed over his chest and his head cocked.

One corner of Stan's mouth lifted in an I-can't-believe-you-just-said-that sneer.

It was bad enough to have one of them proposing a theory so preposterous. Worse to be tag teamed. Especially by these two. See, after the divorce (OK, I'll be truthful, even before I finally got my act together and decided to end my marriage), Kaz was not on the list of Stan's favorite people. That was because Stan is street-smart. He saw right through Kaz's stories and his lies. He wasn't taken in by Kaz's charm and smokin' grin and the whole luscious package that is Kaz.

Not like I'd been taken in.

The fact that they were thinking alike — about anything — was enough to throw me for a loop.

I walked around to the other side of my desk and flopped down in the chair.

I didn't much care which one of them answered, so I propped my elbows on the desk and dropped my head into my hands. "Why on earth would anyone want to run me over with a bike?"

"Why would anyone want to burglarize this place?" Stan countered.

"You need protection," Kaz said.

I groaned, and because my computer was right in front of me, I turned on the screen and clicked over to the Internet. I couldn't get straight answers out of them, and my own brain sure wasn't providing any. At least with the computer to distract me, I didn't have to listen to the disturbing little voice inside my head — the one that wondered if they just might be right.

I hadn't counted on seeing a photo of Kate the Great first thing.

"It's got to be about her funeral." Stan came over and leaned against the desk on my left. "They were talking about it on all the early shows this morning."

Kaz came to stand on my right. "You know all the hoopla's going to die down once they get the memorial service over with, Jo," he rumbled. "You don't want to miss your opportunity. You could be making a bundle off your involvement in all this. I think a woman with your business sense would see that."

I saw plenty, all right. But it wasn't what Kaz wanted me to see.

I sat up straight, barely whimpering at all. At least not too much. "It all started that day Kate came to see me for the first time," I said, more to Stan than to Kaz since Kaz was getting on my nerves. "The burglary, the murder, and now this crazy accident. There's got to be some connection."

"We need a stakeout," Stan announced.

"You need someone to keep you safe," Kaz said.

And me? I hauled myself out of the chair and hobbled to the back room to get my purse and those photos of the mystery button. Thinking, I tapped them gently against my unscraped hand.

What I really needed was answers, and so far, I wasn't being very successful getting them.

Good thing Kaz was right about me being smart.

I was smart enough to know exactly what I was going to do next.

And smart enough to keep my mouth shut about it, too.

The next day, the first thing I did was talk Stan into babysitting the shop again. And yes, I know, a retired cop in a button shop . . . not exactly a match made in heaven. I wasn't complaining, though, mostly because Stan was doing me a huge favor, but also because (let's face reality, here), a button shop doesn't get a lot of foot traffic, not when it's brand-new, anyway. The majority of my orders came in through my website and I could handle those any hour of the day or night. I vowed I'd work twice as hard when I got back to the Button Box that evening and then I spoke to Margot, and once I talked to her, I called one of those bargain-priced hotels over near the Lincoln Park Zoo, the one and only address Margot had for Wynona. Unfortunately for me, bargain-priced translated into nobody answered the phone. Even though I worried that the lowliest of the lowly assistants might have moved on once she got fired, I took a chance. And since I ached too much to hoof it from the nearest El stop, I took a cab, too.

When it came to saying whether Wynona had checked out or was still a guest, the clerk behind the front desk wouldn't confirm or deny. But then, it was the sort of hotel where I imagined a lot of people wanted to remain anonymous. In answer to my plea, he did agree to call up to the room that "Miss Redfern *might* be staying in."

No answer.

Since he was all set to dive into a magazine (it was out on the front desk, and just the title on the cover made me blush), I wasn't surprised when he lost interest immediately and left it up to me to figure out if Wynona was long gone or was still in residence and just out. Or in the bathroom. Or out in the hallway hanging her "Do Not Disturb" sign.

I considered my options, decided there weren't any, and I'd just stepped out of the building when I saw Wynona walking down the sidewalk.

When she caught sight of me, a wobbly smile lit her face. "Ms. Giancola!" She was carrying a dry-cleaning bag, and she shifted it from one arm to the other, folding it over so that she could hang on to it easier. "It's nice to see you. I'm so sorry . . ." The kid's cheeks flamed, and she stared down at the sidewalk. "I read all about it in the papers, of course. I'm so sorry you were the one . . . you know . . . the one who found Miss Franciscus."

It was kind of her to mention it, and I told her so. Right before I invited her to join me for coffee.

Wynona's cheeks reddened even more. "I don't have very much money, and —"

"My treat." There was a Starbucks nearby, and I stepped that way and was relieved when she followed. I waited until we'd ordered and were seated at a table near the window before I eased into the meat of the matter as gently as I could.

"You're new in town," I said, and when Wynona looked at me in wonder, I took pity on her. Yeah, it would have been nice for her to think of me as a genius, but I supplied the easy answer. "You're staying in a hotel and not an apartment yet."

"Of course." I think she would have slapped her forehead if she didn't think it was the wrong thing to do in public, and with a woman she barely knew. I'd bet anything she was thinking about that hotel when she wrinkled her nose. "It's not the best in the city. But the price is right, and it will do until I can find a place that's more permanent."

"Actually, I thought you might not be around at all." I drew in a breath and let it out slowly. I wasn't sure how she'd react when I brought up what I was about to mention, but there was no way around it. "Wynona, I spoke with the other assistants. They told me about how you were let go. And why."

Wynona grabbed on to the table and held on tight, and her voice clogged with tears. "Oh, Ms. Giancola, I didn't do it! Miss Franciscus, she said her pearls were missing and that she was sure I was the one who'd taken them, but honest, I didn't. I didn't even know she had pearls, and even if I did, I'm not that kind of person. Not the kind who steals jewelry. Not from anybody. That's not the way I was raised."

It was hard not to believe a kid who was so darned sincere. I stirred sweetener into my coffee, grateful I'd taken the time to run out to Walgreens the night before. It was tough enough talking about robbery and trying to get to the truth behind a murder. It would have been even harder if I had to question Wynona while I was wearing cartoon-character bandages. The edge of the bandage on my wrist — a plain, old bandage in a plain, old skin tone color — had come loose, and I smoothed it with one finger. "You think someone else took the pearls?"

She shrugged. Even though it was in the nineties outside, Wynona had ordered a hot chocolate, and she sipped and then licked whipped cream off her top lip. "I would never accuse anyone of anything that terrible."

It wasn't what she said, it was the way she said it. I leaned forward. "But . . ."

Her lower lip trembled. "But . . . well . . . somebody must have taken those pearls. And it sure wasn't me. I swear. If Miss Franciscus was going to call the police, I'd already decided that I'd tell them to give me a lie-detector test. Then they'd see. They'd see I didn't do it."

"But she didn't call the police."

She shook her head.

"She fired you instead."

Now she nodded.

"Were you angry? Or grateful?"

Not questions Wynona was expecting. Her gaze darted to mine, then flashed away again. "The last thing I need is a police record. I mean, if I plan on finding another job."

"So it's grateful."

"And disappointed." Her shoulders fell. "That job . . . I thought . . . It was like a dream come true, you know?"

I sipped my coffee. "It didn't look like a dream to me. Not with the way Kate ordered everybody around. The other assistants —"

Her top lip curled. It would have been a far more ferocious look if there wasn't a smudge of whipped cream on her mouth. "You seem like a decent person," she said. "I know I can be honest with you. I'll bet you understand what it's like to work hard and not to have people notice you, to just boss you around and expect you to do things, and then when you're done doing what you're supposed to do and doing it well, they just treat you like you're invisible. I mean you must get the same sort of treatment all the time. You sell buttons." Color shot into her cheeks.

"What you're saying is that nobody would ever notice a button dealer."

She ripped her paper napkin into tiny pieces and kept her gaze on the shreds. "Something like that," she said. "No offense intended."

I wasn't in the mood to offer the all-forgiving *none taken* but I decided to hedge my bets. In the last days, I'd run into two burly burglars, had a customer murdered and discovered the body, and nearly been sent to the final beyond by a mountain bike. It was beginning to look more and more like the button business wasn't for wusses.

But my fragile ego wasn't what we were talking about. We were talking about murder.

Only Wynona didn't have to know that.

"Who are you talking about, Wynona? Who do you think didn't notice you? Miss Franciscus? Or the other assistants?"

"I wouldn't have even gotten the job if that other girl didn't get sick and they weren't desperate." She stuck out her bottom lip. "And I was grateful, don't get me wrong. But that's pretty much the way they all looked at me, kind of as an afterthought. Not that I'm bitter or anything."

This time I calmed her fears with a quick "Not to worry," partly because Wynona was so sweet, I didn't want to see her get upset, but mostly because bitter was exactly what I was counting on. If Wynona was feeling resentful, maybe she'd be willing to spill the beans about her former employer and her fellow employees. If she knew anything worth spilling, that is.

I'd already stirred my coffee plenty, but I gave it another whirl. "You don't seem like the kind of person who's all that into gossip," I told her. "Whatever you think, you

183

can tell me, and I'll know you're not saying it just because you're holding a grudge."

"I went to the zoo yesterday," Wynona said, "and I was watching the hyenas and reading about them, too. That's what they remind me of."

"They . . . ?"

She bobbed her head. "Margot and Sloan and that snotty Blake girl. The minute one of them does something that's the tiniest little bit wrong, the others pounce. You know, like hyenas on a carcass."

It was an uncomfortable comparison, but then, murder is an uncomfortable subject.

"And you think . . ."

She leaned forward. "I can't say. Not for sure, of course. But I think one of them must have taken Miss Franciscus's pearls. I know for a fact, I didn't. And nobody else was around upstairs in those rooms they gave us to use while they were filming the movie. If the pearls were there, then one of the other assistants took them."

Interesting. Before I had a chance to point it out, Wynona leaned closer.

"One of them must have killed her, too, don't you think? They didn't like her, you know. Not one bit. Margot thought she was every bit as good as Miss Franciscus. I mean . . ." Wynona sat back, her cheeks dusky. "I only worked with them for a little while, but it was obvious, you know? Margot, she did what she was told, but I saw her looking at Miss Franciscus sometimes and you know that old saying about how if looks could kill. That's what I thought."

"And Margot doesn't have an alibi for the night of the murder. Neither does Blake."

"Blake and Sloan were just as bad. Once, I heard Blake say something about wanting the bi . . ." Wynona swallowed the word. "Pardon my French, but I have to say it because that's what Blake said and I wouldn't be reporting it right if I didn't use her words. She was talking about Miss Franciscus and she was mad about something, and she said . . ." She lowered her voice until I had to strain to hear it. "She said, 'I wish that bitch was dead.' "

It was damning but hardly proof. And time to get to the heart of the matter.

"Which of them liked buttons?" I asked Wynona.

She went still for the space of a couple heartbeats. But then, it was an odd question, so I couldn't blame her for trying to put it in perspective. Finally, she shrugged. "Well, Miss Franciscus, I guess, since she's the one who came to you to buy buttons."

"What about the assistants?"

She took another drink of her hot choco-late. "Not any of them. Not as far as I know. But then, like I said, I was only there a little while." She set her cup down with a clatter. "Does it matter?"

"Probably not." For all I knew, that was true. "It's just that I found a button. In my shop." The moment the words were out of my mouth, I realized how dumb they sounded, and I added, "I mean, a button that doesn't belong to me."

"My goodness! You know your button inventory that well? You'd really know a but-ton that wasn't yours? When you have so very many of them? It's not that I'm ques-tioning you or anything," she said on the end of another blush. "I'm certain you know what you're doing. It's just so . . ." A look very much like admiration lit her non-descript eyes. "So amazing!"

"It's not so amazing. This is a pretty special button," I said because though I did, actually, feel an affinity for each of the but-tons in my collection, I didn't want to come across looking like a know-it-all. "I'm pretty sure it's handmade. I wondered if you might know something about it."

Her smile faded. "I wish I could help. It matters to you, doesn't it? You must be trying to get the button back to its rightful owner."

"Something like that," I said. Let's face it, Wynona had already admitted that she thought of me as a boring button nerd. If I told her I was helping the police with their investigation, I was pretty sure she'd add *nutcase* to her opinion.

Wynona took another drink of her hot chocolate. "It's sad, isn't it? I mean, about Miss Franciscus. She wasn't . . ." She set down her cup and leaned forward, sharing the confidence. "She wasn't very nice. I mean, not like I expected her to be. I've seen her in so many movies and she's always . . . I dunno . . . always so beautiful and so much of a lady. But for real . . ." Wynona made a face. "She didn't treat us very nice. It's sad to die and that's pretty much all somebody remembers about you."

It was.

Except it wasn't all anybody would remember. Not about Kate Franciscus.

Because the entire world would remember that she'd been murdered.

And the Chicago Police Department would remember that though I was supposed to be one of the foremost button experts in the country, all I ever came up

with by way of information that could help
them was a big old nothing.

CHAPTER TEN

I called Nevin Riley twice that night.

Both times, I got his voice mail.

Both times, I hung up before I had the nerve to leave him a message.

I guess I wasn't ready to admit that though he thought I was an expert when it came to buttons and a bust when it came to having a personality, he was wrong.

It looked like I was a loser at both.

In spite of talking to Hugh, and to the assistants . . . in spite of researching and researching some more . . . in spite of obsessing about it . . . I was no closer to discovering anything about the mystery button.

That depressing thought was still banging its way around inside my head when I left for the Button Box the next day.

I had a load of sorting and organizing to do, and I was down one assistant, remember, so I'd dressed comfortably that morning in jeans and a navy-blue T-shirt that didn't so much complement my coloring as it did match the smudges of sleeplessness under my eyes. I'd been too exhausted to fuss with my hair so I had it pulled back in a ponytail and was wearing a Cubs baseball cap and carrying a giant tote bag filled with research books. Yes, I'd already looked through them a dozen times. Yes, I planned to comb through them a dozen times more. Maybe I'd missed a reference, a photo, a clue that would lead me to information about the boxwood button.

And didn't it figure — no sooner was I out the door of my apartment building than Mike Homolka pounced.

He snapped dozens of shots of me before I even had a chance to say, "There really can't be anyone in the world who would be interested in buying those pictures from you. Nobody cares about me."

"Somebody does." I'd already started to walk away when he darted in front of me and took another shot, just for good measure. "I've got a buyer for these pictures."

It wasn't that I didn't believe him. It was just that . . . well, I didn't believe him. I stopped long enough to give him a look that said as much. "It's too early in the morning to listen to your hogwash." I sidled between a parked car and a delivery truck and crossed the street. Unlucky for me, he followed. He was at my side before I ever stepped onto the sidewalk on the other side of the street. I guess it says something about my rose-colored attitude; I actually tried to reason with the man. "You can't just take pictures of a person and then sell them. I mean, not pictures of just a regular person. It's not like I'm a celebrity or anything."

"Law says I can." The grin Homolka gave me was no more attractive than the rest of him. "As long as I'm on public property." He did a quick little dance step against the pavement. "I can take pictures of anything and anyone I want. You should have learned that by now. Anyone who wants to be a big star someday should know things like that."

"I don't want to be a star."

"But you were a theater major."

I wasn't going to let on about how very disturbing it was that he knew even that little bit about me. "I was a theater major with a concentration on costuming. I wanted to design costumes for plays and movies. It didn't turn out the way I'd hoped. Most producers and directors aren't as interested in historical authenticity as they are in saving a few bucks on their productions and I'm too focused on history and . . . , and it doesn't matter, because I've got the best job in the world and I'm happy doing what I'm doing and owning my own business. If you think there's any more to my story than that, you're wasting your time."

"Not according to the e-mail I got last night. The one offering to pay me in return for pictures of you."

I gave him as careful a look as I could through bleary eyes. I was hoping he'd give me a smirk back, one that proved he was just a sick and twisted joker. Dang! Even my sleep-deprived brain could tell Homolka was as serious as a heart attack.

And I suddenly wasn't as weary as I was wary.

A chill crawled through my insides and lodged between my stomach and my throat. "You're not kidding," I said, my voice raspy thanks to said chill. "Somebody contacted you? About taking pictures of me? Who?"

His shrug said it all. "I'm not one to quibble about the who. Not so much as the how much. All I know is the person wants pics of you e-mailed back, as soon as I get them. He offered me a couple hundred to keep tabs on you."

Good thing a bus rumbled by. That way, he didn't hear my gulp when I swallowed hard. "And you're doing it?"

"You're kidding me, right?" Homolka laughed. "I wouldn't take photos of my own mother at her birthday party for only a couple hundred bucks."

The way I figured it, he'd been created out of a batch of smelly pond scum and didn't have a mother, but I didn't quibble. I was too creeped out by the thought that someone cared enough about me to want to know what I was up to. "You must know who wants the pictures. The e-mail had to come from someone. You can't just work for people when you don't know who they are."

"Hey, it's a cash-and-carry sort of business. When the price is right, I know better than to ask questions."

"And when it isn't?"

His grin revealed a wide gap between his top front teeth. "Delete, delete, delete," he said, moving one finger up and down as if he were tapping the computer key.

Like it was a snake and ready to strike, I took a careful look at his camera. "So why are you still taking pictures of me?"

"You're still news. Or maybe you will be one of these days when you finally decide to talk about Kate the Great's last moments."

I was almost grateful he mentioned the murder. At least if I was thinking about the investigation that wasn't, I didn't have to think about the person who cared where I was and what I was doing. "I don't know anything about Kate's last moments," I reminded Homolka, even though since I'd told him that before, I shouldn't have had to repeat myself. "I wasn't there during her last moments. You know that, because you were right there with me."

"Yeah, and thanks for mentioning that to the cops, by the way." Funny, he didn't sound grateful. "They've been bugging me about alibis and motives and all the rest of that bullshit."

"I was just telling them the truth. You were outside the shop the night Kate was killed. You were there before I got there. You knew she was going to be there because Hugh told you."

"You talked to him, huh?" Homolka didn't look surprised. "First the guy couldn't get it through his thick skull that Kate wanted that prince of hers more than she wanted him. Now all he's doing is whining and crying and telling me not to tell the cops that I was following Kate for him."

"But you have told the cops."

"Absolutely." I was heading toward the El, and I glanced at him just long enough to see one corner of his mouth pull into a sneer. "You don't think I'm going to put my neck on the line for a crybaby like Hugh Weaver, do you? I told the cops he paid me to follow Kate. More than a couple hundred bucks, by the way. Much more. I didn't bother to mention that. No use the feds getting wind of numbers and somebody checking them against what I declare on my taxes. I also told them Weaver knew Kate was going to your shop that night. Yeah, he was the one who told me. And I was waiting there for her. I told the cops that, too, just like I told them that Weaver told me she wasn't supposed to show up until eight. I got there plenty early so I could wait around, relax, have a couple beers. Only she must have gotten there even earlier than me, because I never saw her arrive. I figured I'd just hang out and have a bird's-eye view when she showed up. Then you opened your front door and . . ." His shrug was far too casual a gesture to encompass the horror of what I'd found.

"By the way," he added, "the cops loved hearing about how Hugh Weaver was jealous and how desperate he was to get back together with Kate. They were practically salivating when I told them that little detail."

"I can't believe you talked to them at all, I mean, without being paid for it."

Homolka twitched his wide shoulders. "Me, neither! But cops, they have a way of convincing a guy, huh? Besides, they got no reason to be suspicious of me. For me, Kate was a cash cow. Money from Weaver for following her. Money from the tabloids and the newspapers and the cable TV shows for the pictures I took while I was following her. I was probably the last person on earth who wanted her dead. Now I could make even a little more money, you know, if you'd just talk to me a little. Tell me all about how upset you were when you found the body and how you're helping the cops try to figure out what really happened."

This was clearly a fishing expedition. There was no way he could know about the button or about how this particular button expert was turning out to be a button flop. I knew if I was smart, I'd keep it that way. And if there was one thing I am, it's smart.

Except if I really was all that smart . . .

The photos of the mystery button were in my tote along with all those research books, and just outside the El station, I stopped and cradled the tote in my arms, thinking.

If I told Homolka about the button . . .

If he knew it had been found under Kate's body . . .

And that it might have been left there by

the killer . . .

If I allowed him an exclusive in exchange for getting the pictures published in one of the tabloids he worked with . . .

I drew in a breath, taking the thought to its logical conclusion.

If I did all that, it would create a lot of buzz. Newspapers. TV. Internet. By the time it made its way around the world and back again, the sensation might spark a call from someone who knew something about the button.

In a case that seemed to be out of options, it was a not-half-bad plan, and considering it, I gave Homolka the once-over.

That was all it took for me to change my mind.

I didn't trust the man, not as far as I could throw him, and besides, I'd been wrong to think there were no alternatives. In fact, I thought of one. Just like that. It wasn't perfect, but hey, what's that old saying: better the devil you know than the one you don't.

It was time to swallow my pride and call on the one I knew. I just hoped Estelle Marvin didn't gloat too much when I told her I was ready to transform myself into the Button Babe.

■ ■ ■ ■

"Once the lights are on, you're going to look as pale as one of those ugly little fishes that lives at the bottom of the ocean." Estelle was smiling when she said this. I don't think it was because she was trying to soften her criticism. It's safe to say Estelle doesn't care about anyone's feelings but her own. She waved over a makeup person, who proceeded to plop so much blusher on my cheeks, I was sure I looked like a cheap floozy.

Then again, I was feeling a little like one, too. I'd nearly sold out to Mike Homolka and now here I was, really selling out, all for a chance to show off the mystery button to Estelle's supersize audience.

The makeup girl finished, and Estelle leaned closer for a better look. "You look like a prune."

"I thought I looked like an ugly little fish."

"You looked like an ugly little fish before you got some color in your cheeks. Now you'd better smile because I'm telling you, honey, you look like a prune."

I tried my best. Honest. It wasn't easy considering my insides were filled with rampaging butterflies, my outside was sweaty and shaking, and I was surrounded by all the madness of a just-about-to-be-on-the-air-live TV show.

Cameramen. Production people. A director who looked so on edge, I was afraid the poor woman was going to have a breakdown before the cameras ever rolled.

And Estelle, of course. Queen of the beautiful life. CEO of a media empire. Mover. Shaker. Style maker.

And, if what Hugh had told me was even half true, a woman who was over the moon when Kate agreed to be on the show — and furious when she changed her mind.

I reminded myself not to forget it. This was a little two-birds-with-one-stone investigating, and I had to make the most of every moment of it.

"Remember what you promised," I told Estelle, hanging on to the tote bag where I'd tucked the mystery button. It wasn't easy talking Nevin into turning it over. In fact, he only agreed on condition that I didn't mention that the button had any connection to Kate's murder.

"You said you'd let me show a very special button on air."

"I know. I know." Estelle was slipping shoes off and on, trying to decide which looked exactly right with her fresh-blueberry-colored linen suit. "You going to tell me what this button business is all about?"

"You agreed. If I came on your show —"

"I wouldn't ask any questions." She opted for a pair of taupe peep-toe pumps and snapped her fingers so one of her minions could take away the other shoes. "I just wish you would have given me more time."

I would have liked to have given her less, and when I called Estelle the previous Thursday and told her I'd changed my mind and would be on the show, I wanted to get it over with the next day. That is, until I realized I still had that scrape across the bridge of my nose. Bad enough I was about to be seen live by a couple million people, recorded by a couple million more, and that I'd be part of the show archived on Estelle's website and the couple gazillion DVDs she sold every year. Instead of a Friday appearance, I waited for Monday, and now, the scrape was mostly invisible, and I didn't want to wait any longer. My black pants covered the still-smarting abrasions on my knees. My black jacket hid the bandages I wore on my wrist and elbow. I was as good to go as I'd ever be.

"If we had more time to find just the right cabana boy —"

"That's unfortunate." She didn't believe I was sincere any more than I did, so I didn't elaborate. "But I told you, I need help finding out more about this special button, and I need help fast."

"And . . ." Estelle looked at me long and hard. "You know I don't screw around, Josie. And I don't tolerate lies or double-dealing. If I do this for you . . . ?"

As if it would prove it, I held up one hand, Boy Scout style, swallowing my pride along with my scruples. "I'll come back. I'll be on the show again. I'll be the Button Babe and do the cabana boy segment." She kept staring until I added, "I swear."

"Good." Her smile was sleek. In spite of the "No Smoking" sign above her head, she popped a cigarette out of an antique sterling case, lit it, took a drag, and let out a stream of smoke that floated in my direction. "You are going to tell me what this little mystery is all about, aren't you?" she asked.

I hadn't planned on it. As far as I was concerned, Estelle was as much a suspect as anyone else I'd talked to, and when I pulled out the button and showed it on air, I wanted to gauge her reaction. Then again, she was doing me an incredible favor. And I wanted to bring up the delicate subject of murder before the cameras rolled. This

201

seemed as good a time as any.

"I found the button mixed in with my inventory," I said, avoiding the when and where and sticking to what was, technically, the truth. I pulled out the button and held it up for her to see. "I don't recall buying it, and that's unusual for me." Another statement that toed the line between true and not-so-much. I was getting good at this weaving and dodging stuff.

"It's especially odd that I don't remember because the button is unusual and beautiful," I added. "I want to know more about it for a lot of reasons, but one of them is that I want to find the artist so I can buy more of them." That was a truth I had never admitted to Nevin. I had a feeling he wouldn't approve if he knew my research had ulterior motives. "Your viewers are discerning. They're the type who might know where to find this sort of one-of-a-kind button. I'm hoping someone can help. Your director . . ." I glanced that way and prayed the director wasn't so harried, she'd forget. "She said you could do a crawl across the bottom of the screen with my phone number and my e-mail address."

"Hmmm." Estelle bent to give the button a closer look, but when she puffed out another lungful of smoke, I closed my fingers over it. She shot me a look. "You're overprotective."

"It's a piece of art."

"And you're willing to compromise your principles and be on my show because of it." There was a crystal ashtray nearby, and she tap, tap, tapped her cigarette against the rim of it. With each tap, I could practically see the wheels turning inside her head. "I understand why you want to find the artist and buy more of them," she finally said. "Lord knows, not the button part, I'll never understand that. But I've been taken by an objet d'art a time or two, all feverish to get my hands on more. What I can't understand is why you're so anxious to get the information right this very moment. Unless you've got a buyer for this particular button and you know you could make a killing with a few more of them?"

"It's a possibility."

"Or if you pushed to be on the show today just because you knew it didn't give me time to work on the cabana boy segment."

"There's that, of course."

"Or . . ." Another drag on the cigarette before she stubbed it out. "This has something to do with Kate, doesn't it?"

I was grateful she'd brought up the subject, but I managed to play it cool. Not so easy since behind Estelle, I saw a production person give the set a final once-over, smoothing the cushions on the white wicker furniture where we'd be sitting, fluffing the yellow and blue floral print pillows. We were about to go on the air, and I was about to be what I'd spent my whole life trying not to be — the center of attention. My heartbeat sped up, but my voice was perfectly calm when I asked her, "Why would you say that?"

Estelle gave me one of those smiles that the magic of television made look so friendly and sincere. Too bad it didn't translate when she was up close and personal. This close, that smile was cold, calculating, and as friendly as a cobra.

She didn't say a word, and I knew if I was going to find out anything, I'd have to push. Just a little. "You told me Kate was going to be on your show," I said.

There was a mirror nearby, and Estelle gave her hair a final fluff. "That's what she told me."

"You mean before she changed her mind."

When she turned back to me, her smile was flash-frozen. "You don't know that."

"Come on, Estelle. You're not exactly shy and retiring. Everyone on the set of *Charlie* knew you were mad at Kate, and everyone within shouting distance knew why. You showed up there and pitched a fit about her canceling out on you. You didn't think you could keep that a secret, did you? You lost money when Kate pulled out."

She cocked her head and looked me over, and oh yeah, I knew what that glint in her eyes meant: suddenly, she realized I was more than just a mere Button Babe. Not more good. Just more. "You and Hugh Weaver are friends. He's the only one who could have told you about the money."

"So it's true."

The director appeared, nervously shifting from foot to foot, and Estelle acknowledged her with one tip of her head. "We need to get on the set," she said without another look at me, and she led the way.

She settled herself on one end of the wicker couch and I took the other. I'd told the director that I had a special button to show the audience and she'd provided me with a black-velvet-covered cushion to set it on. I put the button and the cushion on the coffee table where I could easily reach them both when the time was right.

Somebody snapped on the studio lights, and I squinted against the brightness.

"Prune, dear," Estelle crooned in a singsong voice. "Do that, and you'll look like a prune."

I pried my eyes open, smoothed a hand over my pants, and held my breath, waiting for the signal that we were on air. It didn't come in one second, two, or three, and I ran out of air, let go of a gasp, and watched the director make a few last-second adjustments.

With a few extra seconds to work with, I decided to make a few adjustments of my own. "You were angry at Kate," I said out of the corner of my mouth. "Do you have an alibi for the night of her murder?"

Estelle's smile was brighter even than the studio lights. "Of course I don't," she said, just as the director signaled that we were on the air. Her familiar theme music wafted over us along with Estelle's own voice-over that welcomed all lovers of the beautiful life. The intro gave her just enough time to lean toward me. "Once the cameras are rolling, you say one word about how I was angry with Kate or how I was alone the night she was murdered and no one can vouch for me, and my goodness, darling, I will bury you and that sweet little button shop of yours so deep, they'll have to dredge Lake Michigan to find you!"

CHAPTER ELEVEN

I had to return the boxwood button to the cops, of course, so I promised Nevin I'd call the moment I got back to the Button Box after the show. Good thing, too, because while I was at it, I could tell him it looked like somebody had tried to break in again.

"You got that right." He arrived just a couple minutes after my call, which was no easy thing considering late-afternoon Chicago traffic, and now, he bent to examine the scratches around the door lock. "It's an amateur job, that's for sure. Looks like he used a small screwdriver or a nail file. No big surprise." He looked over his shoulder out to North Wells. "He wouldn't have wanted anyone to see him try to pop the lock. He'd have to be standing close, see?" Nevin moved in and his hand hovered just about the door and the note I'd taped to it advising anyone who happened to stop by that I'd be on Estelle's show that afternoon and that they should stop by later when I returned. "The door's still locked?"

"I didn't try it. I didn't know if I should touch anything."

My phone rang from inside the shop, and I reconsidered the wisdom of keeping my hands off the door. "If it's somebody calling about the button . . ." I moaned, and didn't elaborate. Nevin knew exactly what I was talking about.

He stepped out onto the sidewalk, pulled out his phone, and made a call of his own. "I'll have a team come over and dust for prints," he explained while he waited for someone to answer the phone. "But honestly, I don't think they'll find anything. It's weird." By this time of the afternoon, it was probably the end of Nevin's shift, and it looked like he'd put in a hard day. He was wearing a lightweight khaki suit that had been rumpled by the heat, and his brown and beige plaid tie was cockeyed. I wondered if he realized there was a dry-cleaning tag on his jacket sleeve. It offended my sense of order but rather than mention it, I reached over, pulled off the tag, and tucked it in my pocket.

He didn't bother to thank me. But then, I really didn't expect him to.

He gave my shop address to the person

on the other end of the phone. "That last burglary, that was done by pros," he said when he was finished and tucking his phone back into his pocket. "No sign of forced entry. No fingerprints. No muss, no fuss."

"Except the mess they left behind." I peered in the window, but the way the sun was shining, it was hard to see much of anything aside from my own reflection. I prayed the thief hadn't gotten in. As much as I love my buttons, I was getting sick and tired of picking them up off the floor.

"This is such a botched job," he muttered. "It's got to be someone different."

"Two people who want to burglarize a button shop?" It sounded unlikely, even to me. "That's what you meant when you said —"

"Weird." He stared at the door awhile longer. I wasn't sure what he was looking for, but I stared, too, just in case I was missing something.

Finally, he combed his fingers through his hair. It didn't help; he still looked like a poorly groomed puppy. "You did a great job," he said, his gaze on the door. "You know, on that TV show this afternoon."

Not what I was expecting to hear, so of course, I was caught off guard. I covered by mumbling the standard, "Thank you."

"No really. I mean it." He stepped back and leaned against a lamppost next to the park bench where I'd sat the night of the murder. "If I had to be on TV, I'd be terrified."

"Join the crowd." I had stepped onto the sidewalk, too, and I maneuvered my way around a woman with a camera who was pointing at the shop and saying something to the man with her about, "That's where it happened."

"I thought for sure I was going to pass out," I told Nevin.

"Really? You didn't look nervous." When I glanced his way, I saw that he was looking at me. At least until he saw that I was looking at him. Then he looked away. "You were cool and calm. You talked about that button of ours, but you were careful not to say too much. Just that it was beautiful and you were anxious to find the artist. You sounded like you really knew what you were talking about."

He didn't come right out and add *even though you obviously don't* so technically, I shouldn't have bristled. He must have realized it because he added, "I didn't mean —"

"It's true." I shrugged. It was hot, so I took off my black jacket, folded it, and tucked it into my tote. "If I was the expert I'm supposed to be —"

"You've already told us more about that button than we could have found out on our own." He pushed away from the lamp-post. "I mean, think about it; we wouldn't have known what it was made of or that it's handmade. And we sure wouldn't have had the connections to go on Estelle Marvin's show to show it off to the world. You've been really helpful."

"About everything but who made that button and how it ended up here and what it has to do with . . ." The woman with the camera was still nearby. I lowered my voice. "Kate's murder."

"Not to worry." He frowned. "The part about what it has to do with Kate's murder isn't your responsibility. That's my puzzle to figure out, and I haven't been any more suc-cessful than you."

Inside the Button Box, my phone rang again, and I screeched with frustration. "That could be someone calling right now with the information we need."

"And if they are, they'll leave a message or call back."

"But —"

"The crime-scene techs, they said they're looking into a robbery a couple blocks away.

But they're going to be at least an hour."

An hour with my ringing phone teasing me from inside the shop. And me locked outside.

I grumbled some more.

"You want to . . ." Nevin took a couple steps in the direction of the trendy bistro across the street and a couple shops down. "You know, get something to eat or something?"

Déjà vu all over again, and I was too exhausted from my moment in the spotlight.

"I don't think so," I told him.

"I haven't had anything since a bagel at seven this morning." He pressed a hand to his flat-as-a-pancake stomach. "I'm starving."

I made a little shooing motion. "You go. I'll wait here."

"I promise not to take any phone calls from the office while we're there."

I bit my lower lip so he wouldn't see my smile.

"Honest." He fished his phone out of his pocket and held it out to me. "If it rings, you've got strict orders not to give it to me."

As concessions went, it was fairly generous, but there is that whole once burned, twice shy thing. Staring at his phone, I considered my options.

"I suppose we could do coffee," I suggested.

He plopped the phone into my hand. "Coffee, it is."

As it turned out, me holding on to his phone wasn't much of a test of Nevin's resolve. It never rang, at least not until we were almost back at the Button Box. By then I figured it didn't matter, and when it rang, I handed the phone right over to him.

"Team's there," he said, listening to the person on the other end of the phone at the same time he told me what was going on. "That burglar never popped the lock and got the door open."

"Thank goodness." I didn't even realize how nervous I'd been until I heard the news and felt the tension drain out of me. "I can get in and retrieve those phone messages?"

"Only if I come with you."

The hour we spent together had been less awkward than our first date but not exactly scintillating. Nevin talked police work because, apparently, it was the only thing he was comfortable talking about. I didn't want to come across as a boring nerd, so I refused to talk about buttons, and that was the only subject I was comfortable talking about. Long silences are us. I doubted Nevin's offer of accompanying me back to the shop was a come-on.

He didn't want me to think it was, either. That's why he piped up with, "That wasn't supposed to sound like what it sounded like. What I meant is that I don't feel comfortable with you walking into the store alone. Not with everything that's been happening."

"Of course that's what you meant. I knew that." I did. I guess that's why I was disappointed.

We arrived back at the shop just as the crime-scene techs were leaving. My phone was ringing again.

I already had my keys out, and I bounced from foot to foot, anxious to get the door open. The last of the technicians did not share my sense of urgency. She was on her knees smack-dab in front of the door, and she took her time packing her fingerprint powder and her brushes. Maybe it had been a long day for her, too. She looked over her shoulder at Nevin. "No harm, no foul on this one, Riley. No breaking and entering, so obviously, nothing taken. And by the way, no fingerprints, either. I can't imagine why you called us for something this trivial."

Nevin's shrug was noncommittal. "Let's

just say it's something I'm doing for a friend."

She responded with one of those *whatever* looks, and as soon as she moved away from the door, I had it unlocked and opened. I looked around my perfect, orderly, wonderful shop and breathed a sigh of relief.

"You were right," I told Nevin. "They never got in. Nothing's been touched."

"I'm glad." He did a quick turn around the shop, anyway, and when he was satisfied that nothing had been touched — and that no one was hiding out in the back room — he flopped into one of my guest chairs and pointed to the phone. "Why don't you —"

I was way ahead of him. I'd already dialed into voice mail, put in my password, and set the phone on speaker.

"Message number one," the computer voice informed me.

"Josie? Adele here. Adele Cruikshank. Don't worry, I'm not calling to harass you about firing that no-good granddaughter of mine. She's already got another job at some tattoo place down on West Lawrence. Honey, I just called to tell you I heard from Frank. You remember Frank. He's my nephew. He saw you on the TV this afternoon, and he says you looked so much better than you did in those pictures of you I showed him a couple months ago, and —"

I would have hit the delete button if I wasn't trying to move so fast. The way it was, I hit the wrong button and saved the message. I'd give it a more permanent end later.

"Message number two."

"Josie, it's Stan. You looked good, kiddo. We'll celebrate when you get home. Ice cream sundaes at my place."

"Message number three."

"Ms. Giancola, Bernie Hoffman here. Literary agent with Hoffman, Brightly, and Briggs. I saw you with Estelle Marvin, and it occurred to me that you have quite an interesting story to tell. Oh, not about those silly buttons. But Estelle, she mentioned that you know Hugh Weaver, and of course, I know about your connection with Kate Franciscus, and I was just thinking, a book about Hollywood stars and their buttons, that just might be quirky enough to catch an editor's attention. Give me a call. I'm in New York, and the number here is —"

This time, I did manage to find the delete button.

"Message number four."

"It's Mrs. Newman, Josie. From the third floor. You know, Adele's friend from the beauty shop. My grandson was with me when I watched you on TV today. He's just about your age. Well, he will be in a few years, and he'll be out of school by then and —"

"Oh good gracious!" I groaned, and hit delete again. "One more offer from an old lady trying to fix me up, and I'm going to scream."

Not to worry. Message number five, as it turned out, was from Kaz.

He got as far as "Hello" before I deleted him.

"Message number six."

By this time, I was grumbling. "I might as well give up," I moaned. "It's not going to be anyone interesting or helpful, or —"

"Ms. Giancola?" The voice wasn't one I recognized. A man's, the accent somewhere between English public school and that little German car in the commercials. "We must talk," he said, only when he did, it sounded like "Vee must talk."

"This is Roland. Prince Roland of Ruritania."

Nevin sat up fast, and together, we bent over the phone, neither one of us wanting to miss one high-class syllable.

"You will understand, my schedule, it is quite constrained," Roland said. "I arrived from my country just in time for my darling

217

Kate's memorial service in Los Angeles yesterday, and I must leave again soon. I will speak to the police, of course. But you, Ms. Giancola, you were the one who found my dear Kate, and I must . . . I must speak to you about this. I will meet you this evening at seven o'clock. The Ferris wheel at Navy Pier."

He didn't ask if I was available. Or willing. Or if it was convenient.

I guess when you're a prince, you don't worry about things like that.

"What do you think?" I slid Nevin a look.

"I think you're getting way too involved." He tapped a finger against the arm of the wingback chair. "I think you're not a professional, and you have no business getting dragged into this investigation. You're a button expert, and buttons are the only things you should be worried about."

He was right. So I shouldn't have felt like arguing. Except that whether it made any sense or not (and I was smart enough to know it didn't), this case was feeling more and more like mine. I was already involved. Whether I wanted to be or not. And now, I had a chance nobody else was likely to get, an up-close-and-personal with Kate's fiancé, and not one encumbered by some formal setting or diplomatic hubbub. I wasn't sure what Roland wanted from me or what I was likely to find out from him. I only knew I had to try.

I wasn't sure how I was going to support my position. I only knew I had to try that, too. I turned to Nevin, crossed my arms over my chest, lifted my chin, and started in. "But —"

"But nothing. I know what you're going to say. You're going to say this is a once-in-a-lifetime opportunity and that this prince might open up more with you than he's going to when I finally talk to him. And me? I'm going to say that you don't know what you're doing and you shouldn't be involved and . . ." His sigh said it all. Nevin checked his watch. "You'd better get a move on," he said, getting to his feet. "You've got a date with a prince."

I've heard people say that Navy Pier is the most popular tourist spot in Chicago. No wonder. When it comes to things to do, the pier is a lollapalooza. There's miniature golf, a carousel, shops, restaurants. All built onto a gigantic pier that sticks out about three thousand feet into Lake Michigan. In summer, even a Monday evening means swarms of people on the pier.

It would be easy for anyone to get lost in

the crowd of jostling, noisy tourists, but I wasn't worried. For one thing, I was looking for a prince, and believe me, I — along with a couple billion other people — knew exactly what Roland looked like. All anyone had to do was see the news, or a tabloid, or an issue of *People* or *Time* or *Newsweek.* A few times a week (more since Kate's death), there was the prince — all six-foot-two gorgeousness of him — making an appearance at some swanky gala, or off to play polo, or heading up one deserving charity fund-raiser or another. Roland had a lock on the whole tall, dark, and incredibly handsome thing. Just for good measure, throw in a little richer than just about anybody on the planet, more stylish than the cover of *GQ,* and sex appeal galore.

Oh yeah, it would be easy to find him, even in a crowd. In fact, he was so recognizable, I wondered why he wanted to meet in a place so public, but then, I wasn't used to the workings of the rich-and-famous world. Look at how Kate had let the paparazzi follow her like dogs after a meat wagon.

I know, I know. An icky metaphor, but true is true.

"What do you think?" I scanned the crowd around the pier's famous Ferris wheel, looking for limos, crowds of adoring onlookers, or the flash of a jewel-encrusted crown. When I didn't see anything even vaguely like it, I glanced at Nevin.

Yes, he had insisted on coming along. Didn't it figure, the one and only time in my life I was likely to have a date with a prince, and I had a chaperon. With a gun.

"He's not here," I grumbled. It had taken us longer than we'd anticipated to make our way through the crowd, and it was a couple minutes past seven. "He's on a tight schedule. He's come and gone. I'm not going to be able to talk to him."

"Relax." Nevin looked relaxed enough for the both of us. I guess he'd been to this sort of clandestine meeting before, because he insisted on stopping for cotton candy. So he could fit in, he said. "My guess is princes work on a different time clock than the rest of us." He ripped off a chunk of the sticky pink confection and popped it in his mouth. "I've got an appointment with the guy at ten tomorrow morning over at the Ruritanian consulate. You want to bet he keeps me waiting?"

"Yeah, but they'll serve you tea and crumpets while you do."

He poked the cotton candy toward me.

I made a face. "Too sugary."

"I'm a firm believer in sugar." It was the

221

most personal thing he'd ever said, and I wrote it off to the casual atmosphere and the summer breeze off the lake. "Sugar's good for you, and besides —" Nevin swallowed whatever he was going to say along with the last of the cotton candy, brushed his hands together, and tossed the paper cone that was all that was left of his treat into the nearest trash can. "There's a guy over there watching you," he said. Trying not to look too obvious, he tipped his head to his left.

I glanced to my right. The guy in question was obviously watching us. He was wearing sunglasses and standing just this side of the line of people queuing up to ride the Ferris wheel. He was tall and probably dark-haired, though it was kind of hard to tell since he was wearing a White Sox baseball cap. He was also wearing jeans and a gray T-shirt that said "Cubs Baseball" on it.

Talk about mixed metaphors.

Only a complete moron — or a prince from another country who didn't know the first thing about Chicago sports — would commit that fashion faux pas.

Nevin stepped back and waited at the nearest hot-dog cart. I crossed the pier to meet the prince.

It wasn't until I was five feet from Roland

that I wondered if I should bow. Or curtsey. Or something.

He saved me the trouble by sticking out a hand. "It was kind of you to come at such short notice."

He was wearing a gold ring that looked like it weighed five pounds. There was a seal with a lion on it, and I wondered if I was supposed to kiss it, but I opted to shake his hand instead.

His voice was icy when he said, "But I did not tell you to bring along a friend."

I knew he was talking about Nevin so I didn't even bother to look his way. "He insisted." I left out the part about how Nevin was a cop. "You know how guys can be."

"Yes, this I do know." For a moment, a smile relieved his serious expression. At the risk of sounding like one of those tabloid reports about Roland, yes, it was brighter than the lights that twinkled from the Ferris wheel. "In my country, it is considered chivalrous for a man to do things such as accompany a woman to assure her safety. Here . . ." His shrug said it all. "You American women, you would do well to be a little less self-sufficient. The real secret of having a man fall madly in love with you is letting him think you need him."

Oh, I wasn't so sure about that. One smile and a couple sentences in those rounded, aristocratic tones and I was already falling madly in love.

I shook away the thought. There was no use making a fool of myself. He was probably sick of women falling all over him, and besides, it wasn't my style. "You said you wanted to talk."

"Yes, but what I have to say, it is private." He stepped back and waved an arm toward the Ferris wheel. It was the first I realized there were two hulking guys in pin-striped suits standing with the operator. The people in line behind them didn't look the least bit happy when we were ushered to the front of the line. The wheel was full. The operator waited until all the passengers were off and we got the next car. As we entered it, the two burly guys stepped in front of the ride. Obviously, nobody else was getting a turn. Not until we were done, anyway.

Once we started our ascent, Roland took off his sunglasses. "You have been canny, Ms. Giancola. You say little to the press about your experience with my dear Kate. I hope when you publish your book about the experience, you will be kind enough to leave this meeting out of it."

"I'm not going to publish a book."

His eyes were the color of emeralds. Big, expensive, glittering emeralds.

"You are not looking to make a profit from this unfortunate experience?"

"I'm not looking to do anything but find out where this button came from." There wasn't exactly a whole lot of room in the Ferris-wheel car, but I managed to pull the pictures of the boxwood button out of my purse. "Was it Kate's?"

He had years of good breeding behind him, so rather than tell me buttons were far too plebeian a thing for Kate to be interested in, he simply raised his eyebrows.

"I didn't think so." I put the photos back where I'd gotten them. "The button was in my shop," I told him. "Under Kate's body."

He looked away but not fast enough to hide the spasm of pain that crossed his face. "My poor darling. I begged her to let me accompany her on this trip to Chicago for the filming of her movie. She said no, that I needed to attend to the wedding details back in my country. Perhaps if I had been there . . ."

It might have been of the royal variety, but it wasn't all that different from the guilt I'd been feeling at not being at the Button Box when Kate arrived. I comforted him with the same words people had been using to try and make me feel better. "If he didn't kill her that night, it only would have been some other time. I don't think there was anything anyone could have done to protect Kate."

"But why?" We were high in the air now with the city spread out around us, glistening and gorgeous, but Roland was lost in memory, his gaze fastened to the vast expanse of Lake Michigan beyond the Plexiglas window that enclosed the Ferris-wheel car. "Why would anyone —"

"I was hoping you could tell me that."

He snapped his gaze to me. "You are not with the police."

"No. Of course not. But I found Kate. In my shop. And —"

"Yes, of course." He nodded. "You are vested in this mystery. You have every right to be. But you are also a friend of Hugh Weaver's, are you not?"

Either the prince read the tabloids and remembered every little tidbit mentioned there or he had a crackerjack intelligence team. Guess which one I was betting on.

"You know my Kate and Mr. Weaver, they were having an affair?"

Another fact there seemed no point denying. "I didn't know you knew."

"Yes, of course." He brushed aside the

thought as if it were as insignificant as one of the gnats that flew outside the window. "A woman as beautiful as Kate, she is bound to have a past, yes? I knew this from the moment I met her. I knew she and Mr. Weaver were involved, and yes, I knew she continued the affair, even after we were engaged."

"And you were angry."

He barked out a laugh. "My dear Ms. Giancola, a man of my position has no need to get angry. I do not have the time for it. But Hugh Weaver . . ."

From what I'd seen of Hugh when he talked to me about Kate at his hotel, I knew *distraught* was a better word than *angry.* Not that it made much difference in the grand scheme of murder.

"Sure, Hugh might have been angry at getting dumped," I said. "But that doesn't mean —"

"Oh, come now, you cannot deny it. He was mad with jealousy. What man wouldn't be? The most beautiful, the most wonderful, the most kind and generous woman in the world had just chosen me over him." Roland lifted his chin, a way of adding *of course* without saying it. "My sources tell me Mr. Weaver, he does not have an alibi for the night of the murder."

Was the prince looking for me to somehow corroborate Hugh's guilt? "Even if I knew," I said, "I couldn't —"

"No, no. No one is asking you to say anything against your friend." We were at the highest point of the Ferris wheel, and the prince looked around. "It is beautiful, isn't it? I wish I had more time to explore your country and this city, but I must return to Ruritania. I was here only this weekend, only for the memorial for Kate. The world is no longer such a beautiful place as it was when she was in it."

"She won't be forgotten." This seemed appropriate, and far more politically correct than reminding him that not everyone thought Kate spread sweetness and light everywhere she went. Roland obviously believed she did, but then, I guess that's what love is all about.

Of course, that didn't mean I couldn't pry. Just a little.

"Her assistants —"

"Silly girls. I told her to get rid of them long ago. She wouldn't need them once we were married. My papa, His Majesty King Leopold, he would have provided Kate with a staff once she was officially a member of the family."

"And the assistants would have lost their jobs."

"You think this is a motive for one of them to kill her?" I actually might have if Roland didn't make the very idea seem stupid by laughing. We were nearing the ground, and he slid on his sunglasses. "I had every intention of providing for them," he said. "Quite handsomely."

"But there was nothing you could do to compensate Hugh."

Our slow revolution was at an end, and we bumped to a stop. One of the big guys opened the car door, and Roland motioned me to get out first. Ignoring the rumbles of displeasure from all the people still waiting, he took my arm and walked me away from the ride. "Kate, she said nothing to you before . . . Did she have a message for me? Or did she say something about the person who did this terrible thing to her?"

I didn't need to see his eyes to know he was in pain. At the risk of creating an international incident, I put a hand on his arm. "She was already dead when I found her," I told him. "She never said a word."

Oh, he made it look nonchalant enough, but Roland had apparently had this sort of thing happen before with commoners. He stepped back just far enough to be out of my reach. "And your friend, Hugh, what does he say?"

"That he didn't do it. That he's broken up about what happened. That —"

"He was paying someone to follow her."

"I know."

"And yet you believe he is innocent."

"I believe . . ." Prince or no prince, what did the man expect me to say? Since I didn't know, I patted my purse. "You've never seen that button before."

"I told you I have not."

"And you don't think it was Kate's."

"I told you it was not."

"And you think —"

"It does not matter what I think." He said that in a way that made it clear that of course, it mattered. He was a prince, after all. Roland lifted his chin. "What matters is the truth, and the truth is that Hugh Weaver was mad with jealousy." Roland snapped his fingers and as if by magic, the two bodyguards appeared. "Hugh Weaver killed Kate," he said. "I am sure of it. You can tell him for me, Ms. Giancola. You can tell him I will see him pay for his crime."

CHAPTER TWELVE

The last person I was in the mood to see was Kaz.

Out on West Schiller, I didn't so much breeze by him as I did stomp. Even that was too subtle for Kaz. He fell into step beside me.

"I was just coming to see you," he said.

I wouldn't have stopped at all if there wasn't a delivery truck blocking the street I needed to cross. "Don't," I grumbled.

When I darted around the truck, Kaz darted with me. "Don't come to see you? I don't need to. Not anymore. I'm seeing you now."

"Don't push me, Kaz." The look I shot him should have told him I was serious.

Which gave him zero excuse for grinning. "You're cute when you're mad," he said.

"No. I'm not." We made it safely to the other side of the cross street and I continued on my way, heading toward the Button Box.

It was Tuesday morning, early, and I had a copy of the day's newspaper tucked up under my arm. I swear, I could feel it burning a hole in my skin. "I'm not in the mood to be messed with," I told Kaz.

"I can see that." Apparently not well, because he leaned over and peered into my face. "What's up, Jo? You're fuming."

I was surprised he recognized anger when he saw it. I pulled the newspaper out from under my arm and waved the front page under his nose. "This is what's up. Hugh Weaver's been arrested for Kate Franciscus's murder."

"So?"

"So . . ." We got stuck at another cross street and I screeched my impatience as well as my inability to explain why just looking at the headline made my temperature shoot past the boiling point. "It's not that I think he's innocent," I said. "I mean, it's not that I think he's guilty, either. And it's not that I care. I mean, of course I care because I've known Hugh for years and it would be terrible if he really did kill Kate. If he's guilty, of course he should be arrested, but . . ." As soon as I could, I got moving again.

"So this old friend of yours is a scumbag." Kaz always had a way of distilling a problem down to its essence. Like I said, subtleties escape him. Like the emotional investment of friendship. Or the fact that a woman who's divorced her no-good husband probably doesn't want to see him again. "So that's over and done with. Time to get on with life. And my life . . ." He glanced over his shoulder and lowered his voice. "There are some things I need to talk to you about, Jo. Important things."

"That old friend of yours with the job problems and the kids and the wife and the —"

Kaz's mouth thinned. "This time, I'm as serious as a Lifetime movie."

"You always are," I reminded him. I would have launched into more of a lecture if I wasn't so busy grumbling all over again. But then, that's because when we neared the Button Box, I saw that Nevin was just about to walk up to the front door.

I turned on the afterburners and closed in on him before he knew what hit him. It was his turn to have the newspaper waved in front of him. "Why didn't you tell me?" I demanded. "I saw you last night; why didn't you mention that you were going to arrest Hugh?"

"You saw him?" Kaz propped his fists on his hips and gave Nevin the once-over. "Last night?"

233

Nevin ignored him. He did a pretty good job of dodging out of the way of the flapping newspaper, too. "I was just coming to see you. Can we talk? Privately?"

He didn't have to come right out and say that Kaz was intruding. There's something about a guy in jeans and a T-shirt staring down a cop in a wrinkled suit that says that all by itself.

I stepped toward the shop. "Good-bye, Kaz."

"But Jo . . ." Kaz came with me. "If I could just talk to you for a second and explain . . ."

"Don't say a word," I warned him. "The answer is no."

Nevin stepped up. "Is this guy bothering you?" he asked.

I wasn't looking to get Kaz in trouble so I said no; then because Kaz lit up like a Christmas tree at the prospect of having hornswoggled me again, I said, "Yes. He's bothering me. He always bothers me. But you don't need to do anything about it," I told Nevin. "This guy, I can handle on my own."

I unlocked the shop and walked inside.

So did Kaz.

And Nevin.

"If I could just talk to my wife in private,"

Kaz said, taking my arm.

I took it back.

"You have a husband?" Nevin asked.

I groaned. "Ex-husband."

"And he's bothering you." Nevin stepped forward.

"You're both bothering me." I zoomed into the back room to deposit my purse and the lunch I'd brought with me, then completed my usual morning routine, turning on the lights, adjusting the spotlights above the display cases to make sure they were pointed just-so, checking my e-mail for any messages from other dealers or orders from customers through my website. I was hoping by the time I finished, they'd both be gone, but rather than let them know, I ignored Kaz and Nevin completely.

Eventually, I heard the shop door open, then close. Had one of them left? Or both? I pretended I didn't care and started going through the mail that had come the afternoon before.

A moment later, Nevin shifted from foot to foot in front of my desk. "I didn't know about it, either," he said, and he didn't have to elaborate. I knew he was talking about Hugh's arrest. "Not until early this morning. Not until I got the call to go pick him up."

"Just like that?" I slapped my electric bill on the desk. "You're the lead investigator on this case, and you're telling me someone else made the call? All right, the only police work I know is what I see on *Law and Order,* but still, even I know that sounds fishy. If it's your case, you should have been the one who —"

I bit off my words, and my tongue while I was at it. "Roland," I said.

His hands clutched behind his back, Nevin walked over to a case where I'd arranged a lively display of molded glass buttons from Czechoslovakia. Finished there (it didn't take him long), he went over to the door, grabbed one of the red-and-white-striped mints in the bowl on the table, unwrapped it, and popped it in his mouth. "That's not the official word."

"But that's what you think."

"I'm not paid to think. Not when it comes to politics."

"But that's what you think."

He crossed the shop, back to my desk. "We've got a strong circumstantial case against Hugh Weaver."

"Still, you're not convinced that arresting Hugh was the right thing."

"Weaver was crazy with jealousy. He admits it. He and Kate Franciscus were

236

involved, and she dumped him. He was paying someone to follow her, and he knew she was going to be here that night. And we got a look at her e-mails. He sent her one that said that if he couldn't have her, then nobody would."

"So you do think you arrested the right man."

Nevin pulled in a breath and let it out in a minty huff. "I doubt that kind of evidence is strong enough to hold up in court."

"But you made the arrest anyway."

"I did what I was told to do, and I wanted to be the one to tell you about it except you didn't give me a chance."

We looked across the desk at each other. "I just thought that if you knew yesterday . . ."

"I didn't. Honest. I would have mentioned it to you."

I had no choice but to believe him so there was no use not getting over it. "Do you think he really did it?"

"I really can't discuss the case." Nevin sat down. "Do you think he did it?"

"Hugh's always been self-centered and egotistical. These days, you can add phony to the list, too. But he's not a murderer."

"Then who do you think killed her?"

He had me there. I propped my elbows

on my desk and cradled my chin in my hands. "There were a lot of people who were mad at Kate for one reason or another. Hugh, yeah, sure. He was one of them. But the assistants were going to lose their jobs, and they each had personal problems with Kate, too. And Kate had just fired Wynona, so she had her reasons, too. So did Estelle Marvin, because although she denies it, Hugh says she lost a ton of money because of the show Kate pulled out of, and I know she was angry enough to go to the set and confront Kate. And then there's Mike Homolka; we can't forget about him. He was in the area at the right time, but why he'd want to kill the woman who was making him so much money . . ." I spread out my hands. "It's a pretty wide-open field, and remember, Kate had just increased security, too, right before she died. She was afraid of someone. It might have been one of the people we're looking at, or it could be someone we don't know a thing about yet."

"And just because Weaver's behind bars doesn't mean I'm going to quit looking for that someone."

Kaz wouldn't know subtle if it hit him over the head. Nevin? He was all about nuances. Just the way he said *I'm not going to quit looking* made me sit up and take notice.

"You didn't say *we're* going to keep looking. You said *I'm*. As in, you alone. As in no support from the department. They've told you to back off."

"There's been an arrest made in the case. If we keep digging, Weaver's attorney will get wind of it, and that will deep-six our case against him. Officially, I'm off the case and on to other things."

"Unofficially?"

He tapped a finger against my desk. "If we could just find out more about that button . . ."

It was all the reminder I needed that I had yet to check my voice-mail messages. I did just that and found they consisted of a marriage proposal from a man in Peoria I'd never met but who'd seen me on TV and was sure I was the woman of his dreams, a reminder from Estelle that I'd promised I'd make another appearance on her show and the good news (or was it a threat?) that she'd found the perfect cabana boy for me, and a call from a woman.

"Hi! Ginger Lasky here. I'm a big fan of Estelle Marvin and I saw yesterday's show. That button you were asking about, I can't be sure, of course, but I think it looks familiar. If you could just give me a call. I'm on the West Coast, so it's Pacific time and the number is . . ."

I wrote it down as fast as she could say it and made sure I saved the message. "What time do you suppose it is on the West Coast?" I asked Nevin.

He checked his watch. "Early."

I made the call anyway.

Ginger Lasky was the answer to my prayers.

Sort of.

She'd seen buttons similar to my boxwood hawk, she told me. In fact, she owned six of them, though hers were carved in the shape of trees, not birds. (Just for the record, I feel it is important to point out that hearing this, I still managed to keep strong and focused and did not ask right then and there if I could buy the buttons from her. I did, however, put her phone number in a safe place so that when a sufficient amount of time passed and I didn't look too eager, I could call her and make her an offer.)

But back to the matter at hand.

The buttons, Ginger told me, were given to her when she graduated from elementary school in a little town called Bent Grove, West Virginia. They were part of a tradition, she said. Each year, each graduate of Bent Grove Elementary School got a set of six buttons, and each year, the motif was different. Birds one year, trees the next. There was even a year she recalled when the buttons were little pickup trucks.

Who said West Virginia was almost heaven? It sounded to me like the real thing.

Unfortunately, Ginger had left Bent Grove many years earlier, and she couldn't say if the buttons were still being made and given to students. She did remember that the woman who carved the buttons was known around town as Granny Maude.

"Maude." Nevin spoke slowly and carefully into his phone. "Yes, that's right, M-A-U . . ." Apparently, he was less than impressed with the person he was speaking to from the county sheriff's department in Bent Grove. He rolled his eyes. "Yes, I did say I was from Chicago. Detective Nevin Riley. And I'm looking for this Granny Maude and —" A muscle at the base of Nevin's jaw twitched. "Yes, I do understand you can't be too careful, and I have heard about identity theft, but I'm investigating —" He held the phone in his right hand. His left curled into a fist. "That's an awfully long time to have to wait." His expression was stony and his teeth were gritted when he added, "Yes, of course I understand and I appreciate your help. Good-bye."

I knew better than to jump in and start

241

peppering him with questions, but let's face it, I'd been on pins and needles since he made the call. I jumped in and started peppering him with questions. "Well? You told them about Granny Maude and the buttons, right? And they said —"

We were in the back room of the shop, where I was supposed to be sorting buttons as a way of trying to get rid of some of the nervous energy I'd had since I spoke to Ginger Lasky. Nevin set his phone on the work table. "You pretty much heard what he said. Except the part about how he had to confirm my identity before he'd provide me with any information. Since I've been told to back off on the investigation, I don't want him talking to my lieutenant. We're kind of at an impasse."

Not what I wanted to hear. I made a face.

"It gets better." I'd made a pot of coffee while Nevin was making the call, and he went over to the corner of the room where there was a sink, one of those dorm-sized refrigerators and a coffeemaker, and poured himself a cup. "Even if he decides I'm on the up-and-up and he can help me, the town's Home Days celebration starts tomorrow," he said. Maybe he added as much sugar as he did in an attempt to get rid of the bitterness in his voice. "The sheriff says he's going to be very busy with Home Days going on. So even if I decided to take my chances and give him my lieutenant's name, I'd have to wait until the fair is over. The long and short of it, he says he can't possibly look into the Granny Maude thing until next week sometime. Earliest."

"But —"

He downed his coffee. "He sounds young so I'm willing to cut him at least a little slack. He's just going by the book, the way he's been trained. He did admit he doesn't remember anyone named Granny Maude, but that could be because he's not old enough. He says he'll make some inquiries."

"Did you tell him it was important?" As soon as the words were out of my mouth, I cringed by way of apology. "I know; I'm sorry. I heard everything you said, and I realize how frustrating it was."

"You got that right." He finished his coffee, rinsed out the mug in the sink, and set the cup down next to the coffeemaker. Before he'd made the call, we'd looked up Bent Grove, West Virginia, on the computer, and I'd printed out a map. It was on my work table and Nevin studied it. "I suppose I could try to contact someone with the West Virginia State Police, but you know how these cops are in small towns. Well, maybe you don't. Let's just say I'm pretty sure that if I ruffle this sheriff's feathers, he's going to stonewall me. We've got no choice but to sit tight and wait. I'll call him again next week."

"Or we could go to Bent Grove and make the inquiries ourselves."

If I gave him the chance, he probably would have told me it was a half-baked idea.

I didn't give him the chance.

"It's an important case, isn't it?" I asked.

"You know it is, but —"

"And you're going to look like a hero when you solve it."

"I would, but —"

"So why not go where the clues lead?"

"Because we've got Hugh Weaver under arrest for one thing, and that means my superiors aren't going to take to the idea of me heading out to God's country. Oh yeah, they'll be all for me tracking down the button lead. But not if it means overtime hours. If I ask to go to West Virginia, I guarantee they're going to tell me I'm wasting my time, and they're going to tell me to sit tight. I told you, Josie, as far as they're concerned, the case is all wrapped up, neat and tidy. The button is just a bump in the road. No way they're going to give me permission to go chasing after a lead about it in some middle-of-nowhere place."

"You're right." I'd already snapped off the overhead lights in the back room so I grabbed my purse, and headed for the door. "But that doesn't mean I can't."

Yes, I was concerned about the case.

Yes, I wanted to get to the bottom of things and help Nevin out and get back to my boring, ordinary, wonderful pre-murder-investigation life.

These were all good reasons for me to close up shop for a couple days and take off on a road trip.

But, truth be told, there was another reason, too. One I am not ashamed to admit to.

I was in the grip of button fever.

It's not a disease that will ever be listed on one of those medical diagnosis websites, but to a button collector, it's as real as any case of the chicken pox.

There were buttons out there in Bent Grove, West Virginia. Beautiful buttons. They were realistics, that is, buttons that looked like real things — trees, and birds, and pickup trucks. They were handmade in sets of six. Limited editions of the most glorious kind.

And oh, how I wanted to get my hands on them before some other collector caught wind of them and beat me to it!

When I packed my overnight bag, I made sure I threw in my checkbook.

Chicago to Bent Grove is approximately a ten-hour drive, and rather than deal with traffic, I took my time, organizing and planning to leave that evening. I gassed the car, then loaded it with my suitcase, my laptop so I could check website orders while I was gone, and a cooler that contained some bottles of green tea, a couple of sandwiches, and a few apples. Since I am a just-in-case sort of person, I threw a blanket into the backseat along with my roadside emergency and first-aid kits. Just in case.

The shop was officially closed, and I changed my voice-mail message to tell customers I'd be back in a few days, but I made sure Stan still had my extra set of keys. Just in case.

By nine, convinced that there would be less traffic to deal with at night, I was ready to set out. It had started to rain, and between that and the gathering darkness, I had all I could handle to maneuver my way out of the Chicagoland area and onto I-65 in Indiana, a route that would shoot me south to where I could then head due east.

I was almost in Indiana, my windshield wipers slapping out the minutes, when I heard a rustling sound in the backseat.

Oh yeah, I had anticipated all the just-in-case scenarios I could think of.

Someone hiding out under the blanket in the backseat of my car wasn't one of them.

CHAPTER THIRTEEN

Which came first?

The shrieking?

Or the veering off to the shoulder and slamming the car into park?

No matter.

In the spirit of not embarrassing myself completely, let's just say that within a couple seconds of hearing the first rustlings from beneath the blanket in the backseat, I was stopped by the side of the road, my hands in a death grip on the steering wheel, my heart pounding louder than the eighteen-wheeler that rumbled by.

One second.

Two.

Three.

I didn't dare wait any longer.

One by one, I pried my fingers from the steering wheel and fumbled with the electronic locks, ready to bail.

That's when a hand clamped down on my

248

shoulder.

"Don't panic! Don't panic, Jo! It's just me."

My gaze flashed to the rearview mirror and when I saw those chocolate-colored eyes looking back at me . . . well . . .

Can anybody blame me for starting to shriek all over again?

"All right, calm down!" I'd already turned in my seat and swatted Kaz, so I guess I couldn't blame him for scooting as far away as he could to get out of the path of my flying fists. "I didn't mean to scare you. Just calm down!"

"Oh, I'll calm down, all right. When you get out of my car!" I was breathing hard, part adrenaline rush, partly because I'm short, and it was a stretch for me to reach all the way into the backseat. I gave it my best shot, anyway, just to get in another whack. As long as I was flopped over the seat like a hooked-and-landed fish, I figured I might as well make the most of it; I groped for the handle, and heedless of the rain that spattered that side of the car, I threw open the back door. "Get out!"

"In the middle of nowhere? In the dead of night? In the pouring rain? Come on, Jo. You wouldn't do that to me."

We were in the middle of nowhere. And it

was a dark and rainy night. Always conscious of safety, I punched the button that turned on my hazard lights, and while I was at it, I exhaled one long, exasperated sigh. My wild heartbeat ratcheted back. So did my blood pressure. "What are you doing in my car?" I asked.

Kaz sank back against the gray upholstery with its not-very-convincing-imitation-leather trim. Between dodging my flying fists and the fact that I'd actually managed to connect with a couple earnest but hardly lethal blows, his hair was a mess, and he combed his fingers through it. "I needed to get out of town for a few days," he said. "I tried to tell you this morning, but you wouldn't listen."

I was turned in my seat, so it actually hurt a little when I strained a muscle to pound my left hand against the steering wheel. The pain was inconsequential, and better that than starting to scream again. "So this is my fault?"

"I didn't say that."

"You said I wouldn't listen to you so you had to stow away in my car and nearly give me a heart attack."

"I said I was sorry for that part."

"No, actually, you never did. And besides, sorry wouldn't help a whole lot when I got so freaked out that I drove into a tree and killed the both of us."

His smile flashed in the seventy-mile-an-hour glow of the lights of an oncoming SUV. "I knew that would never happen. You're . . ." He searched for the right word. "Sensible. I knew you'd do exactly what you did. You'd pull over and —"

"And tell you to get the hell out of my car?" Just in case he'd missed it, I gave the open door a telling look. My timing was off. If I was hoping for him to slide across the seat and get out, I shouldn't have picked the exact moment thunder rumbled overhead and a flash of lightning lit up the rural landscape.

I groaned. "What, you couldn't take a Greyhound bus out of town? Or did you just have a sudden itch to go to West Virginia?"

"Is that where we're headed?" He didn't look interested. Or disappointed. Just relieved to be anywhere but Chicago.

This time, my groan was louder than the last. But that's because the reality of what I was dealing with finally dawned. "Somebody's after you."

"I never said —"

"You don't have to. It's the same old same old. It always is. You owe somebody money.

251

That's why you wanted to hide out at my place, and when that didn't work out, hitching a ride with me worked out even better. I'm guessing this time, they must be planning on kneecapping you. Or worse. What's wrong, Kaz — you losing that magic touch of yours? You can't charm these guys like you do everyone else?"

He raised his eyebrows. "Do I? Charm you?"

It wasn't what we were talking about. It wasn't even what I was thinking about. Then again, maybe he figured that flash in my eyes wasn't just a reflection of the bolt of lightning that split the night. Maybe he didn't realize it was really anger. Or maybe he just needed to be hit over the head with the truth. Maybe if I did it often enough, one of these days it would actually sink in.

Maybe.

"Get a clue. You don't charm me, Kaz. You used to. But not anymore. Exactly because of things like this. And one of these days, you're not going to be able to talk yourself out of these messes you get into. You want to spend the rest of your life hiding out in people's cars so you can sneak out of town so you don't get your legs broken?" Another thought hit, and I added, "How did you get in here without me noticing, anyway?"

"You should never leave your car unlocked in the big city," he said, so matter-of-factly it boiled my blood. "And you should have looked in the backseat after you came down from saying good-bye to Stan. You can't be too careful, Jo."

"I'll remember that." My smile was tight. But then, my teeth were gritted. "But I guess what happens in the big city won't matter to you anymore since you're getting out of the car here and living out the rest of your days in Indiana."

He slid a look at the open door and the rain that pattered just beyond it. "West Virginia sounds like a better option. Why are we going there?"

"*I'm* going to check out some buttons."

"Because of the one you talked about on that TV show."

"Maybe."

"My guess is that's the same button you were asking Kate Franciscus's assistants about."

"It might be."

"Which means you're being the resident expert." Like this was no big surprise, he nodded. "That explains it."

I knew better than to ask, but let's face it, when somebody says something that vague, it's impossible not to be curious. "Explains what?"

Kaz shrugged. "That cop who was waiting for you outside the shop this morning. You know, the one who looked like he'd slept in his suit. If you're helping out with the investigation . . . I mean, that explains why he was so anxious to see you. Why else would he be hanging around?"

Of course, the button was the only reason Nevin was hanging around. I knew that. Kaz didn't have to rub it in.

"Thanks for nothing," I grumbled.

"Oh, come on, Jo!" What, I expected an apology? For once, Kaz didn't disappoint me. "You know what I meant."

"What you meant was that no guy could possibly be interested in a button nerd."

"I always was."

I didn't dare look at him. I knew his eyes would be gleaming, and damn it, I was in no mood for gleaming.

Instead, I turned in my seat and counted the times the wipers swished the windshield before I was calm enough to speak. "That door's still open."

"Yeah, it is." He slid over and slammed it shut, but he didn't get out.

I didn't have the heart to make him. After all, it was raining.

■ ■ ■ ■

Bent Grove, West Virginia, is as big as a minute. In the gray morning light, I drove through the center of town and saw one bank, one mom-and-pop grocery store (the hand-drawn sign in the window featured a fish screaming "Live Bait!") one school, one place to stay.

It was Home Days, the man behind the check-in desk of the Debonair Motel informed me, and it was clear I should have known this because he looked at me as if I had two heads. He had only one room left.

I took it, and I was shameless enough — not to mention exhausted enough — to let Kaz carry my suitcase in from the car.

"It's adequate," I said, stopping just inside the door and taking the suitcase out of his hand. The room was tiny; from where I stood, I had no trouble plopping my suitcase down on the green and blue paisley bedspread. "It's reasonably clean. That's all that matters."

Just on the other side of the threshold, Kaz yawned. "That, and a hot shower and a chance to sleep in a nice, comfy bed for a couple hours."

"My plans exactly." I swung the door closed.

"But, Jo!" He shot out an arm to keep the door from closing in his face. "I thought —"

"The car's open." I didn't bother to add that I wasn't stupid so I didn't leave the keys. "You want to sleep, you're going to have to do it there."

"But, Jo, I —"

"See you later, Kaz."

He deserved it, so I didn't feel guilty for keeping Kaz out of the room. Besides, there is only so much an ex-wife should have to put up with. Sharing a bed with the man who used to be the man of her dreams wasn't one of them.

But though I am firm, I am not heartless. By the time afternoon rolled around and I'd slept for a while, then showered and dressed, I was feeling a little more generous. I let Kaz in to take a shower.

Mistake. But then, I never expected him to be so bold as to saunter out of the bathroom wearing nothing but a threadbare Debonair towel around his waist and a sheen of shower steam on his skin.

"I didn't have time to pack much." The room wasn't very big, and he had to reach around me for the backpack he'd brought along. "If we're going to investigate —"

"Who said anything about we?" He smelled like soap and my herbal shampoo. I sidestepped away from him. "I'm going to head out and see what I can find out about Granny Maude, the woman who might have made the button. You —"

He stepped in front of me. "I can help. I mean, maybe not so much with this crazy button business, but you know if you need me, Jo . . ." He took a step closer, checking out my jeans and the sky-blue T-shirt I was wearing. "You know, for anything . . ."

I am a strong woman, but this close, even I couldn't resist skimming my gaze down Kaz's muscled body. Oh, those abs! Oh, those pecs!

Oh, the heartache he'd caused me over the years!

I turned around so I could grab my purse and a sweatshirt, just in case the evening turned cool. "If you're coming," I said, "you'd better get dressed. Fast."

It didn't take long to find the fair or to see that, at least for the rest of that week, it was the center of activity in Bent Grove. Main Street was cordoned off and lined with pop-up tents that featured dealers selling

257

everything from arts and crafts to home-made pies and jellies and the usual assortment of funnel cakes, hot dogs, and lemonade. The street ended at the high school, and the parking lot there was filled with amusement rides and games of chance. I parked the car (and paid two dollars to the Boy Scouts who were using the lot behind the city hall for their annual fund-raiser) and got my bearings. Before I left Chicago, I would have assumed the logical place to start was the sheriff's department, but I had heard how reluctant that sheriff was to help out Nevin when he called, and I was not feeling up to trying to cajole information out of him. I already had Kaz to deal with, and he was all the blarney I could handle.

Instead of heading for the building up ahead with the "Sheriff's Department" sign outside it, I looked up and down Main Street and made up my mind. "I'll see you later," I told Kaz; then before he could decide to tag along, I sidestepped my way through the crowd and headed for the nearest craft vendor.

No luck there, but then, her stock was pretty much limited to crocheted toilet-paper-roll covers and bookmarks.

The second vendor I stopped to talk to was no more help, even though the woman knitted fabulous scarves and hats. Obviously, there wasn't much call for buttons on fabulous scarves and hats.

The third tent was set up right outside the Bent Grove Barber Shop and belonged to a quilter named Hetty, and just looking at the quality of her products, I perked right up. Her fabric choices were gorgeous. Her work was detailed and meticulous. In addition to meeting a kindred spirit, I was hoping I hit pay dirt.

I knew it for sure when I checked out the quilt hanging at the back of her display and drew in a breath of pure wonder. It was one of those crazy quilts — bits and pieces of fabric sewn together along with scraps of lace and pieces of ribbons and strips of velvet, then embellished with embroidery stitches in all shapes and sizes and colors — along with hundreds and hundreds of buttons.

I knew I was going to like Hetty, even before I introduced myself and showed her a photo of the mystery button.

"That's one of Granny Maude's, surely." Hetty was as thin as a green bean, a seventy-something woman with soft creases in her cheeks and a head of riotous silvery curls. She smiled and nodded. "Maude, she made them buttons and passed them out to the children over at the local school when they graduated from eighth grade. Can't be another person anywhere 'cept Maude who makes buttons as fine as those." She gave me a sly glance. "You lookin' to buy?"

She'd confirmed the Granny Maude theory, and for that, I owed her at least part of the truth. "I might be. What can you tell me about her and her buttons?"

"I've got a set." Hetty grabbed my arm and piloted me to the crazy quilt. "See here. They was apples the year I graduated."

Close inspection showed a quilted tree cobbled together from scraps of different green fabrics and topped off with six fabulous apple buttons.

"You're not from around here," Hetty said, while I was still staring, openmouthed, at the detail — including a tiny stem and leaf — on each apple button. "If you was, I'd know you. Everyone in these parts knows everyone else. So I'm guessing you think we're a little funny turned, gettin' all excited about buttons as graduation gifts."

"Not at all. I think buttons . . ." I already had a hand out, ready to run my fingers over a quilt square dotted with dozens of earthenware buttons shaped like turtles and fish and seashells, and I caught myself just in time. I pulled my hand to my side. If quilters were anything like button collectors, they loved it when someone admired their work, but they also appreciated a little courtesy. It's always best to ask permission before touching.

"Buttons are the best," I said, and when a grouping of tiny calicos caught my eye, I bent closer for a better look. "Anybody who gives buttons as a graduation gift must be a real genius."

Hetty laughed. "I s'pect that's not the way folks looked at it that first year Maude made her buttons and showed up with 'em at graduation. She was a little touched in the head, see. At least that's what folks always said about her. Me, I do believe buttons, they were her way of letting that artistic spirit of hers fly free."

"Her work is wonderful."

"That it is. And after the first couple years, when she insisted on giving the kids her buttons, the school board gave in just so's Maude wouldn't put up a stink. Well, that's when folks in these parts realized how valuable them buttons were. Not because they were fixin' to sell them, mind you." I knew she'd added this caveat for my benefit. "But Maude, she started with her buttons way back during World War II. She figured if she gave them at graduation and it became somethin' of an honor to receive 'em, then the kids, they'd stay in school."

"Did they?"

Hetty shrugged. "Some did; some didn't. Sometimes, the boys went off and joined the army even before they finished their schoolin'. You know, lied about their ages and all. Sometimes, makin' sure there's food on the table is more important than anything, even special buttons."

I wasn't so sure about that, but it hardly mattered.

"So, Granny Maude . . . She's been making these buttons for a long time."

"Died years ago, bless her heart." Hetty's smile was bittersweet. "Probably just as well. Can you imagine kids these days carin' about a thing like buttons? It's best that Maude was givin' the buttons away years ago, back when people still appreciated things made by hand."

It was more than I knew when I'd begun my Kaz-complicated trip to West Virginia, and I was grateful. But still not satisfied. "These buttons that look like hawks . . ." I held up the photo. "You don't happen to know what year they were made, do you?"

Hetty cocked her head, considering. "Not back when I was a kid, I can tell you that much. Me and my brothers and sisters —

there was thirteen of us — we all got them buttons from Maude. My goodness, how proud my mother was to know all her little 'uns had gone through eighth grade. If any of us had gotten them bird buttons, I'd surely remember. Must have come later."

"And Maude, she's been dead since . . ."

Thinking, she pursed her lips. "Seems to me it was that same summer the river up near Carrysburg flooded over its banks. Bunch o' folks was killed. That would have been . . . oh my, a good ten years ago at least."

"And that's when the button tradition ended?"

"I suspect so. I'm pretty sure my grandson . . . that would be Bo, Bo Clarence Johnson . . . I'm pretty sure he got a set of them buttons. And he's nearly forty."

It wasn't much, but it was a lead, and I tried not to look too enthusiastic. There was no use letting Hetty think that I, too, was funny turned. "Maybe if I could talk to Bo . . ."

She shook her head. "Livin' up in Wheeling. Has been for years. Workin' at some fancy school teachin' fancy kids such as they don't appreciate homemade things any more."

My heart sank, and I guess Hetty knew it,

because she patted my arm.

"Not to worry. Plenty of Bo's friends still live here in town." She checked the Timex on her wrist. "You come back when I'm done with my dinner break, say, five o'clock, and I'll get some of the boys Bo went to school with over here to meet you. Sound good?"

It sounded better than good. I promised Hetty I'd see her in a couple hours and went back out into the street.

I wasn't exactly looking for Kaz.

But then, it was pretty hard to miss the commotion coming from the tent with the sign above it that said beer could be purchased there. A loud bump. A crash. Voices raised in anger.

A second later, my ex came flying onto the street.

CHAPTER FOURTEEN

Kaz was airborne for a couple seconds. That is, right before he crash-landed next to a garbage can.

I didn't exactly race over to see what was going on. I more like strolled, partly because I could see he wasn't really hurt (well, except for his pride, but that was Kaz's problem) and mostly because I wondered if whatever had happened inside would be continued outside. If it did and if — as I suspected — Kaz was in the center of things, the last place I wanted to be was at his side.

People streamed out of the beer tent and gathered around to see what was going to happen next, but thank goodness, nobody threw any punches.

That was my go-ahead signal. I excused myself through the knot of people gathered around Kaz and offered him a hand up, but not until I got in the dig I was sure he deserved.

"What, you were hitting on somebody's wife?"

"That's not a fair question and you know it." Kaz dusted off the seat of his jeans. The left sleeve of his shirt was ripped, and he gave it a disgusted look before he turned the same expression on me. "Come on, Jo, whatever I did to you, you know I was never unfaithful."

It was true, but that hardly excused a brawl in a strange town. Especially a town where we were supposed to be cozying up to the locals to get information.

Just to see how bad things really were, I leaned back, peeked into the tent, and saw that one table was overturned and a couple of plastic cups of beer were spilled and scattered on the floor. The commotion was definitely over, and there didn't look to be any major damage and nothing happening except for the man wearing an apron, cleaning things up and grumbling.

"So . . ." I waited for an explanation, and when Kaz didn't offer one, I went right back to filling in the blanks. "You drank a couple of beers, right? Then you informed them that you couldn't pay."

"What kind of guy do you think I am?" Ignoring the curious onlookers, Kaz limped across the street, putting some distance between himself and the ego (and butt) bruising. Once he was gone and the excitement was over, the crowd broke up, some of them going back in for beer and others continuing on their way through the fair. "I was chatting it up with the bartender," Kaz said. "And not for any other reason than that I was trying to help you out, asking about that Maude lady and her buttons. You know, minding my own business." He stretched and winced. "And this big guy walks right behind my seat and jostles me."

The picture was starting to come into focus. I crossed my arms over my chest and stepped back, my weight against one foot. "So you challenged him to a throw down."

"Hey, you know me better than that, Jo. I'm a lover, not a fighter!" His smile reminded me of exactly that.

Which is why I turned around and walked away. For all his faults (and lord, there were many!), Kaz had never been a brawler. I knew that, and I shouldn't have jumped to conclusions. Then again, I doubt anyone could blame me. It was hard to think the best of a man who'd put me through the special hell on earth that is life with Kaz. And harder still to apologize, even when I knew I owed him.

Hard, but not impossible.

"Sorry," I mumbled when he'd caught up and was walking at my side. "I shouldn't have assumed —"

"No. Really. That's OK. I guess I can't blame you." We were standing near a booth that sold kettle corn, and Kaz loves kettle corn almost as much as I do. He ordered an extra-large bag, then patted his pockets and looked to me for assistance.

I rolled my eyes and pulled out my money, and once we had our popcorn, we stepped to the side.

"So . . ." I didn't realize how hungry I was until I smelled the delicious combined scents of fresh-popped corn and sugary coating. I got down to business, finishing a couple handfuls before I continued. "What did you find out from the bartender?"

"About Maude? Nothing. I never had a chance." He tossed a handful of corn into his mouth and chewed. "The first time that big guy walked by and bumped me, I figured it was just an accident, you know? It was crowded in there, and I figured he wasn't paying any attention. But the second time . . . Well, you can't blame me for saying something to the guy."

"Which was . . . ?"

He shrugged and chewed. "Nothing inflammatory, that's for sure. I know better than to get on the wrong side of the locals in a place like this. I said something about how he should watch where he was going. That's it. That's when . . ." He grabbed another handful of corn and winced when he chewed. "The big guy didn't say a word. He just threw a punch."

"And you punched back."

Kaz's shoulders shot back. "I tried. But . . ." He touched a hand to the spot on his jaw that was already turning purple. "Did I mention he was big? He picked me up and threw me right out of the tent. How humiliating is that? If word ever gets back to the guys at the port about this . . ."

I knew what he meant, but embarrassment might be the least of our worries. My adrenaline wasn't on overdrive; I was thinking more clearly than Kaz. "Could that big guy have followed you from Chicago?"

His hand in the bag of popcorn, Kaz froze. "You mean, was he sent by the guy I owe money to? No way! Nobody knew I was coming here. Nobody knew you were coming here, right?"

"Well, you managed to figure it out."

"Yeah, but . . ." He glanced around; then, so it didn't look like he was nervous or worried, he twitched his shoulders like it was no big deal. "There's no way. Really. Think about it, Jo. I had my backpack packed, sure, so somebody who saw me with it could have assumed I was going somewhere, but it's not like I dragged a suitcase out of my apartment or anything. I wasn't even sure where I was headed, and I only stopped over at your place on the spur of the moment. You know, to ask for help. One more time. I figured if you caved and gave me a couple thousand, I was home free. If not, then I was going to . . . I dunno. I was going to hop a bus, I guess, and just make myself scarce for a little while. I took a couple days off from work, and I thought maybe I'd go to Toledo and spend some time with my cousin there. But just as I was walking up to your building, that's when I saw you throw your suitcase in the car. It was just luck that you were leaving town, and nobody could have known I'd be with you. Believe me. I would have known if somebody was on my tail. No way." He was convinced and took another handful of kettle corn. "No way anybody followed me from Chicago."

His logic was impeccable. Feeling better about a random bar fight than I would have if this was some calculated get-Kaz ambush, I grabbed some of the popcorn, too. "Then the guy was just a jerk. Or a drunk. Or both.

We won't worry about it. I've got to head back and see Hetty at five. Until then, we've got some time to look around. Let's head . . ." I turned around, the better to size up the tents lining Main Street.

And that's when I saw him.

He was a full three hundred feet away, but that didn't matter, seeing as he was as big as Wrigley Field and impossible to miss. But then, so was the laser gaze the man aimed in our direction. My heart stopped — I swear it did — then started up again with such a clatter, I jumped.

Kaz was at my side, and without taking my eyes off the big guy, I groped for his arm and gave it a pay-attention jab. "That guy who came after you in the beer tent? Was he wearing jeans and a black T-shirt?"

"Yeah, but why . . . ?"

By the time Kaz caught on, the big guy had moved behind a tent, where two guys in pioneer-style fringed leather coats were doing a blacksmithing demonstration.

Kaz narrowed his eyes and looked where I was looking. "You think you saw him?"

I wasn't sure, and oh, how I wanted to be. I strained my eyes, waiting for the big guy to come out on the other side of the black-smith tent, but he never did.

Kaz craned his neck. "You think . . ." He

gulped down his kettle corn. "You think he's still watching me?"

"I'm pretty sure he's not." I wasn't so hungry anymore. I shoved the bag of kettle corn at Kaz, brushed off my hands, and kept an eye out for the big guy. Sure, he was wearing jeans and a T-shirt that day, but I swear, I'd know those supersize shoulders anywhere. If he was dressed in a black leather jacket and a ski mask . . .

My heart bumped out a funky rhythm, and my brain toed the edges of don't-go-there.

I was pretty sure I was right when I told Kaz he had nothing to worry about and no one had followed him from Chicago.

But that didn't mean someone hadn't followed *me*.

It was weird. Not to mention disturbing. My brain flashed back to the early morning burglary at the Button Box. Right before it turned to mush.

Truth be told, I probably would have hopped in my car right then and there and gotten out of Bent Grove if not for Hetty.

And Granny Maude's buttons.

Oh yeah, the siren call of those glorious buttons had me in its grip. So much so that

I was willing to indulge in some serious denial.

I was imagining the whole thing. That's what I told myself. Sure, the guy who took out Kaz was big, but the world is a big place, and there are plenty of big guys in it.

No way this particular big guy was one of the goons who'd ambushed me at the shop.

No way he could have followed me to West Virginia.

No reason.

No how.

Thus encouraged — even if I was a little delusional — I never said a word to Kaz about my concerns. Number one, they were completely irrational and I knew it, and when it all turned out to be a big old nothing, I didn't want to look silly. Number two, in spite of all his shortcomings, I knew that if he thought I was afraid — of anything — Kaz would go all superhero on me.

I had enough problems trying to find out about Granny Maude and the buttons. I didn't need to throw a macho man into the mix.

I kept my fears to myself, and at five o'clock, Kaz and I went to Hetty's tent. She was back from dinner, just as she'd promised she'd be. But she was alone.

"I'm just as sorry as can be." Hetty was

wringing her hands, so I believed her. "I called my grandson, Bo. I told him how you wasn't from around here and you needed to learn more about Maude and those buttons of hers, and so you had to talk to him and his friends, but . . ." Her feeble shrug said it all. "Bo, he called and talked to his buddies on your behalf, but this just isn't the kind of place where folks are likely to open up to strangers. I hope you understand."

"I do." True. Sort of. I hid my disappointment well. Or at least I thought I did.

"It's not the end of the world." Hetty patted my arm. "I didn't just sit and do nothin' but chew on pot roast after I talked to Bo." She'd tucked her straw purse under the table, where she kept her sales-ticket pad and cash box, and Hetty went and got it and pulled out a piece of paper. "I made a few calls of my own," she said. "About that there button of yours."

Hetty bustled across the tent to where a two-seater wicker couch had been set up and covered with quilts. She carefully removed each one, set them on a nearby table, and touched a hand to the seat beside hers.

"1987," she said after I sat down. "That's the year that button of yours was made. Hawks was given in 1987."

I was so grateful for the information that I would have hugged Hetty if she didn't stop me with a smile that told me there was more to come. "There was eight in the graduatin' class that year. Don't look at me like I'm livin' in some Land Before Time, young fella," she added for Kaz's benefit when he opened his mouth to say something I'm sure would have amounted to, "You've got to be kidding me!"

"This ain't the Big Apple," Hetty said, as if we needed the reminder. "Our elementary school classes was small back then. The high school, that's where all the elementary classes from all around the county were combined. These days, the kids is bussed from miles and miles around and all mixed in together early. The school board claims it saves money, but I'm not convinced. Back when that button you're askin' about was made, our schools was small. Those kids, they got plenty of attention."

"So eight students each got a set of six hawk buttons." I did a quick calculation. It meant that aside from the button now in the possession of the Chicago police, there were forty-seven more hawk buttons out there. "Do you have any idea who —"

"I surely do." Hetty smiled. "Like I said, I made a couple calls while I was waitin' on you. Once I learned about the class of 1987, it was easy to get the names of every one of them students." Hetty cleared her throat and read from the paper in her hands. "Homer Ketch. Tiffany Chatham. Mike Crowell. Tommy Hames. Lois Buck. Gil Johnson. Mary Katherine Rosman. Sharon and Ron Porter."

"That's nine," Kaz piped up. "You said eight."

Hetty waved away the discrepancy as inconsequential. "That's on account of how Sharon and Ron, they's twins and they did just about everything together so everybody just thought of them as one."

"But that means one more set of buttons." This comment, of course, came from me, and Hetty nodded, confirming my theory. I was already doing new calculations.

"This will help you?" She held out the piece of paper to me.

"Absolutely." I took it and thanked her. "The people from that class, do they still live in the area?"

She glanced at the note again. "Can't say for certain. Not about all of 'em. They's all younger than my grandchildren and I didn't know them well. I can tell you that Tommy died in a truck wreck a year or so ago. But his mama's still here, that's for certain. I s'pect she'd be only too happy to talk to you about Tommy. Nice boy as I remember."

"I'll get right on it." I tucked the note in my purse. "And Kaz, he can help me and . . ." I stood and turned to where he'd been standing only to find that Kaz was gone.

Rather than grumble and have Hetty think I was less than grateful, I thanked her again. While I was at it, I tried to talk her into letting go of that crazy quilt.

Not a chance.

Yes, I was disappointed. But hey, if it were mine, I wouldn't have sold the crazy quilt either. I bought a pretty lap-sized quilt, instead. Hetty told me it was made from reproduction flour sacks from the 1930s. Not a button in sight, but the reds, greens, and sparkling yellows were cheery; the floral patterns were cute; and the quilt would look just right thrown over the back of the rocking chair in my living room. Besides, I owed her.

I also owed it to myself not to have to trudge around the fair looking for Kaz with a quilt slung over my arm. I went back to the car and stowed the quilt in the trunk, and I'd just turned to head back toward Main Street when I felt a prickle along the back of my neck.

Hardly scientific, but an unmistakable sensation.

Someone was watching me.

I refused to look. Just like I refused to panic, even though the Boy Scouts were long gone and there was no one else around. Here behind city hall, the sounds of the fair were distant echoes: music, laughter, the *scratch, scratch, scratch* of one of those game-of-chance wheels spinning around and around. I was surprised I could hear any of it above the sudden, frantic beating of my heart.

I was surprised I could think clearly, too, but somehow, I managed. I knew if I hesitated or if I ran, I'd only look as scared as I felt. And that, I knew, would be a major mistake.

Instead, I threw back my shoulders, lifted my chin, and calmly crossed the parking lot, heading toward Main Street. But hey, I'm not a complete imbecile. My head might be high and my footsteps assured, but while I was walking, I was also groping in my purse for my keys. I nestled my key ring (it was a giant button) in the palm of my hand, the keys poking through my fingers like a weapon.

Just in case.

I made it past the town's recycling bins

and the parking places marked "Staff Only," and I was nearly to the sidewalk when my courage cracked. I didn't want to do it, I swear. But I couldn't help myself.

I glanced over my shoulder.

The big guy in the jeans and the black T-shirt was fifty feet behind me.

I walked a little taller, a little faster, and at the sidewalk, I turned right. Another block away was Main Street — and the crowds of people I was sure would keep me safe. I crossed the street. Still safe, I told myself. Just a hundred more feet. Still safe.

But a little confused.

In my rush to get out of the parking lot, I'd lost my bearings; the street I cut up was cordoned off where it met Main Street. The carousel was just on the other side of the yellow tape with the black letters that warned "Do Not Cross."

I am all about following the rules.

Usually.

This time, I threw caution to the wind. I ducked under the tape, sidled between it and the spinning carousel, and squeezed myself through the space between a generator throwing off about a million degrees of heat and a stand that sold cotton candy and snow cones. When I stepped onto Main Street, I allowed myself a look over my shoulder.

The big guy was nowhere to be seen.

Deep breaths. Deep breaths.

I swallowed down the lump of panic in my throat and glanced around to see where I'd ended up.

While I was at it, I called Kaz's cell. No, I didn't have the number stored. I'd erased it the moment I decided to divorce him. But that didn't mean it wasn't indelibly etched in my brain. Damn it.

And damn it again, because there was no answer.

I told myself not to worry, that I'd call again in a minute. Or find Kaz somewhere in the crowd. As Hetty had so eloquently put it, Bent Grove was not the Big Apple. Sooner or later, I was bound to run into him.

Keeping to Main Street and with the crowd, I walked as far as the high school. There was another beer tent set up at that end of the fair, and though I didn't think Kaz would risk a repeat of the afternoon's trouncing, I had to be sure. I ducked in and looked around. No Kaz.

When I came back out, the sun was full in my eyes. I squinted against the brightness but not for long. But then, that's because the hulking shape of a guy with shoulders bigger than all of Bent Grove was directly across the street, blocking the light.

This close, there was no mistaking him. It was the same man I'd seen outside the beer tent where Kaz had been involved in the free-for-all, the same man who followed me out of the parking lot.

Oh yeah, I was sure of it now. But then, it's hard to tamp down a memory that terrifying. Or the clear-cut look I had from here of that scar slashed just above the rounded neck of his T-shirt.

It was one of the men who'd paid that early morning visit to the Button Box.

Panic knocked against my ribs, and my brain went into overdrive. I had enough sense to look up and down the street for a police officer, and when I didn't see one, I dialed Kaz again, left him a voice-mail message that pretty much went, "Call me back. Right now," and kept with the crowd. There were fireworks scheduled for just after sundown, and people were already streaming toward the high school football field. I went right along with them.

"Where are you, Kaz?" I mumbled, as surprised as I could be that I suddenly couldn't wait to see the very man I'd sworn a year earlier that I never wanted to lay eyes on again. Disgusted, both at Kaz for his disappearing act and at myself for caring so much, I followed the crowd around the Ferris wheel, past the Tilt-A-Whirl, toward where the street narrowed and dead-ended into the athletic fields.

With every step, I was getting farther from the parking lot and my car, and I wondered how smart that was.

I hesitated for a second.

It was one second too long.

Someone bumped into me from behind, and I turned and would have apologized for slowing down traffic if I didn't find my nose against a black T-shirt and a chest that didn't look as much like a piece of anatomy as it did a cement wall.

"Going somewhere?"

Oh yeah, the shoulders were familiar, but the accent was unmistakable. When the big guy shot out a hand to grab my arm, I ducked, dodged, and took off like a shot.

Note to self: a short woman in sneakers should be able to sidestep in and out of crowds faster than a big guy with a phony Schwarzenegger accent. That should have been the good news. The reality? It seemed no matter how fast I walked, the big guy was just a few steps behind me.

Near the pony rides, he made another move to grab me, and this time, I didn't hesitate, and I didn't bother with walking, either. I took off as fast as I could, darting in and out of the crowd and not bothering to excuse myself. I was back to the area where the craft tents were set up, and I headed for Hetty's. A seventy-year-old woman might not be much help in a fight, but I figured there was safety in numbers. Her display was a few hundred feet up ahead, and I kept my eyes on it. Better to focus on getting there than to think about how my lungs burned and my leg muscles screamed for me to stop.

There was a clown making balloon animals almost directly in front of Hetty's display. I raced around him, turned —

And smacked right into Kaz.

"Hey, I've been looking for you. I thought for sure you'd still be here with Hetty." He wound an arm through mine. "Come on, we've got a date over at the Dew Drop Inn."

CHAPTER FIFTEEN

Did I mention the big guy to Kaz?

I did not. There was the whole thing about worrying what he might do, of course, but honestly, the real reason I didn't say anything was that after he told me we were going to the Dew Drop Inn, he told me why.

And my button fever went from red-hot to raging.

It seems while I'd been chatting with Hetty and then getting chased around the fair by the burglar from Chicago, Kaz had been making phone calls (which explains why he never got my voice-mail messages). He couldn't get in touch with all the people from the class of 1987 who Hetty mentioned, but he got through to most.

Go figure.

Remembering what Hetty had also said about how strangers weren't exactly welcomed with open arms in these parts, Kaz had played his cards right. (And just as an aside here, playing his cards right isn't something Kaz always does. Hence the fact that he owes so much money to so many people.) His story was that we were leaving town bright and early the next morning, so we had to talk to them soon. He mentioned that I was buying — the drinks, that is, as well as their buttons if they were willing to sell them.

Let's face it, with the thought of those buttons tempting me like a snake in an apple tree, I wasn't going to risk Kaz running off and tracking down the big guy in black. No way, no how. When it comes to buttons, I am willing to take chances, and make sacrifices, and keep my mouth shut. At least until we were finished with our meeting at the Dew Drop Inn. Then, I promised myself, I'd spill the beans.

I am not, however, completely nuts. Or careless. I let Kaz drive, but I made sure I looked behind us a couple dozen times when we left town. I told him I was admiring the scenery when what I was really doing was making sure we weren't being followed.

Within fifteen minutes, we parked outside a little place just beyond the town's water-filtration plant, a miniature golf course, and a junkyard. The Dew Drop Inn looked as if it had been there for more years than I'd been alive, a ramshackle place with a roofline as steep as the hills that surrounded it. Its paint was weathered to a shade of gray that matched the quickly gathering evening light, and the building would have blended right into the night if not for the glowing neon beer signs in each of its windows.

From the looks of the gravel parking lot, it was obvious not everyone in town was interested in the festival. The place was packed with more pickup trucks than cars, and from inside, I heard the jukebox wailing country music. I'm a city girl and no expert. It might have been Patsy Cline.

"Now, don't just charge in there and start talking buttons." When we got out of the car, Kaz looked at me over the roof. "Remember what Hetty said. If people don't trust us —"

"What's not to trust about a button collector?" I practiced my friendliest smile, the one I was planning on using on the class of 1987. "Besides . . ." I said as I rounded the car, and side by side, we headed for the door, "if I keep the conversation to buttons, they won't suspect I'm really talking about murder."

Inside, the Dew Drop Inn reminded me of the neighborhood saloons that are so plentiful in Chicago. There was a long wooden bar with a mirror behind it against the wall to our right and across from it, booths against the far wall and tables and chairs in between. The place was cozy without being crowded, dimly lit without being too dark, and decorated with a collection of hunting trophies, football memorabilia, and old license plates.

A few of the tables in the center of the room had been pushed together, and there were six people gathered around. Midthirties. Looked like locals. I knew we'd found the people we were looking for even before one of the men waved us over. He was balding and paunchy, and he stood when I got to the table and extended a hand.

"Homer Ketch, ma'am," he said. "We understand you're looking for information about our class back from when we was all in elementary school."

At the same time I nodded hello to the people around the table, I remembered Kaz's caveat. I sat down across the wooden table from him, with Homer on my right at the head of the table and the woman who introduced herself as Tiffany Chatham Dubois directly to my left. She smelled like gardenias, and my nose twitched. "Let's order drinks first before we talk business," I suggested. "And something to eat?"

After the lone waitress took orders for burgers and beers, I got down to brass tacks. I explained that I was a button collector. I told them about my shop. Fortunately, nobody connected me with the button lady whose face (and butt) had been splashed all over the tabloids along with pictures of Kate Franciscus, so I was able, without being too specific, to say I'd come across one of Granny Maude's buttons and I was eager to learn more about her and her artwork. It was a hawk button, I told them.

Tiffany perked right up. She had a head of bleached hair, a bowed mouth coated with startling red lipstick, and a bright smile that made me bet that back in the day, Tiffany was considered the cutest girl in Bent Grove. She turned that smile on Kaz. "Hawks was our year," she purred, tracing an invisible pattern against the table with one finger and leaning forward just enough to expose the cleavage that peeked from the V-neck of her too-tight camisole. Still smiling at him like she was a beauty-pageant contestant and he was one of the judges, she took a sandwich bag out of her purse and plunked it on the table. Yes, I had been restrained. And as professional as all get-out. But I couldn't help myself. The moment that bag touched the table, I slid it closer for a better look.

There were hawk buttons inside.

Six of them.

Since Tiffany wasn't paying the least bit of attention to me, I was able to slip the buttons out of the bag, the better to admire them, while she said, "Betcha think it's silly, a whole town gettin' all het up over some buttons."

Sure, she was talking to Kaz, but I answered anyway. "You forget, buttons are my business. I think they're the most interesting things in all the world. So, of course, I don't think it's silly at all. You all . . ." The buttons cupped in my palm, I looked around. "Do you all still have your hawk buttons?"

"Not with us!" Sharon Porter laughed. She didn't have any front teeth. "Me and Ron . . ." He was sitting next to her, and when Sharon nodded, Ron did, too. "We had our buttons framed years ago. You know, on account of because they're real special. They're hanging in my living room and in Ron's, too, even though Cindy, his wife, she ain't all that fond of them."

Three sets of buttons accounted for.

"I love it that you all appreciate the artistry of Maude's work," I said as the beers arrived, and I waited for the waitress to pass them. I took a sip. Truth be told, I'm not much of a beer drinker. It was a small sip. "How about you?" The man sitting at the other end of the table was tall and thin, and he'd been pretty quiet. "Do you still have yours?"

"I would if my wife would let me near 'em." He chuckled and introduced himself as Mike Crowell. "Used them on a sweater she knitted. Said they were too pretty to keep packed away. Says once that sweater wears out, she's gonna put them on the next one she knits."

"Really? All six of them?" I hoped that sounded as casual as I meant it.

Mike nodded. "Every one of 'em. And Gil, that wife of yours, she used yours, too."

"On her wedding gown." Gil still couldn't believe it. He rolled his eyes. "She cherishes that ol' thing, even though we've been married close to twenty years now."

Again, I hoped for casual. "All six of the buttons on a wedding gown? That's amazing!"

Gil nodded. He was seated next to a stick-thin woman with inch-long nails painted Barbie pink who'd been chain-smoking since we walked in. I wasn't sure if she was Lois Buck or Mary Katherine Rosman.

Turned out I was wrong on both accounts. She was Betty Hames, the mother of the classmate who'd died in a truck accident the year before. Even from where I sat, I could catch the cloying scent of her rose perfume. "Got Tommy's buttons, too," she said, and she blew a long stream of smoke into the air and eyed Kaz like he was a ham on a buffet table — and she was starving. "Kept all of Tommy's things, of course."

"Amazing." It really was, so it wasn't much of a stretch to dig just a little deeper. "And Mary Katherine and Lois . . ." I looked around the table. The two women were obviously missing, and I hoped someone knew something about them.

"Mary Katherine, she's living up in Pittsburgh. I talk to her once in a while," Tiffany informed me. No easy thing since she was busy batting her eyelashes at Kaz.

And my ex? He was taking all this female attention in stride, sitting back in his chair, his chest puffed. As far as I knew, he'd been telling the truth when he said he'd never been unfaithful when we were married. But I couldn't help but wonder what Kaz had been up to since our divorce was final.

And oh, how I hated myself for even thinking about it!

I washed away the thought with a gulp of

bitter beer. Kaz wasn't my problem. Buttons were. Buttons and murder.

If I was smart, I wouldn't forget it.

"I don't suppose you and Mary Katherine ever talk about the buttons?" Oh yeah, it was a stretch, but hey, I was paying for burgers and beers; I might as well get my money's worth. "Do you think she still has hers?"

"I know she does." Tiffany skimmed a finger across her collarbone. "Mary Katherine, she makes her own necklaces and bracelets and such. She told me she used them buttons as part of a necklace."

I cringed at the thought of such sacrilege. But not for long. That left only one class member, and my hopes lifted along with my anticipation.

"Lois Buck." I looked around the table. "Nobody's said a word about her. Or her buttons."

"Lois." Tiffany's bowed lips puckered even more. "Worthless."

"Was she?" I sat up, interested. "You mean —"

"Tiffany's still jealous!" Homer laughed, and so did the others around the table. All except Tiffany. "Still hurts, don't it, Tiffany? After all these years?" He looked my way. "Lois stole Rand right out from under

Tiffany's nose, and we were all surprised at that. Lois, she was about as ugly as a mud fence. Never made much sense, Rand givin' up Tiffany for a girl like that."

Tiffany was not amused. "No accountin' for the taste of a sixteen-year-old boy," she said. "And it's no mind to me, anymore. You can be sure of that. I tell you, I'm not the one who lost out in that deal." She tipped her head toward the bar and the man who was sitting on a stool at the far end of it. "I guarantee . . ." She was smiling again. Smiling and looking at Kaz. "If Rand Jones didn't dump me for Lois, he wouldn't be sittin' there now lookin' so sad and lonely all by himself. I know how to keep a man out of the bars and happy at home."

While the others oohed at this good-naturedly, I took a chance to glance over my shoulder at Rand Jones. He was a little older than the rest of us, and his dark hair was shot through with silver and streamed over his collar. He was dressed in worn jeans and a stained T-shirt, and his craggy jaw was coated with a couple days' growth of beard.

"It's just as well you never hooked up with Rand," Betty said. She kept her voice low enough not to be heard at the bar. "Betcha even with the tips you get over at the salon, you couldn't keep up with his bar tab. I swear, I don't know where that man gets his money. Says he works hard over at that gas station of his, but it's hardly ever open, and I never see him do hardly a lick of auto-repair work. He's always off huntin' or fishin'. And did you see that new truck of his out in the parking lot? Is there a female version of a sugar daddy? That would explain everything. Maybe Rand's got a sugar mama!" She squealed with laughter, then clamped both her hands over her mouth, just in case Rand might know what she was laughing about.

"So this Rand . . ." I glanced over my shoulder again and saw that Rand was lost in his own world, his hands clutched around a rocks glass and his gaze on the amber liquid in it. "He and Lois . . ."

"Oh, they were an item!" Sharon giggled. "Remember how Lois got put on suspension in eighth grade?" she asked her friends. "Mrs. Greer, she found Lois and Rand out on the playground together when Lois should have been in class and Rand should have been over at the high school. They was behind the bushes by the softball field doing . . . well . . . you know!" Her face flushed a color that matched the flashing scarlet beer sign over her left shoulder.

Interesting, from an oh-my-gosh-what-is-the-world-coming-to standpoint, but off subject. I gently nudged us back in the right direction. "So Lois and Rand were dating, and Lois was in your class, so she got a set of the buttons, too. But she couldn't make it here tonight, so what can any of you tell me about her buttons?"

One by one, they either shrugged or shook their heads. "Nobody's seen Lois in years," Homer said. "Since that summer right after graduation, in fact." He leaned closer. "Been stories that Rand there, he killed her and buried her out behind his shed."

I was appropriately shocked and didn't even try to hide it. "Do you believe it?"

Homer waved to the bartender for another round of beers. "Her parents never did. That's for sure. I mean, they never called the sheriff or anything. I know that for a fact, 'cause my ma, she was the dispatcher for the sheriff's department then."

"But then . . ." Tiffany had her purse open. She peered into a tiny mirror, added another coating of lipstick, and looked at Kaz before she smacked her lips together. "From what I hear, those parents of hers, they didn't much care if Lois was here or gone. My mama always said Lois was raised by wolves. Those parents of hers was heartless and thought they was better off without her."

"Which means we have no idea what happened to Lois's buttons."

Nobody else caught the undercurrent of despair in my voice except Kaz. He tossed me enough of a look to commiserate before he went back to sliding his gaze between Tiffany and Betty. Betty? Honestly? The woman had to be forty-five. A well-preserved forty-five, sure, but forty-five nonetheless.

Fortunately, our dinners arrived, and the burgers were far more appetizing than my current train of thought. I waited until we'd all finished (it took Sharon a while, but then it's hard to eat a burger without teeth) before I made my next move. "So your buttons . . ." Tiffany's were still on the table and I made sure my hands were perfectly clean before I put a reverent finger on them. "Like Kaz told you when he contacted you this afternoon, if any of you are interested in selling, I'm more than interested in buying."

"My wife would kill me," Mike said. "Not a chance!" Gil and Homer and Sharon and Ron and Betty all nodded in agreement.

Which left Tiffany.

She hesitated.

I was already prepared to offer a more-than-fair amount, and I wondered if it would sweeten the pot if I threw Kaz into the deal.

She didn't give me the chance.

"I'm not ready to make a decision," she said, scooping up the buttons and stowing them back in the plastic bag. "Not right at this very moment, anyway. But I will think about it and maybe we can . . . negotiate."

Do I need to say she wasn't looking my way when she said this?

I wasn't sure if I was more disappointed or disgusted. I told myself neither emotion was going to get me anywhere, thanked everyone for coming, and as they were just getting up to leave, asked, "What about Lois's parents? Do they still live nearby?"

"I see them around," Homer said. "They live in that house on the street that backs right up to the high school, the house with the big oak tree in the front yard." He grinned. Which made me think that Homer was pretty savvy. At least when it came to buttons. "You think maybe they got Lois's buttons and they'll be willing to sell?"

"Well, I'd certainly like to know," I said and gave Kaz a meaningful look. "I mean, I'd like to know if they have Lois's buttons."

That was a good enough answer to satisfy

them. One by one, I thanked everyone and wished them good-night, and they left. Homer was last out, and I'd just barely said good-bye to him when Kaz walked over to the bar. I opened my mouth to tell him I really wasn't in the mood to hang around, then snapped it shut again when I saw that he'd gone over to sit next to Rand Jones.

With a look, Kaz told me to keep quiet; he'd do the talking. "Buy you a drink?" he said to Rand.

This close, Rand smelled like cigarettes and motor oil. He sat back, sniffed, and looked Kaz up and down. "Don't know you."

"Not yet." Kaz signaled the bartender. I slid onto the bar stool on one side of Rand. Kaz took the one on the other side. "We're visiting Bent Grove and —"

"And you been talkin' to all them losers who were in school together." He glanced at the mirror behind the bar, and from where we sat, I could clearly see the table where we'd had dinner with the class of 1987. "What do you want?"

The bartender deposited two shots in front of Kaz. He slid one Rand's way. "Just a little information," Kaz said.

Rand downed the whiskey. "About what?"

Since Kaz was busy slugging down his

own shot, it gave me a chance to get in on the conversation. "Lois Buck."

Rand wiped the back of one hand across his mouth. "Don't know who you're talking about."

"Oh, come on!" I'd already sat up, all set to challenge him, when Kaz signaled me to shut up.

"I must have misunderstood Tiffany," he said. His smile was all about keeping things light and casual. "We were talking over there . . ." He tipped his head back toward our dinner table to make it clear that he knew Rand knew who we were talking to. "And she said she used to be crazy about you. And Lois stole you away."

"Oh, that Lois." Even though Kaz didn't offer it, Rand signaled for another shot. "Haven't seen her in years. Nobody has." He drank down this shot as quickly as the first. "You gonna ask me if I killed her? I know for sure those losers you were havin' dinner with mentioned it. Everybody knows that story."

"Don't be silly." I could be cool and casual, too. Yes, I'd been told to keep quiet, but I figured one pointed question wasn't going to hurt. "Do you suppose her parents know where she is?" I asked Rand. I did not add, "and her buttons." But then, Rand didn't look like the type who would care about buttons.

He laughed so hard, he started to cough. "You can surely ask," he said, pounding his chest. His smile made my skin crawl. "But I'm tellin' you now, lady, you're wastin' your time. I can guarantee you . . . Red and Masie Buck, they got no idea where their little girl's gone to."

I was going to tell Kaz about the burglar at the fair on the way back to the motel, but I never had a chance. For one thing, we were too busy going over everything we'd learned from the class of 1987. It wasn't much, but there were some interesting details to consider, the most important of which was that Lois seemed to be our only hope. If all the other buttons were accounted for, then maybe one of Lois's was the one I'd found at the scene of the crime.

Unless Granny Maude had made who-knew-how-many-other hawk buttons and kept them for herself. Or sold them. Or given them to Halloween trick-or-treaters.

If I sound sullen, it's because I was. I felt as if we were getting nowhere with the case. That was problem number one. Then there was also the fact that in between discussing our case, Kaz asked me what I thought of

Tiffany. And Betty.

He had to be kidding, right?

My mood thoroughly soured, I didn't confess how nervous I was knowing the big guy in black was in Bent Grove. Instead, when we got back, I took a good look around my motel room, and once I said good-night to Kaz and locked the door, I pushed the couch in front of it. My car was parked right outside, and for the second night in a row, Kaz was sleeping in it. If anyone tried to kick down my door or smash through my window, he'd hear for sure, and he could have his chance to play Superman.

We'd decided to visit the Bucks the next day, so once I was up and dressed, I fully expected Kaz to come knocking, asking to use the shower.

All the more reason I was surprised when he finally did show up and he looked as fresh as the proverbial daisy.

"You ready?" he asked me. "I'm starving. Let's get out of here and get breakfast."

"You don't want to . . ." I looked toward the bathroom.

"Let's get going and talk to these people." He grabbed my keys from the bedside table and headed out to the car.

We were almost there when I stopped and

sniffed the flowery scent that perfumed the air.

"Is that — ?" I bit off my question because I already knew the answer.

What I smelled all over Kaz was either gardenias.

Or roses.

Either way, I didn't want to know.

CHAPTER SIXTEEN

"Can't figure why all of a sudden, people is so worried about Lois and those infernal buttons."

These were the first words spoken to us by Masie Buck after we got to her front door, introduced ourselves, and told her why we were there, and hearing them, I perked right up.

Just in case he missed the significance of the comment, I poked Kaz in the ribs with my elbow to get his attention. He'd been preoccupied (and humming softly to himself, by the way) since we left the Debonair, and I really, truly did not want to know who — or what — he was thinking about. "Someone else has been here asking about Lois? And the buttons?" My throat tightened around a ball of anticipation, and I squeaked, "Who?"

Masie was a beefy woman with faded red hair and a tattoo of a butterfly on her upper left arm. Her eyes were rimmed with red, and her jeans weren't zipped. It was already close to noon when we rang the bell at the house behind the high school, but I had a feeling we'd woken her up.

That might explain why she wasn't quite getting it. "Who what?" she asked.

I stifled a groan of exasperation, the better to keep my smile firmly in place. "Who came by and asked about Lois and the buttons?"

"Ain't seen Lois in years. And good riddance to her." Masie was half in and half out of the front door, and from where I stood facing her, I could see into the living room. It was just as well we hadn't been invited inside. The place was a pack rat's dream, a maze of boxes and stacks of newspapers. A black-and-white cat darted between Masie's legs and raced across the porch and down the front steps. "Girl was never nothin' but trouble from day one. Never did a lick of work around here. All's she ever cared about was party, party, party. Surprised she even made it out of the eighth grade."

"And after that . . . That's when she disappeared." Since I had no children, there was no way I could fully understand a mother's love. Still, it was impossible to

304

imagine that any parent wouldn't still be frantic, even after all these years. "You never heard from Lois after that? Aren't you worried?"

"Sheriff come around when school started that year. Somebody there musta wondered where Lois was. They looked." She shrugged. "The way I figure it, if she was dead somewhere, we woulda got her body back by now." Masie took a step back into the living room and the door inched shut.

I knew we were going to lose her if I didn't act fast.

I wedged my tennis shoe against the inside of the door. "So that other person who was here asking about Lois . . . ?"

"Wasn't nobody here. I never said there was. Don't you young people pay any attention? A man called a few days back and asked about Lois, of all people. Never said who he was or why he wanted to know, but he asked about them buttons of hers, too. Just like you did. He the one who sent you?"

"That's right." Needless to say, a lie that smooth and easy could only flow from Kaz's lips. At least it proved he was paying attention and not lost in thoughts about . . . whatever. "He asked us to stop by and —"

"Told him already, told him I didn't know nothin' about them buttons, and he said to take some time, like, and think on it some more. Damn if I'm gonna waste my time on such nonsense. That's what I told him. But I guess the mind, it's a funny thing. There I was last night, just sittin' and watchin' *American Idol*. That's when I remembered."

"You found Lois's buttons?" I sucked in a breath to calm my suddenly racing heart. Sure, another piece of the puzzle that was Kate Franciscus's murder might be chunking into place right before my very eyes, but let's face it, I had other things to be excited about. It was obvious Masie Buck didn't give a damn even about her own daughter, so unlike the people we'd met at the Dew Drop, she might not give a damn about the buttons, either. That meant . . .

My fingers itched. My palms were damp. I scraped them against the legs of my jeans. "Can we see them?" I asked Masie.

"Them buttons? Humph!" It was clearly a tremendous favor to ask, but at least she didn't say no. Instead, she disappeared into the labyrinth of the living room, and it was a good thing she wasn't gone long because I held my breath the entire time. When she came back to the door, her right hand was fisted.

I tried not to look too anxious when I held out my palm and one by one, she dropped the gorgeous hawk buttons into my hand.

One.

Two.

Three.

Four.

Five.

"So this means Lois is still alive, right? And that she killed Kate Franciscus?"

Kaz was smarter than that. He didn't always show it, but I knew he was. I cut him some slack seeing as how his brain was still apparently mushy from what he'd been up to the night before. If I was a betting woman (and believe me, I wasn't, but then, Kaz had always done enough of that for the both of us), I would put money on the fact that he hadn't gotten a wink of sleep.

"We don't know that," I said, out on the street in front of the Buck house and sliding back behind the steering wheel of the car. "We only know that one of Lois's buttons is missing. But if you saw that house . . ."

"Creepy, huh?" A shiver snaked over Kaz's broad shoulders. "I'm surprised she was able to find the buttons at all."

"And I'm surprised she wasn't willing to sell them." Yes, I was grumbling when I said this. Like anyone could blame me! The hawk buttons in my hand and hope springing in my heart, I'd made Masie an offer that wasn't just fair, it was generous. She'd declined. "Something tells me she's holding out for even more money."

Kaz chuckled. "I'm surprised you didn't make her an offer she couldn't refuse."

"Oh, I'm planning on it," I admitted, starting the car. "I just didn't want to look too eager. If I call her again in a few hours, it will give me an excuse to ask about the buttons again. And about the guy who's also asking for information about them."

"Who do we think that is?"

I wished I knew, and I told Kaz that. "There's Hugh, and Roland, and Mike Homolka . . . They're all guys, obviously, and they all have a connection to the case." I sighed with exasperation. "The real question is how anybody got as far as we did and even knows about Lois. Unless . . ." It wasn't a new thought that hit; it was just one I hadn't had time to worry about. I drummed my fingers against the steering wheel, following it to its logical conclusion. It went something like this . . .

Unless someone followed us.

Like it or not, I knew it was time to tell Kaz about the guy who chased me through the fair.

I did.

Predictably, he freaked.

"You should have told me, Jo. You could have been in danger. At least if I knew you were worried about that guy, I could have —"

"What? Stayed outside my room last night to make sure no one broke in?" I sounded whiny. And like I cared. I regretted it instantly. "I'm sorry. Whatever you did last night . . . Wherever you went . . . Whoever you were with . . . It's none of my business."

He didn't ask how I knew. He just slid me a look. "I didn't mean to upset you."

"I'm not upset. Why would I be? We're not married anymore. I have my life and you have yours."

"Sure, and that's great and all, but if you still care —"

I poked the car into drive and turned onto a side street I thought would take us around the Main Street festival detour. "I don't. Not like that."

"Then maybe like a friend would care."

We were on a dead end street. I grumbled and turned around. I took the first left turn I came to, and we found ourselves in the parking lot of Bent Grove Elementary School.

I grumbled some more, but truth be told, deep down inside I was grateful for the diversion. Driving through an unfamiliar town was a lot like maneuvering my way through this conversation: frustrating, exasperating, maybe even dangerous if I wasn't careful.

When we stopped at a red light, and I took the opportunity to look up and down the cross street and saw the sign for the local library, I regained some of my legendary control. I remembered seeing the library the evening before. I knew we were back on track. "It's none of my business," I said.

"Sure. Like that cop back in Chicago is none of mine."

I turned to face him. Not such a good idea considering I was driving. I told myself not to forget it, got my eyes back on the road, and glanced at him out of the corner of my eye. "Nevin and I aren't . . . It's nowhere near the same."

"Then how is it?"

"We're working together on this case. Because of the button. That's it."

"Then it's not like me and —"

"No. Not at all." Perfect timing. I honestly didn't want to know if Kaz was going to name Tiffany or Betty, so when we got to the library, I turned into the lot and parked.

Apparently, Kaz was relieved to get away from personal and back to business, too. He got out of the car when I did and followed me inside. "We're here to . . . ?"

"See what we can find out about Lois Buck, of course."

As it turned out, that wasn't very much.

There were no yearbooks for the elementary school, so there was no finding Lois there, and though she was mentioned a couple times in the town newspaper and there should have been photos to go along with the articles —

"Somebody's cut out every one of them." I pointed a finger toward the hole in the newspaper and the caption that said Lois Buck was at the top of a cheerleader pyramid pictured above. "Somebody doesn't want us to know what Lois looked like. Why?"

Kaz stuck his entire fist through the gaping hole in that newspaper page, then flipped to another edition of the newspaper, where Lois's name was mentioned in connection with the spelling bee at Bent Grove Elementary School in 1986. According to the article, seventh-grader Lois Buck had received a ribbon for third place. Maybe she was proudly displaying that ribbon in the picture. Hard to say since all that was left of that page above the caption was a jagged edge where the paper had been ripped.

Kaz sat back and folded his arms across his chest. "Maybe we could ask her mother for a picture of Lois," he suggested, but he knew he was barking up the wrong investigative tree even before the words were out of his mouth. He made a face. "No way that nasty woman would have kept a picture of the girl. Not with the way she feels about her own daughter. Can you imagine anyone being like that? I mean, think back to when we talked about having kids. We never would have —"

I wasn't going there. "Lois has been missing for nearly twenty-five years," I said, my mind on the case and not on the misguided plans I'd once had for a happily-ever-after with Kaz. Still thinking through the scenario, we left the library and went back to the car. "She'd be an adult by now. If she's still alive. Why would it matter to anyone if we find out what she looked like?"

Good thing Kaz's cell rang. It kept us from dwelling on the fact that neither one of us had any answers.

He brightened up as soon as he heard the voice on the other end of the phone. "Hey, Tiffany!"

Well, that answered one question.

"What's that?" Listening, Kaz held up a finger to signal that whatever she was saying, it was something important. "Really? That's terrific. What's that you say? You're off at three? Sure, we can be over there then." A truck rumbled by, and Kaz pressed one hand to his right ear and asked, "What's that?" He listened some more, turning his back on me. Yeah, like that could actually keep me from hearing when he said, "No, it's her car so she's got to come along." When he looked back at me, his smile teetered between nervous and embarrassed. "Yeah, we'll see you later," he said and hung up.

"You've got a date with Tiffany. At three."

"*We've* got a date with Tiffany at three, and that means we've got time for lunch first. Good thing." He wound an arm through mine. "I'm starving."

We'd finished breakfast not too long before, but I wasn't about to argue. I needed a chance to sit down and process everything that had happened. We were close to Main Street, so rather than driving, we walked to the nearest greasy spoon. "So . . ." I waited until we were seated at the Formica table and had ice teas in front of us, biting my tongue to remind myself to keep on track — and off anything that even smacked of me sticking my nose into Kaz's personal life. "We're going to pay a call on Tiffany just to be sociable?"

"Never underestimate the power of my charm," Kaz said. Grinning, he added sugar to his tea. "Tiffany tells me she was thinking about what we talked about at the Dew Drop last night and that got her reminiscing about the good old days. She spent some time going through her old school things this morning. She says if we're interested, she's got some stuff set aside for us. Including pictures of good ol' Lois Buck."

I let Kaz drive, and don't think I didn't notice that even though he didn't ask Tiffany for directions when they talked on the phone, he knew exactly how to get there, anyway. He took us out the same street we'd been on the night before, past the Dew Drop and onto an impossibly twisted road up an even more improbably steep mountainside.

Tiffany's house sat at a V-shaped kink in the road, a neat, white bungalow with a long drive, a garage out back that looked big enough to hold a semi, and a brick walk up to the maroon front door. There was a well-tended plot of veggies just off the driveway to the left of where we parked, and the front walk was lined with marigolds. Tiffany did not strike me as the gardening type. Go figure.

We were only halfway up that walk when the door swung open, and Tiffany raced out. "Oh, Kaz!" She threw her arms around him. "I'm so glad you're here. Oh, Kaz, honey . . ." She grabbed his hand, dragged him into the house — and left me standing there like the last wallflower at the high school dance.

OK, so I remembered Kaz's bedroom technique as being stellar but not being able to wait even long enough to say hello . . . This seemed a little extreme, even to me.

"Uh, Jo!" Maybe Kaz wasn't all excited about Tiffany getting her clutches into him and getting him all to herself. Just inside the front door, he waved me closer.

I can't say I was all that thrilled, but I followed him into the house. The first thing I saw when I stepped into the living room was that though the outside of the house was as cute as a picture out of *Good Housekeeping,* the inside left a lot to be desired. In fact, it rivaled Masie Buck's in the disaster category. The cushions were off the couch. The flat-screen TV was tipped. There were magazines strewn across the powder-blue carpeting, and the drawers of a nearby desk were pulled out and emptied on top of them.

"It was like this when I got home." Tears streamed down Tiffany's face. Funny, all that water didn't keep her from batting her eyelashes. "Oh, Kaz, honey. I'm so scared! What if the burglar's still in here?"

It was a good question, and I, for one, didn't want to find out the answer. I pulled out my cell.

"Oh, I already called the sheriff," Tiffany said. Bat, bat, bat. "I'm brave like that."

I don't care. I don't care. I don't care.

The mantra floated through my head while I watched Kaz take a look around. "Is anything missing?" he asked Tiffany.

She shrugged. "It's kinda hard to say. 'Cept for the stuff I had out on the table over there. You know, the stuff I told you about."

My heart sank, and believe me, it wasn't because Tiffany grabbed Kaz's hand. "The photos of Lois Buck?" The words were bitter in my mouth, and I gulped them down. "They're gone?"

Tiffany nodded. "Can't imagine why anyone would take those silly old things." She was a pouter of epic proportions, and she pouted for all she was worth. "There's plenty more valuable things here. But 'cept for the mess, it looks like nothing else has been touched."

Kaz extricated himself from Tiffany's death grip and rubbed one hand across the back of his neck. "Well, we'll find out more when the sheriff gets here."

As if on cue, we heard the sound of a car in the drive.

Tiffany went to the door, and her face turned as pale as the skintight white top she was wearing with her cutoff shorts. "It ain't the sheriff," Tiffany wailed. "It's Buzz. My husband!"

"Husband?" Kaz's expression turned as sour as his voice. "You didn't tell me you had a —"

Tiffany was not in any condition to discuss the matter. She grabbed onto Kaz and tugged him across the room. She threw open a closet door and braced her hands on Kaz's back to shove him inside. "Oh, Kaz, honey, you better hide!"

He locked his legs. "I'm not going in there. Besides . . ." He whirled away from Tiffany and scooted to my side. "There's no reason for me to hide. Buzz doesn't know —"

His reasonable comment died in a groan when Tiffany nodded.

"He does." Tiffany wrung her hands. "You

317

see, Buzz, he wasn't supposed to be home from his over-the-road drivin' job for another couple days yet. And when he's gone like that from me . . . Well, I sometimes tell him about the guys I've been with. You know, as a sort of way of making Buzz real anxious to get home to me. I talked to Buzz this morning and —"

"Told him everything?" Kaz's face went green.

Another nod from Tiffany. "Includin' a real good description of you, I'm afraid."

The back door slammed shut, and a man's voice called out, "Who's that parked in our driveway, Tiffany? If it's that no-good, wife-stealin' city man you talked about, he better know I got my shotgun here and —"

We didn't wait to hear any more. In seconds, Kaz and I were in the car. A quick stop at the Debonair for my suitcase, and we were on the road back to Chicago.

CHAPTER SEVENTEEN

"Really, Jo, you don't have to do this."

It wasn't the first time Kaz had said that. Like the last time and the time before, I ignored him — and the little thread of relief in his voice that told me he was saying one thing and hoping for something else — and kept on writing the check. I ripped it out of my checkbook and handed it across my desk to him.

"Let's get this straight. I'm not paying your gambling debt," I said. There was no way I was going to establish that sort of precedent. "I'm paying you for helping me out in West Virginia. For your time. And your effort. It's a business arrangement, nothing more. What you do with the money is up to you, though if you were smart, you'd use it to make sure you don't get kneecapped. But don't think you can come to me every time you need —"

"No worries!" Kaz folded the check and

tucked it in his pocket. His smile was as bright as the Chicago sunshine. "You're the best, Jo."

"Not the best at figuring out what I'm supposed to be figuring out." When I got to the shop the morning after we returned from West Virginia, I'd made two lists: one of what we knew about the case and one of what we didn't.

Guess which one was longer.

I nudged the legal-pad pages spread across my desk. "None of it makes sense," I grumbled.

"Except that we're sure Lois Buck killed Kate Franciscus."

Kaz's use of the word *we're* was poetic license. On the drive from West Virginia to Chicago, he'd decided this was the one and only valid explanation, and he was sticking to his conclusion.

Me?

"I wish I knew for sure," I said.

"What we need to find out is who Lois Buck really is. That's the key to this whole thing, Jo. Obviously, she's living under an assumed name. That's why we can't find her anywhere on the Internet." Kaz knew this for sure because I told him how I'd tried searching every which way and sideways and had come up empty. "We also know that she knows we're onto her. That's why she got rid of all those pictures at the library and why she broke into Tiffany's home and took everything Tiffany had set aside for us. She doesn't want us to recognize her."

"But how did she know that Tiffany was going through her old stuff and pulling out pictures of Lois? And what about the guy who followed us from Chicago?"

Kaz's shrug said it all. He wasn't even going to consider these things, because if he did, they would blow his theory out of the water. Instead, he stuck to his guns.

"Think about it, Jo," he said. "Lois was in eighth grade in 1987. That means she's in her thirties." He'd been standing, and he dropped into my guest chair, the better to give me a searching look. "Who do we know who fits the bill?"

"Besides me?" His expression told me he wasn't going to let me off with a smart-aleck answer, so I actually took some time to think. "Wynona and Blake are too young," I said. "And Estelle Marvin . . . My guess is she's too old, even though I bet she'd never admit it. She's too well known, too. If she was Lois, someone would have noticed by now. But Margot and Sloan . . ." I thought about the two assistants. "They're both about the right age."

"See?" Kaz perked right up. "It's not such a crazy theory after all, is it? Think about it! Lois Buck leaves Bent Grove and changes her name. That's why she doesn't want us to find any pictures of her. Because if we did, we'd recognize her as one of Kate's assistants."

I thought this through. "OK, so if we think it's possible —"

"We know it is!"

I stayed on track. "If we think it's possible, then the next question we need to ask is why did Lois kill Kate?"

"Come on, Jo, there must have been plenty of reasons for either Margot or Sloan to hate Kate. You said it yourself. She treated them like they were unappreciated servants."

"And they did each have a personal grudge against Kate." It wasn't that I hadn't thought of it before; it was just that I was reconsidering. "Margot, because Kate had ruined the vacation plans she had with a man, and Sloan, because of some silly mix-up about lipstick. It was nothing, really, but Kate embarrassed Sloan in front of the production crew, and before it happened, Sloan was planning on applying for a job on Hugh's staff."

"Which means the nothing was really something." Kaz was all fired up. "See, Jo, we haven't gotten nowhere. We've got something to go on. All you have to figure out is if Margot or Sloan is really Lois Buck."

"All." He missed the significance of that one little word. In fact, Kaz looked at his watch and popped out of the chair. "I've got to get going," he said. "And about that check . . ."

I waved him away. He didn't need to say thank-you again, and I didn't need to hear it.

Once he was gone, I did a turn around the store, dusting off the display cases and making sure every button in them was shown to perfection and while I was at it, I thought about the murder. I wished I could be as sure as Kaz was about Lois Buck. But there was still the matter of the big guy. And the button.

Too preoccupied to sort and pack the order I'd gotten in that morning from a dealer in Honolulu who had a customer interested in an entire collection of sweet calico buttons, I went over my list again.

And got to the same old nowhere I'd been to before.

My disheartened sigh echoed in the silence

of the shop.

I spent a few minutes wandering and thinking and a few more minutes helping out a customer (hallelujah, foot traffic!) who bought four lovely enameled buttons for a jacket she was making and promised she'd tell her friends who sewed all about the Button Box. Once she was gone, I settled down and looked through the press clippings that Stan had assembled pertaining to the case. Still doing his best to prove he wasn't washed up, he went over all the details each day and gave me an envelope full of the articles he found in various and sundry newspapers and magazines not only about the crime, but about Kate's life and her work as an actress. With nothing else to do (except for those buttons getting the aloha, and I promised myself I'd get to them as soon as I was finished), I read through the clippings, steadfastly ignoring the ones that included that picture of me with my butt sticking out from under the desk.

I found nothing new.

Nothing helpful.

Nothing.

I tapped the articles into a neat pile and would have slid them back into the envelope they came out of if the item at the top of the stack didn't catch my eye. *Actress, Art-*

ist, the headline read, and I knew the piece was a retrospective of Kate's career because I'd just read through it. What I hadn't done was paid a whole lot of attention to the photo that went along with it.

It was taken on the set of *Charlie* a couple days before Kate's murder, and it showed her looking like a dream in a costume that included elbow-length kid gloves and a white off-the-shoulder gown with puffed sleeves. But it wasn't the star who caught my eye in the photograph; it was the little slice of behind-the-camera activity that showed in the background.

There was Hugh, watching the filming and looking miserable, his gaze on Kate. There was the director, signaling to a cameraman who was giving him the high-sign back.

And behind them all, there was . . .

I sat up like a shot and since I was sitting at my desk toward the back of the shop, I got up and carried the clipping to the front near the display window so I could take a better look.

It wasn't as crisp as I would have liked, but then, it was a black-and-white newspaper photo. Still, it was just possible to make out the man who stood far back in the shadows.

The one in the sunglasses who was wearing a White Sox cap and a Cubs shirt.

Yeah, that's the one.

The prince who swore he wasn't even in the country until after Kate's murder.

I was in luck. Roland was still in Chicago. In spite of the fact that he was in "deep mourning" (or so his quote in the morning paper said), he was hosting a fund-raiser at the Field Museum that evening.

No, I hadn't been invited.

But I'd just gotten a big, fat royalty check, remember. I could afford to be a five-thousand-dollar donor.

And according to the website of the charity benefiting from the event, five-thousand-dollar donors had the honor of being presented to the prince.

My closet wasn't exactly a fashionista's dream, so I made a quick trip to Saks and spent as little as I could for a dress I thought was appropriate. It was basic black (hey, if I was spending that kind of money for a dress, I wanted to wear it time and again), strapless, with a nipped-in waist and a slightly flared skirt.

"Cute."

I knew Stan meant it as a compliment, but "cute" wasn't exactly what I was going for. I wasn't used to running around with

326

bare shoulders, and I tugged at the top of the dress to make sure it was right where it was supposed to be. At the same time, I glanced out the car window to the imposing facade of the museum, with its gigantic columns and the colorful banners that announced the royal fund-raiser. "You sure I'm going to fit in?"

"Hey, you've got a chauffeur like these other highfalutin types, don't you?" Stan laughed. He'd insisted on driving me to the event, saying that nobody who was dressed the way I was should be riding the El. "There you go, kiddo." He stopped in front of the building and a valet moved to open my door. "Call me when you're done. I'll pick you up right here."

I was inside in a matter of minutes, and after showing the appropriate identification, having my evening bag looked through, and being wanded, I was in the royal reception line.

Not the ideal way to interrogate a suspect, I told myself for about the hundredth time. But at least it gave me access to Roland. I knew I might only have a moment to speak to him, so I pulled out the folded newspaper clipping that had been tucked in my sparkly black evening bag. When I was three from the front of the line, I got waylaid by a woman with a sharp expression and an eagle eye who looked me up and down. "You will curtsey when you are introduced to His Royal Highness," she said in an accent that matched Roland's. "You will not speak unless you are spoken to. You will not, by any means, solicit His Royal Highness on behalf of any charity or cause. You will not be too familiar or too forthcoming, nor will you call him by his first name. You will extend your right hand and touch it to his, but you will not close your fingers over his. He is a prince, not a rock star. You will smile. You will not gush or carry on. You are being given exactly thirty seconds of His Royal Highness's valuable time, and you will certainly appreciate his generosity and thank him. You understand all this?" Her smile was as fleeting as her instructions were terse. "That is all very good. Have a nice day."

And I moved up another place in line.

There was a couple in front of me, and I watched them follow the woman's direction to a tee. She curtsied. He bowed. They spoke to Roland in hushed tones for exactly thirty seconds, after which it was my turn.

"Ms. Giancola!" Apparently, rules don't apply to princes. He did, indeed, close his fingers over mine. Like we were old friends.

Or like he was trying to schmooze me. I told myself not to forget it. Not so easy a thing, considering that the man I'd last seen in jeans and a T-shirt was decked out like the hero in an old swashbuckling movie. Oh yeah, Roland had it all: the pseudo-military uniform, a chest full of medals, even a cummerbund and a sword. Considering what I had to talk to him about, I hoped it was just ceremonial.

"How kind of you to come and support the cause." Roland's smile dazzled. He was a handsome man, and he had the whole rich and powerful thing going for him. I might have been caught in the spell — if I didn't remember why I was there.

And if a movement from behind the nearest pillar didn't catch my eye.

I glanced over just in time to see a man move back behind the column, where he'd been hidden. Dark suit. Grim expression. Shoulders as big as —

"Hey!" I darted forward. Not so good an idea when there are more big guys in black suits guarding a prince. They came running, and I had a feeling I would have been hogtied, gagged, and on my way to a Ruritanian prison if Roland hadn't flashed them a signal that said all was A-OK. By this time, it was pretty pointless for the big guy behind the pillar to stay hidden, so I pointed right at him.

"He was in my shop," I told Roland, though at this point, I figured this was no big surprise to him. "And he followed me to West Virginia."

"Yes, yes. This is true." Roland spoke quickly and quietly, the better to send the message that this was what he wanted me to do, too. "You must not hold it against him. Wolfgang was acting on my behalf."

"Burglarizing a button shop?" I was pretty sure my thirty seconds was up, but then, I'd wasted a lot of mine getting almost apprehended by Roland's security team. Behind one hand, the protocol maven coughed gently. Roland shot her a look that said this one time, he would be the one who set the limits.

I stepped back and gave him a searching look, and since he didn't bother to answer me the first time, I said again, "Burglarizing a button shop?"

Roland's smile was sleek. So was the way he slipped one arm through mine. "You will excuse us for just one moment," he told the waiting crowd, and with that, he led me across the wide gallery and behind one of the massive pillars.

No doubt, I was about to make the tabloids again. As the prince and I walked away, a dozen cameras snapped. In the interest of keeping away as many of the sensational headlines as possible, I waited until we were far from the crowd before I batted his hands away.

"You're ignoring my question," I said. "You said Wolfgang and that hulky friend of his were working on your behalf. Why?"

Roland sniffed. In a very aristocratic way, of course. "They were protecting my best interests, of course."

I folded my arms over my chest. "And killing Kate, was that in your best interest?"

Roland didn't look surprised. Or outraged. In fact, a smile twinkled in his eyes. "Don't be a silly woman," he said. "I loved Kate. Everyone knows that."

"But not everyone knows you were in town when she died."

He froze. So did his thousand-watt smile. One heartbeat. Two.

"You cannot possibly know that," he said.

I showed him the picture.

Roland's top lip curled over his perfectly straight and impossibly white teeth. "That could be anyone."

"But it isn't. It's you."

"And so you think this proves something?"

"I think it proves you lied. To me, and to

the police, I'll bet. And if you had reason enough to lie —"

His laugh cut me short. "You Americans, you read these wonderful romantic books. And you watch fantastic, romantic movies. And you think the royal life, this is what it is really about. The lowly reporter meets the princess and falls in love with her. The commoner captures a king's heart. An actress . . ." I knew who he was talking about now, even though he never said Kate's name. "An actress meets a prince and they fall in love and live happily ever after."

"Unless the prince kills the actress."

"Yes, this could be a possibility. But it is not. You see, my dear . . ." Once again, Roland wound an arm through mine. As if we were entering a royal ball, he led me back to the reception line, where a gaggle of onlookers was oohing and aahing and wondering what we were up to. "I would never have killed Kate, you see," he purred into my ear, depositing me back where we'd started and making it clear that I could find my own way to the door. "As I said, I loved her. But I love my jet-setting life even more. Don't you see, you foolish woman, I would never do anything to jeopardize my royal title."

■ ■ ■ ■

"So that's what true love is all about!"

Nevin was not exactly the person I wanted to discuss the ins and outs of love and devotion with, and my guess was he wasn't exactly thrilled to be on the receiving end of my moaning and complaining, either. Too bad for him. Since he was the only one with me in the shop the next morning, he had no choice but to listen — whether he wanted to or not.

I was holding a copy of that morning's *Tribune,* and the picture on the front page showed me and Roland, arm in arm. I side-handed the paper, and it skittered across my desk. "How can anyone be so callous?"

Nevin had quick reflexes. With one hand, he kept the paper from landing on the floor. "You look great!" he said.

"I do?" Believe me, I don't do coy well, so I wasn't playing games here. But how I looked at the fund-raiser wasn't what we were talking about. And I was surprised Nevin noticed.

I cocked my head and took another look at the picture. If I didn't know better, I'd think that ol' Roland and I were actually having a good time together. He was smiling graciously like . . . well, like the prince he is. I was looking up into his eyes. "I can't believe he had the nerve to say that, about how he loved Kate but he loves his title more."

Nevin set the paper down. "I can't believe you spent five thousand dollars just to get to talk to him again!"

"It was for a good cause; plus, it's tax deductible."

"Always thinking." Nevin said this like it was a good thing. He'd brought a cup of Starbucks coffee to my office with him (and one for me, too, by the way, but since he wasn't clued in about my Caffè Misto obsession, it was Komodo Dragon Blend, the flavor of the day). "Unfortunately, you spending five thousand dollars and talking to Roland . . ." He didn't blow on his coffee or even sip it, just popped the top off and took a big swig. "It doesn't help. I heard at the office this morning that now that the fund-raiser is over, Roland's headed back home sweet home. And by the way . . ." He took another drink. "There is no extradition treaty between this country and Ruritania."

"Which means Hugh takes the fall for a crime he didn't commit." Disheartened, I dropped into my desk chair. "That's just wrong."

"It might not be the end of the world. Like I told you, there's a circumstantial case against Weaver, but a jury won't buy it."

I was a coffee sipper. I took a careful taste, and since the coffee was as hot as blazes, I set the cup on my desk right next to the list of web orders I'd gotten in that morning and would be packing and shipping later in the day. "If you can't prosecute Roland and you can't convict Hugh, that means Kate's murder goes unpunished. *That's* just wrong."

"That it is." He took the seat across from mine. "But once you're in this business as long as I've been in it, you learn that what's right and what's just and what's fair . . . Well, it doesn't always happen."

"And we're just supposed to accept that?" I, for one, wasn't willing. Too upset to sit there and think about it, I got up and did a turn around the shop. The bowl of mints on the table near the door was almost empty (since I hadn't had that many walk-in customers, I wondered how many were in Nevin's pockets), and I went to the back room, got a new bag out of the supply cabinet, snipped it open with the scissors I kept in my top desk drawer, and refilled the bowl. "It's wrong," I said. No big surprise, taking care of the mints hadn't done much for my mood. Or my anger.

Even though it didn't need it, I straightened the guest book on the table with the mints. I tidied my desk. I glanced into the back room and realized there were still buttons I hadn't gotten around to cataloging and rearranging since the break-in engineered by Roland and carried out by his two goons.

"So why would Roland send his bodyguards to mess with my buttons?" I'd given Nevin all the details as soon as he got to the Button Box that morning, so this wasn't a surprising question. "What did they have to gain?"

"You got me there!" Nevin stretched out his long legs. "It might have delayed the wedding, I suppose. I mean, if Kate was as fussy as you say, and she couldn't find the exact right buttons she wanted . . ."

"Crazy." So was the jumpiness eating at my insides. Desperate for something else to do, I looked around and caught sight of the briefcase that contained the buttons Kate had taken to her designer. When I retrieved it from the set of *Charlie,* I'd checked to make sure all the buttons were present and accounted for, but I hadn't had time to put them away.

It was something. And something might

help soothe my nerves.

One side of the briefcase was smashed from where I'd fallen on top of it, and I struggled with the latch. Nevin got up, popped it open, and handed the case back to me, and I removed the cards that contained the buttons.

That's when I realized there was something at the bottom of the case.

"Look. A photograph." I took out the five-by-seven picture of a girl with red hair and bad teeth and tipped it so Nevin could see it. "It's Wynona. Why on earth would her picture be in with my buttons?"

"Humph." It was as much of a comment as Nevin was willing to make. He took the picture from me and looked it over. "It looks like a school picture. Like maybe she's, what, twelve or thirteen? Why would Wynona want Kate to see a picture of her at that age?"

"Unless she was trying to prove a point . . ." I took the picture out of Nevin's hands and walked to the window with it, the better to check out Wynona's please-don't-take-my-picture expression, her orange braided hair, and her neat white blouse.

"Wynona always said she didn't steal those pearls, that Kate fired her unjustly. Maybe she wanted Kate to feel sympathetic. You know, to see that she was a real person with a real past and that —"

I took another look at the picture and my words dissolved.

"What is it?" Nevin hurried the length of the shop to stand next to me.

I bet when I looked up at him, my eyes were shining. But then, I was feeling pretty proud of myself when I said, "Nevin, look at the buttons on her blouse! I know who did it."

CHAPTER EIGHTEEN

Estelle Marvin arrived first, a vision in a short-sleeved print dress in fresh pinks and greens. She had a beaded shawl draped artfully around her shoulders, and she slipped it off and tossed it to Kaz just inside the door of the shop.

"I can't imagine what's so important," she said, breezing past Kaz (but not, it should be noted, until she gave him an appreciative once-over). "Unless you called so we can schedule your next appearance on my show."

"Yes, of course. I promised I'd do the show, and I will. But that's not why we're here tonight." Kaz and I had arranged my desk chair, my guest chairs, and some chairs I'd borrowed from Doctor Levine in a circle as wide as my narrow little shop could accommodate, and I motioned Estelle to sit. She just so happened to take a seat facing the one Kaz dropped into. She was busy sparkling at him when I told her, "We'll get started in just a couple minutes. As soon as —"

Margot and Sloan walked in. Clearly, they were just as confused by my invitation as Estelle was. Lucky for me, they were also curious and had decided to show.

In fact, within a couple minutes, I was feeling pretty proud of myself. In addition to Estelle, Margot, and Sloan, I'd also managed to get Mike Homolka into the Button Box. He had strict orders not to bring a camera, but I had no doubt he was taking copious mental notes. Unlike Margot and Sloan, and even Estelle, Homolka didn't have a personal stake in this case. But he did have a professional one. If what he did could be called a profession. He was there for one reason and one reason only: he smelled a story. With any luck, I'd be able to give it to him.

"We'll get started in just a couple minutes," I told them, and behind my back, I crossed my fingers. If things went exactly as planned . . .

They did. The next time my door opened, Hugh Weaver was standing outside.

"What's he doing here?" Estelle had taken out a cigarette, but at a death look from me, she'd refrained from lighting it. "Aren't you . . ." she pointed at Hugh with the cigarette, "supposed to be in jail?"

"I'm not supposed to be. But I was." Hugh kissed me on the cheek, and it wasn't until after he took a seat that I realized that Wynona had walked in right behind him. Then again, Hugh had always been a little larger than life, and Wynona was . . . Well, in jeans and a Hello Kitty T-shirt, she looked younger and more vulnerable than ever. Just inside the door, she did a little nervous dance step on the hardwood and wrung her hands.

"Come on in." I waved her closer. "We've got a lot to talk about."

"I don't know what." Wynona's voice was breathless, and her eyes were as big as saucers. She back-stepped toward the door. "I don't think I belong here. Not with all these important people."

"Of course you do." Before she could bolt, I took her arm and piloted her to the chair between Margot and Sloan, where I figured she'd be most comfortable.

"So, it's like one of those old mystery novels, right?" Homolka practically salivated. "You've got all your suspects assembled, and you're going to reveal who done it."

"Not all my suspects." I mumbled these

341

words and saw Kaz check the button-shaped clock that hung on the wall just above the doorway to the back room. He didn't have to say a word. I knew Kaz was thinking exactly what I was thinking. Honestly, did I expect him to show?

A moment later, a sleek limo pulled up in front of the shop, and my hopes climbed. That is, until the shop door opened and Giant #1 and Giant #2 stepped inside.

Flashback! My breath caught in my throat. My heart thrummed. Instincts are a funny thing, and mine advised me to run. I tensed, and good thing I was standing right behind Kaz. He reached up a hand and grasped mine. Like I said, instincts are a funny thing. Just like old times, Kaz's touch calmed and relaxed me.

At least until Roland walked in.

Even though I hoped he'd come, I can't exactly say I was expecting him, so I was thrilled.

Everybody else? I think it's fair to say they all just about dropped their teeth.

Except for Hugh.

He glared at Roland, who gave him a royal glare back. Right before he waltzed over to the last empty chair. No jeans and T-shirts for the prince tonight. He was dressed in a perfectly tailored suit, a blinding white shirt,

and a dark tie, and yes, he did look smash-
ing.

"I trust this will not take long." Roland
propped one royal arm casually over the
back of his chair. He sized up first Margot,
then Sloan. I guess it goes without saying
that he passed right over Wynona without a
second glance. "My private jet is waiting at
the airport, and I am anxious to get home
and put this unfortunate trip behind me."

"I'll bet you are," Hugh growled.

And I knew I couldn't let things get out
of hand. I ignored the ugly undertone.
"Now that we're all here . . ." I looked
around at the curious expressions of my
guests. "Yeah, it does feel like a scene in
one of those old movies, I admit it. Hugh,
you, especially, should appreciate that."

"I appreciate being out of jail." He sat
back and crossed his legs. Hugh's complex-
ion was pale; no tanning booths in lockup, I
suppose.

"I'm not trying to be dramatic," I told
them. "And I apologize if that's how this is
coming across. But you've all got a stake in
this case, so I thought you should all be here
when I tell you what really happened."

"You know?" Estelle's voice caught. "But
how —"

I held up one hand. "I'll explain every-

343

thing. You see, it all comes down to the buttons." I signaled to Kaz, who handed me the photo of the Granny Maude button I'd found the day after the murder right about where I was standing now. I handed the picture to Estelle, who gave it a look and passed it around the circle. "Without that button, we would never have gotten on the right track, and we never would have found out who killed Kate Franciscus."

"Well, it's about damned time." Hugh harrumphed and crossed his arms over his chest. "Better His Royal Highness here should be doing time than me."

"Ridiculous!" Roland's outburst was monumental. "I had nothing to do with Kate's murder. Ms. Giancola, she knows this. And I have nothing to hide."

"You're right. You don't. At least not from us." I stepped into the middle of the circle, but I kept my eyes on Roland, the better to gauge his reaction when I said, "But Kate did."

Homolka perked up, and the prince shifted uncomfortably in his seat.

"Do you want to tell them?" I asked His Royal Highness. "Or should I?"

He, too, crossed his arms over his chest, the posture so like Hugh's I wondered if the men knew they were mirror images of each other.

I guess I had the floor, and I glanced around.

"It's like this," I said. "Kate Franciscus wasn't really Kate Franciscus. I mean, she was. Of course she was. But Kate Franciscus was nothing more than a wisp of beautiful imagination. A woman created out of necessity, a whole lot of cosmetic surgery, and the daydreams of a girl named Lois Buck."

I waited for this little bit of news to sink in before I looked back at Roland. "That's what it was all about, right? That's why your buddies here . . ." I looked toward the bodyguards at the door. "That's why they burglarized the shop. You knew that Kate, being as particular as she was, wouldn't let the wedding go on if everything wasn't perfect. If she couldn't find just the right buttons, that would do it. And nobody but me . . ." I didn't blush. Why should I? After all, it was true. "Nobody but me was going to be able to provide those buttons for her. For the longest time, I couldn't figure out why you'd want to delay your wedding, especially when you claimed you loved Kate."

Roland's shoulders shot back. "Yes, this is true. I did love her." He aimed a look at

Hugh. "More than anyone else ever could."

"But . . ." I wasn't going to let him get away with it — not in the room where Kate had taken her last breath. "But you admitted to me last night that you loved your royal title even more. I have no doubt that your operatives checked into Kate's background, and I bet they found out who she really was a lot faster than Kaz and I did. Once you knew that everything she'd ever told you about her life was a sham—"

Roland jutted out his royal chin. "What I knew did not matter."

"Of course!" Homolka's cackling laughter left His Royal Highness in the dust. "There was that lingerie model a couple years ago. And the rock star." He rubbed his hands together. "Word on the street is that Prince Roland here made his royal papa very unhappy with his indiscretions. In fact, I have it on good authority that the king told him if he took up with another woman with even a hint of scandal to her name, he'd be disinherited, and Roland's younger brother would eventually get the throne." He swung his gaze to the prince. "You have anything to say about that? On the record?"

Roland sniffed. "This does not mean I killed Kate. On the record . . ." He drew out the words, as if Homolka might not be smart enough to understand. For all I knew, he wasn't. "On the record, you can tell the common rabble who read your tabloids that I did not kill Kate. I simply needed to push back the day of the wedding. That is all. Until I could get things sorted out and decide how to break this news to my father. He would not be amused to find out that this wonderful actress with an impeccable background was not who she said she was. A girl from some little mountain town?" A shiver snaked over the royal shoulders. "Really!"

"Which explains the burglary. And why your goons . . ." Oh yeah, I looked at the two big guys when I tossed out the insult. For what they'd put me through that one terrible morning, I owed them. "That's why they followed us to West Virginia and that's why they picked a fight with Kaz at Home Days. They wanted us to leave town before we found out anything. When we didn't up and run . . . When we got on the trail of Lois Buck, they had to destroy all the pictures of her. They didn't want us to know who she really was and who she'd turned into."

"This certainly does not make me guilty of murder," Roland mumbled. "Even if it does mean I am guilty of having poor taste in women."

"You son of a —" Hugh was out of his seat in an instant, and I swear, he would have had his hands around Roland's throat if I didn't stop him. The burly bodyguards might have been willing to put up with a lot, but when it came to their boss's safety, I knew they wouldn't fool around. By the time I clamped a hand on Hugh's arm to hold him back, one of the bodyguards already had a hand inside the jacket of his dark suit coat. Good thing Hugh got the message and backed off; I didn't want to see what the bodyguard was going to pull out.

Hugh was trembling when he glared at Roland. "How dare you say Kate wasn't good enough? She was the most perfect, the most wonderful woman. She was . . ." His voice broke, his shoulders slumped, and I handed him off to Kaz, who led him back to his seat.

"I guess you see what that proves," I said to no one in particular. "Hugh couldn't have killed Kate. He loved her too much. In fact, I'm betting he was the only one who ever really did. Too bad Kate wanted the publicity of a royal wedding and that title more than she wanted true love. She would have been better off with you, Hugh."

"Yes." He hung his head and wept softly. "Yes."

Ever practical, Estelle refused to be caught in the undercurrent of emotion. "But how do you know any of this?" she demanded. "How can you prove it?"

"The proof? That's easy." I had the photograph I'd found in the briefcase with the buttons, and I held it up for all to see. "It all comes down to this one picture."

"It's me," Wynona gasped.

I nodded. "I found it in with the buttons I'd given Kate to show her designer. You know that, Wynona. You're the one who put it there. And you were the one who was trying so hard to get it back. That day outside the mansion where the movie was being filmed, that was you on the bicycle that slammed into me. You were hoping to snatch the briefcase, and you missed. So you had to try and break in here. News flash: if you're looking for burglary lessons, these guys . . ." Once again I looked toward the bodyguards at the door. "They're way better at it than you."

"But why . . . ?" Margot looked from Wynona to me. "Why would Wynona give Kate a picture of herself?"

"I think Wynona's the only one who can answer that."

Wynona's face flushed a color that rivaled the pink in Estelle's print dress. "I don't know what you're talking about," she said, so gosh-gee honest, I would have believed her if I didn't have that picture in my hands. "I didn't put that picture in with Kate's things. How could I? And I didn't hop on a bicycle and knock you down. Ms. Giancola, you know I'd never do anything like that."

I wasn't about to argue. But then, I didn't have to. I strolled over and handed the photo to Wynona. "Then explain."

She didn't bother to look at the photograph; her eyes were filled with tears. "I don't know. I don't know what you mean. I have no idea what you're talking about."

I pointed. "I'm talking about the buttons."

Wynona froze and I took the opportunity to pluck the photo out of her hand. One by one, I took it around to each of my guests. "Notice anything?" I asked. "About the buttons on the girl's blouse?"

At that point, Hugh had the photograph and he squinted at it. "They're small and dark," he said. "But other than that . . ."

"They're little plastic raisins." I had a magnifying glass on my desk and I handed that to Hugh, too, who peered through it, checked the picture, then handed both the glass and the photo to Estelle, who did the same thing. "California Raisins, to be exact. Those of you who are a little older than Wynona here will remember —"

"They were a huge hit, back in the eighties," Homolka piped up. "Animated raisins that sang and danced and sold raisins. It was pure advertising genius. Everybody knew the California Raisins."

"Even some button manufacturers," I added. "There weren't many made, but there were actually plastic buttons made to look like the raisin cartoon characters. Now, Wynona here is maybe what, twenty-three or -four? And the girl in the picture is thirteen or so. Which means if that's a picture of Wynona —"

"There's no way she'd be wearing a blouse that old. Or one with buttons on it that were that old." This from Kaz, who, although he'd been a good enough sport to say he'd be there that evening, didn't know the ins and outs of what I had planned. "I tell you what, folks, Jo may think I don't pay attention when she talks about those buttons of hers, but I hear plenty. I know that if that photo is only a few years old and that girl is wearing those raisin buttons, they'd be collector's items and worth a mint. Nobody would use them on a kid's shirt. That means —"

"The picture is old." Estelle nodded. "And the girl in it —"

"Is Lois Buck," I said.

"But she —" Never one to waste time, Estelle popped out of her seat and took the picture from Margot. "This Lois Buck is the spitting image of Wynona."

"Actually Wynona is the spitting image of Lois. But that's not surprising, is it, Wynona?" I stared her down. "The girl who used to be Lois Buck transformed herself into Kate Franciscus. She was your mother."

If everybody wasn't so busy talking all at the same time, we might have heard Wynona start to sob. The way it was, it wasn't until my guests settled down before we heard her whimper. "I didn't know," she said. "Not until just recently. My mama got sick, and she died, and at the funeral, one of the neighbors, she told me my mama loved me like I was one of her own." Wynona raised shining eyes toward me. "Like I was one of her own! It was the first I knew I was adopted."

So far, so good. "How did you put the pieces together?" I asked her.

"It was that button. The one made by that Granny Maude lady. I . . . I had it since I was a baby, and once I found out I was adopted, I got to wondering and I did some looking and some digging, and I knew my parents — my adoptive parents — I knew they lived in Bent Grove before I was born."

"So that's how you ended up where we did."

Wynona bobbed her head. "I talked to everyone about that button, and I ended up talking with Rand Jones, and from what everybody told me about him and Lois . . ." At least Wynona had the sense to shiver when she spoke. "I was pretty sure he was my daddy. Only he insisted he didn't know what I was talking about. But I didn't believe him, and that night when I went to see him and he told me he couldn't help me find my mother, I . . . I waited outside the house instead of leaving right away. He . . . He thought I was gone, and he made a phone call. I heard him leave a message that said, 'Our baby girl is all grown up, and she's looking for you.' That's when I knew for sure."

"Good old Rand." Thinking back to the surly man at the Dew Drop, I made a face. "The guy who barely works and has all the money in the world. He obviously had Kate's number. In more ways than one. He called her because my guess is that she was paying for his silence."

"As was I." Roland nodded. "Even once

Kate was dead, I couldn't let the truth be known. Not about who she was, where she came from. When her payments to this Mr. Jones ended —"

"Yours started up. He's got quite a nice little racket going there!" This from Kaz, who, of everyone in the room, surely knew the most about a nice little racket when he heard about one.

"That explains about the pearls!" Margot stopped just short of slapping her forehead and looked to Sloan for confirmation. "We found them! The pearls Kate said Wynona had stolen? We found them when we were cleaning up Kate's things. They were in a purse she used the morning she died. So we figured she must have known they weren't stolen. Even so, she fired Wynona. That didn't make sense. Until now."

"Because Kate saw that Wynona looked just like her. At least just like her before the cosmetic surgeons took over," I added, for those who weren't quite getting it. "That's why Kate needed an excuse to get rid of Wynona. She realized the girl who was working for her was her daughter."

When he looked at Wynona, Hugh's top lip curled. "Kate used to look like that?"

"Impossible!" Estelle snorted.

"But think about it, and it makes perfect

sense," I pointed out. "I don't suppose we'll ever know for sure, but my guess is that Lois had her baby . . ." I looked at Wynona. "And maybe she left that button with her as some sort of souvenir, something to tie the two of them together. Lois abandoned the baby and left Bent Grove, and the only one who knew her secret was Rand. That's why Lois had to pay to keep him quiet. She was a smart girl, and she knew a thing or two about chutzpah, that's for sure. My guess is she had a string of lovers who paid for this cosmetic surgery and that cosmetic surgery, and before anyone knew it . . . voilà! Kate Franciscus was born. It's exactly what your version of the Secret Service found out, wasn't it, Your Royal Highness?"

"Yes." Roland's jaw was tight. "Yes, you have the story essentially correct. How the woman could have had the gall to lie. To me!"

"The only one who really knows what happened after that . . ." I swung around the other way, "is Wynona."

"Yes." She was crying all-out now, great big tears slipping down her ruddy cheeks. "I waited until the next day, after that night I went around and talked to Rand. I waited until he was out of the house, and nobody in Bent Grove locks their doors, so I went

355

in and I checked the redial feature on his phone. And I got . . ." Even now, she could barely believe it. Wynona choked over the words. "I got Kate Franciscus's private line. She said she was in Paris with . . ." She glanced at the prince. "With him. She said she was buying a gown for the Oscars and . . ." Wynona's chest heaved. "I just couldn't believe it. Kate Franciscus! I loved her movies. She was so beautiful and so glamorous. She . . . She was my mother!"

"So you tried to get in touch with her." Another right-on point from Kaz.

Wynona nodded. "Well, sure I did, because I was sure she'd be thrilled to find me, just like I was thrilled to find her. I even had proof, see, because I found that picture of her . . ." She looked toward the photo of the girl wearing the blouse with the California Raisin buttons on it. "I found that picture at Rand's, and I knew right away that it proved Kate was my mother because we look so much alike. So I . . ." She gulped. "I admit it. I stole the picture. And because I knew there was no way Kate could deny our relationship once she saw it, I starting calling and leaving messages, and well, I guess she never got them because she didn't return my calls. So I wrote her letters."

"Well, that explains the beefed-up security," Sloan muttered.

I'm not sure Wynona heard. Then again, the kid was on a roll and so upset that her words combined with her tears and fell like rain. "I read about the movie in the newspaper, the one that was going to be filmed here in Chicago, and I came here, and I . . ." Her cheeks were ashen when she looked at me. "I did a terrible thing," she said.

Estelle clasped a hand to her throat. "Oh! She killed Kate. You heard her! She said she killed Kate."

"Except that's not what Wynona is talking about," I told Estelle before looking back at Wynona. "Right?"

She nodded. "I kept an eye on all of you." She glanced from Margot to Sloan. "All of you assistants. And I went into the restaurant where that Shawna was having lunch. And my mother — I mean, my adopted mother — she used to use a lot of herbs. You know, natural remedies she learned about back in West Virginia. And I slipped some herbs into Shawna's lunch. I didn't want to hurt her, just make her sick. And I did, and then you needed another assistant and there I was, like magic!"

"And Kate never paid the least bit of attention to you." I knew I was right on the money when I pointed this out because Wynona's face turned an unattractive shade of red. "Why would she? You were just a lowly assistant. I bet when she finally did, she was shocked to see a younger version of herself looking back at her."

"I slipped that photograph into the briefcase with those buttons you gave Kate, and still — still, she didn't see. Still, she didn't say she knew who I was and she was so happy to see me. Then I finally had a chance to talk to her alone. I came right out and told her who I was and —"

"And after all your effort and all your time and all your trouble, what did you get in return?" I stared Wynona down. "Your mother didn't want anything to do with you, did she? In fact, she fired you. That's why you followed her here to the shop that evening."

"Yes." Wynona was crying so hard, she could barely speak. "Yes, but what happened after that . . ." She leapt to her feet and looked around the circle. "I told her that if she had acknowledged me as her daughter, maybe I would have had the money to keep my mama — you know, my adopted mama — alive. My daddy and I, we wouldn't have lost our home and all we had because of mama's medical bills. And

Kate . . ." All the color drained from Wynona's face. "She laughed at me."

"And you picked up that buttonhook and —"

"It was an accident," Wynona screamed. "A terrible accident. She came at me, you see, and she pushed me. And I knocked against the table, and I didn't know how to defend myself. And I didn't know what that hook thing was and I just grabbed it, and I hit Kate with it and —" Reliving the scene, she stared down at her empty hands. "I didn't know what happened until I saw the blood."

"That's all I need to hear!" Mike Homolka hopped out of his seat and headed to the door. So did Margot and Sloan. His Royal Highness, it goes without saying, had heard enough. He stood, raised his chin, and marched out. It took Hugh a little longer to collect himself. Shaking, he plodded to the door, stopping only long enough to give Wynona a searching look and ask, "Why?"

That left me and Kaz. Me, Kaz, and Wynona. I signaled him that it was OK for him to leave. "I'll wait outside," he said.

Wynona and I were alone.

"Oh, Ms. Giancola!" she wailed. "I'm so sorry. I never meant any of this to happen. I feel so terrible, but I didn't know what to do. After I realized Kate was dead . . . Well, I messed up your store. A lot. I figured I needed to make it look like someone had been looking for something, like maybe Kate had walked in on a robbery or something. I didn't know what to do. I had to keep it all a secret. That's why I tried to get the picture back." Wynona hung her head. "I'm so sorry I hurt you that day I was on the bike. It's why I offered that horrible Mike guy money in exchange for taking pictures of you. So I'd know where you were and when you were out of the shop and I could come here and get the photograph. But Mike . . ." She curled her lip and wrinkled her nose. "He laughed at me, too, and when I tried to break in here . . . Well, that didn't work, either. I've made some terrible mistakes, and I've really messed things up. What's going to happen to me?"

I put a reassuring hand on her shoulder. "You're going to talk to the authorities, and you're going to tell them exactly what you told us all tonight. And they're going to take it all into consideration, Wynona. About how upset you were, about how Kate came at you first and you had to defend yourself. The important thing now is just to get the truth out in the open. They're going to understand."

She raised shining eyes to mine. "You'll come with me?"

"Yes, of course." I patted her arm and stepped aside so she could get to the door. "And we'll go right now. That way, you won't be able to talk yourself out of it. And don't worry, Kaz and I will be right there with you. We'll help you explain."

She had her hand on the doorknob when I added, "Only there's one thing I can't help with because I don't understand it myself."

Wynona froze and looked at me over her shoulder.

"The gloves," I said.

Her eyelids fluttered. "Gosh, Ms. Giancola! Gloves? I don't know what you're talking about."

I smiled. But then, Wynona had already stabbed Kate with a buttonhook. I didn't want to get on her bad side. "They were one of the pairs of gloves Kate wore in the movie, those gorgeous, elbow-length gloves, right? There were so many pairs, nobody would miss one. And gloves . . . That explains why there were no fingerprints the day you broke in here to try and get the photograph back. More importantly, you brought those gloves with you the night Kate died. And you wouldn't have done that by chance, Wynona. You didn't want to leave any evidence. Because you planned on killing Kate that night."

Wynona's smile was sleek. Her voice wasn't breathy any longer. It was as hard-edged as that silver buttonhook. "Nobody can possibly understand how much I hated that bitch. She had everything. A glamorous career and that damned prince of hers, and all the money in the world. And she wouldn't share any of it. She wouldn't even acknowledge me as her daughter. I showed her, didn't I? You see, I inherited more than just that stupid button from Kate. I'm as good an actress as she was. Little ol' me? A cold-blooded killer? Once I turn on the waterworks, everybody's going to be convinced that what happened here that night was a terrible accident."

"Except for me, and a jury." When Nevin walked out of my back room, Wynona's mouth fell open. She spun around just in time to see him raise the digital tape recorder in his hands. "And once they hear what you just said . . ."

Wynona's animal scream cut him short. She was on top of me before I even saw her coming, her face red and distorted, her hands around my neck.

"You tricked me, you bitch!" She squeezed

362

and stars exploded behind my eyes. "How could you —"

As quickly as it started, the pressure on my neck eased. But then, like I said, Nevin had great reflexes. He had Wynona face-down on the floor and his handcuffs out even before Kaz came running.

CHAPTER NINETEEN

The cabana boy really was wearing a loin-cloth — and as far as I could tell, nothing else.

I gulped down my mortification, mumbled some word of thanks for the tray of buttons he set down on the table in front of me (the one that also had a glass of wine on it), and got to work.

Realistic buttons.

My topic on Estelle Marvin's show was realistic buttons.

And I swear, I know a whole lot about realistic buttons.

All of which would have been easier to remember if the more-than-half-naked, dark-haired, dark-eyed, incredibly gorgeous hunk wasn't grinning at me.

To this day, I don't remember what I said or how I filled up the five-minute time slot Estelle had allowed for the "Button Babe" segment.

I only know that when it was over and we cut for a commercial, I felt as if I'd been wrung out and hung up to dry.

"You did great!" The hunk bent down and gave me a peck on the cheek before he disappeared back toward wardrobe, where he would, no doubt, do the world a disservice by clothing that incredible body.

"You need to get your butt out of there!" This, of course, was from Estelle, who shooed me out of my chair. "We've got another segment to do, and you're not in this one. And by the way," she added when I pulled myself onto my rubbery knees and made a move to leave the set. "You weren't half bad. You'll come back for another appearance, won't you? Of course you will!" she decided before I could. "Anybody as savvy as you knows a good business move when she sees one, and my show, honey . . ." Estelle barked out a laugh. "This is as good as it gets!"

When the director signaled for silence, I dashed to the sidelines, where Stan was waiting for me.

"Good work, kiddo," he whispered. He put an arm around my shoulders and led me to a spot where he knew we'd be far enough away from the cameras to talk. "You looked fabulous. You're good at TV and at solving murders, too. You're a real pro!"

"The only thing I want to be a pro at is buttons." Our hot Chicago weather had breezed out on the tail of a cold front and it was a gray, chilly afternoon. I grabbed my raincoat and headed for the door. "From now on, that's all I'm going to worry about. Buttons, buttons, and more buttons."

"I don't know about that." Nevin stepped out from behind a piece of scenery. It was a good thing I didn't know he'd come to the show because I would have been more nervous than ever. "Stan's right," he said. "You're pretty good at this TV thing, and Stan . . ." Nevin was carrying a Starbucks bag, and he shifted it from one hand to the other. "I want to thank you for all your help, sir. It was good of you to share your experience." They shook hands. "We couldn't have done it without you."

Whether that was true or not was anybody's guess, but at that moment, it didn't matter. Stan's shoulders shot back, and rather than let things get maudlin, Nevin got down to business. He opened the bag and handed around cups of coffee.

I breathed in the fabulous aroma rising from my cup. "Caffè Misto. How did you know?"

Nevin smiled. "Hey, I am a detective!"

"And I'm a third wheel." Stan went ahead of us to the door, and Nevin and I left the studio, too. We were already out in the hallway when Kaz zipped around the corner.

"Hey!" One look at Nevin, and Kaz stopped short. "I wanted to see you do the show. Is it over? Dang! I would have been here sooner, but I had to stop at home for a couple things."

It wasn't until I looked him over that I noticed he was carrying his backpack. "You're going away?"

Kaz's smile was swift and sweet. "For a little while."

It was a week after I'd gathered my suspects together at the Button Box, a week since Wynona's arrest, and now that the case was wrapped up and my appearance on Estelle's show was over, I was free to get back to my normal life. I'd been walking on a cloud. Until that very moment. The familiar twinge of disappointment soured my mood. "You didn't use that money I gave you for what I thought you were going to use it for, did you?" I asked Kaz.

He made a face. "I had this sure thing going, and I just knew, this time, it was going to work. But hey . . ." He checked his watch and headed back the way he'd come. "No worries! There's always next time. I've got a cab waiting. If anybody happens to call and ask about me, you'll do me a favor, won't you, Jo?"

"And tell them I don't know who they're talking about? You bet!"

Outside, Nevin and I were just in time to see Kaz hop into a cab.

Nevin shook his head. "Trouble, huh?"

I sighed. Right before a smile relieved my somber expression. "Something tells me you didn't have to be a detective to figure that out. Kaz always has been trouble. He always will be. And me . . ." I toasted Nevin with my coffee, and since I'd waited long enough, I popped the lid and took a sip. "I'm never going to let myself forget it."

"Good." He moved his paper cup from one hand to the other. "So maybe we could . . . I dunno . . . I was thinking . . . dinner?"

What was that Estelle had said? I was smart enough to know a good move when I saw one?

Maybe when the subject was business. When it came to Nevin . . .

I looked him over and decided that like appearing on TV — and solving murders — there was only one way to find out.

"Dinner," I said. "But no pizza."

"Agreed."

"And I promise not to talk about buttons," I told him. "If you promise not to talk about murder."

"Oh, I don't know!" Nevin put a hand on my shoulder to usher me down the street. "When it comes to murder . . . Josie, I think we finally found something we have in common."

BUTTONS 101

Whether you're looking through Grandma's button box or attending your first-ever button show, you'll find there's a world of information to learn about buttons. There are dozens of different materials used to manufacture buttons, from metal to porcelain to rubber, and collectors who specialize in each style and design. If you'd like more information about the history of buttons, collecting, and button clubs all over the world, check out the National Button Society at www.nationalbuttonsociety.org.

BOXWOOD BUTTONS

Granny Maude isn't the only artisan who's made buttons out of boxwood. The wood is hard, has a smooth texture, and retains its sharp edges, which makes it perfect for details and for intricate carving. Boxwood colors can vary from dark yellow to brown to a reddish hue. The wood is mellow, and in the hands of a skilled carver, it can almost glow. You'll find boxwood buttons in the shape of everything from dragons and mermaids to dogs and bees.

To clean boxwood or other wooden buttons, gently polish them with a soft cloth and a little furniture polish or mineral oil.

The employees of Thorndike Press hope you have enjoyed this Large Print book. All our Thorndike, Wheeler, and Kennebec Large Print titles are designed for easy reading, and all our books are made to last. Other Thorndike Press Large Print books are available at your library, through selected bookstores, or directly from us.

For information about titles, please call:
(800) 223-1244

or visit our Web site at:
http://gale.cengage.com/thorndike

To share your comments, please write:
Publisher
Thorndike Press
10 Water St., Suite 310
Waterville, ME 04901